Praise for Eileen Watkins and her
Cat Groomer mysteries!

Gone, Kitty, Gone

"Enticing. . . . Distinctive characters, all of whom contribute to the
crime-solving in one way or another, drive the well-paced plot.
Cat cozy lovers will be enchanted." —*Publishers Weekly*

"Feline-focused, perhaps to the detriment of human characters—
and what's more cat than that?" —*Kirkus Reviews*

Feral Attraction

"This entry is a cat lover's delight." —*Publishers Weekly*

"Watkins' series is distinguished by the incorporation of facts
about cats relating to each case, making her writing educational
as much as it is entertaining." —*Kirkus Reviews*

"This delightfully cozy mystery is a perfect rainy day read.
So curl up with your cat and dig in!" —*Modern Cat*

The Bengal Identity

"A first-rate sequel to *The Persian Always Meows Twice*. It doesn't take
a cat lover to fall in love with this perfectly crafted cozy series."
—*Publishers Weekly* (starred review)

The Persian Always Meows Twice

"A fantastic thriller that is sure to make your pulse race,
The Persian Always Meows Twice is an awesome mystery
debut from Eileen Watkins." —*Modern Cat*

"The purrfect mystery to curl up with for a lovely cozy read,
preferably with a cup of tea, cuddly cat optional but recommended."
—**Leslie Meier**, author of *Irish Parade Murder*

"[A] delightful first novel and series opener." —*Publishers Weekly*

"*The Persian Always Meows Twice* is a delightful debut mystery. It's
smart, well-plotted, and features a cast of characters—both human
and feline—that I want to see more of. This book will be catnip
for cat lovers." —**Laurien Berenson**, author of *Game of Dog Bones*

Books by Eileen Watkins

THE PERSIAN ALWAYS MEOWS TWICE

THE BENGAL IDENTITY

FERAL ATTRACTION

GONE, KITTY, GONE

CLAW & DISORDER

NIGHT OF THE WERE-CAT

Published by Kensington Publishing Corp.

Night of the Were-Cat

EILEEN WATKINS

Kensington Publishing Corp.
www.kensingtonbooks.com

KENSINGTON BOOKS are published by

Kensington Publishing Corp.
119 West 40th Street
New York, NY 10018

ISBN: 978-1-4967-2302-4 (ebook)

ISBN: 978-1-4967-2299-7

First Kensington Trade Paperback Printing: March 2022

10 9 8 7 6 5 4 3 2 1

Printed in the United States of America

For Mia, my faithful lap cat, for keeping me company and keeping me inspired during the early days of the COVID-19 pandemic.
Don't know what I'd have done without you!

Acknowledgments

My beta readers, Chelle Martin and Nicki Montaperto, helped keep me on track and "psyched" throughout a difficult, early pandemic season; other members of Sisters in Crime Central Jersey provided much-appreciated "virtual" company and support.

Thanks as always to my agent, Evan Marshall, and my Kensington editor, John Scognamiglio.

I also need to acknowledge the photographs by Robert Sijka (Felis Gallery) of some astonishing male Maine Coon cats, which provided the inspiration for this story.

Chapter 1

Still in his walking harness, the exotic creature—the size of a small collie—sprang to the top of a three-foot-high, carpeted tower. He sat there immobile and surveyed us three humans with a lordly expression.

"Holy—!" I sputtered. At Cassie's Comfy Cats, I handle all types for a living, but this one actually made me back up a step. It was his stature, his bearing . . . and that face.

My assistant Sarah let out something between a gasp and a chuckle. "That is one scary-looking animal."

Nancy Whyte, the somewhat pudgy, middle-aged blond lady who held his leash, grinned broadly. "This ol' sweetums? He wouldn't hurt a flea. Well, maybe a flea . . . if he sat on it!"

I dared to pet the creature's thick, soft fur. His dark gray head sprouted two large, pointed ears; extra-long tufts at the ends gave them the look of devil horns. Though he was purring—I could feel that as well as hear it—there was something un-catlike about his whole demeanor. That long nose, that heavy chin. Those golden, hooded eyes. The wild ruff around his neck, charcoal shot with silver.

"I guess a lot of male Maine Coons have these heavy features," I told Sarah. "Nancy's other boy, King, has kind of a long face, too. But this guy . . . he hardly looks like a cat at all. He looks . . ."

My sixtyish assistant finished the thought. "He looks like a wolf!"

Sarah was right. But not just any regular, doglike wolf.

Like the Big Bad dude that ate Little Red Riding Hood's grandma!

Far from offended, Nancy beamed. "Doesn't he? When Angie was showing him, people often said that. In fact, one sore loser complained to a judge that he couldn't possibly be a purebred, and had to be part lynx. Of course, all Angie had to do was produce his papers. And as you can see, he's got purebred manners." She hugged the dignified beast, burying her nose in the thick fur of his neck. In response, he rubbed his head against her shoulder.

I laughed. "You're right, I can't see a wild hybrid acting like that."

"Handsome is as handsome does, I guess," Sarah said. As if gaining courage from Nancy's demonstration, she also stroked the animal's dense coat.

"So, is he yours now?" I asked our visitor.

She sighed. "It's a little up in the air. Poor Angie has been very ill lately from her diabetes, so she's gotten out of the breeding business and has sold off most of her cats. Quentin always was one of her favorites, though; she had him neutered and has been keeping him as a pet. But now, even lifting him into his carrier or taking him for walks has become too much for her to handle, so she asked if I could keep him for a while."

Nancy looked up to the challenge. She radiated cheerful energy today, with her short, messy golden curls—which I'm sure would have shown some gray without assistance—and her cherubic pink cheeks. To wrangle the big cat, she had dressed in loose jeans and a tunic sweater patterned with autumn leaves.

I knew that Nancy, a former breeder herself, still had two Maine Coons of her own. "How is he getting along with King and Jessie?"

"There was a little growling and hissing the first day or two. But all three of them grew up in households with other show cats, so they adjusted pretty quickly."

Meanwhile, Sarah regarded the sinister-looking feline with a twinkle in her dark eyes. "She named this one 'Quentin'?"

"That's right." Nancy exchanged a knowing glance with my assistant.

I sensed I was missing something. "Sounds kind of nerdy for such an impressive fellow."

"You'd probably have to be closer to our ages to get the joke," Sarah said. "You're not even thirty, too young to remember *Dark Shadows*."

"I've heard of it," I said. "An old TV series, right?"

Nancy explained. "It was kind of a spooky soap opera, about a wealthy old Maine family, the Collinses. They had *real* skeletons in their closets. One very handsome young man, Quentin Collins, happened to be a werewolf. Every full moon, he went on the rampage—so embarrassing for the rest of the family."

"I'm sure." I grinned, wondering if Nancy might even have suggested that name to her friend. Her own male cat's full handle was "Stephen King"—also appropriate, since the author resided and set many of his thrillers in Maine.

"Anyhow," Nancy said, "Angie hasn't been able to keep up with Quentin's grooming lately, so I thought I'd let you two shape him up before I bring him home with me."

"Glad to," Sarah said, though her tone remained wary. "As long as he's not half as demonic as he looks."

"He's not, but as you can see, he is a big boy," our customer cautioned us. "And strong!"

"Sarah and I should be able to manage him." My assistant was on the petite side, but I stood a little taller than average, and over the year and a half we'd been running this business, we both had built up some muscle. Good thing, because I guessed Quentin must tip the scales at a good twenty-five pounds. And that was at his trim, fighting weight!

I took his leash and led him back to our cat condo area, which featured one extra-large enclosure set somewhat apart from the dozen others. The Maine Coon came along as obediently as a show dog. He remained just as cooperative while I opened the door to the closet-sized condo, unfastened the Velcro straps of his harness, and ushered him inside.

"This should help him feel at home." Following us, Nancy handed me a round, red plush bed, already decorated with a few wisps of his dark gray fur, that probably had been marketed for a medium-sized canine. I slipped it onto the second shelf of the three-level enclosure, and His Majesty curled up in it contentedly enough.

"Looks like he'll get along here just fine," I observed, latching the door. "Sarah and I will make him all handsome in time for Halloween. Say, Nancy, you should enter him in the pet parade in the park. This guy wouldn't even need a costume!"

She looked surprised. "I hadn't even heard about that. Is it something new?"

"This is just the second year. It's a fundraiser for FOCA, the Friends of Chadwick Animals."

"They have a shelter downtown, right? I passed it on my way here."

Sarah disappeared briefly to the front sales area of our shop and returned with a flyer. Its border showed photos from the previous year's event, with pets of all sizes and species in crazy Halloween garb. The centered text proclaimed:

2ND ANNUAL CHADWICK HALLOWEEN
PET PARADE
SATURDAY, OCT. 24, 11 A.M.—2 P.M.
ENTRY FEE $10
PROCEEDS BENEFIT THE FRIENDS OF
CHADWICK ANIMALS,
A NO-KILL SHELTER

The flip side featured an entry form.

"Plenty of time to enter," Sarah told her, with a smile. "It's still a few weeks off."

"This does look like fun, and it's certainly a good cause," Nancy admitted. "Don't know if it would be good for Quentin, though. I'm just taking care of him for Angie, so I wouldn't want to stress him out or put him in any danger. From last year's pictures, it looks like most of the entries were dogs."

"That's true," I said. "I guess dogs tend to be better sports about getting dolled up in costumes and paraded around in public. Of course, Quentin does walk on a leash . . ."

She laughed darkly. "But if he got agitated—or God forbid, a dog actually went after him—I would not want to be responsible for the outcome."

Sarah grimaced. "I can see why. Though the dog might get the worst of it!"

"You're completely right, of course," I told Nancy, feeling a bit chastened. "It was just a funny idea."

The three of us returned through the playroom—where our boarders could take their exercise on an array of multi-level trees and wall shelves—to the front of the shop. At my hot-pink-and-black sales counter, I wrote up an estimate for

Nancy that included the grooming job and a couple of days' board, until she could pick Quentin up again. She left us some of his usual food for the stay, and his carrier. It also could have accommodated a sheltie-sized dog and could be pulled on wheels.

We parked it close to Quentin's condo and gave him some food and water to help him settle in. Sarah and I sent Nancy off with good wishes for her friend's health to improve.

Sensing it was nearly time to close up, I stole a look at the playroom wall clock, which had pawprints instead of numbers. Sarah noticed my glance and guessed, "Tuesday night . . . Got a movie date with Mark?"

I smiled at her perceptiveness. "Yeah, we'll be hitting the Paragon later. It's *The Haunting* this time." Though Chadwick's restored movie theater also needed to show a few first-run films just to stay in business, it screened oldies on Tuesday and Thursday nights. My veterinarian boyfriend and I, never having seen most of the vintage films, tried to get to at least one a month.

"Ah! I caught that one on TV, many years ago," Sarah said.

"I only read the book, *The Haunting of Hill House*, in college," I told her. "I really liked that."

"You probably would, having studied psychology. The main character is something else!"

"She is. You start out liking her and feeling sorry for her, but as the book goes on—"

"Julie Harris does a wonderful job in that role, you'll see." Sarah shed her grooming apron for the day and tossed it in our laundry hamper. "Sounds like the Paragon's already getting into the Halloween spirit."

"In a big way. The owner, Avery Lathrop, seems to like themes. He ran corny beach movies from the sixties this summer, and everything from *Miracle on 34th Street* to *A Christmas Story* last December."

"I've heard other people mention Lathrop. He revamped The Firehouse restaurant, too, didn't he? I gather that he's older, at least my age, and has big bucks. Have you ever met him?"

"Yes and no," I admitted. "He dressed up as Santa to greet people in the lobby before one of the Christmas shows, but all I could tell for sure is that he's rather tall. I'm willing to bet, though, that he doesn't have rosy cheeks and a long white beard the rest of the year. Probably not a big belly, either."

"If he's that into costumes, could be interesting to see what he does for Halloween."

"It should. For that whole week, the Paragon is showing a marathon of werewolf movies."

My assistant feigned a shudder. "*The Haunting* is more my style. Very spooky, but no real gore or violence." She shrugged into her dark green suede car coat, shouldered her purse, and started for the door. "Anyway, you and Mark have a great time."

"I'm sure we will. See you tomorrow."

I locked the front door behind Sarah and set the alarm system, which I'd installed about six months after I opened the shop, following an attempted break-in.

Now that the sun was setting, the shop had grown cool. I turned up the thermostat, something I seemed to be doing more often these days. In response, I heard a dull bang, followed by rattling noises, from the cellar. *Just the thing to set the Halloween mood!*

I did not envision a bloody ghost dragging chains across my basement, but the reality could be almost as worrisome. My furnace had come with this eighty-year-old, two-story

building. Nick Janos, the handyman who'd helped me reno-
vate the place, had warned in the past that the unit might be
on its last legs. No doubt even to repair it would cost me a
couple thou, and to replace it much more.

While my business brought in enough to cover my
monthly expenses—most months—it was hard to maintain a
cushion to cover emergencies. Summer tended to be a flush
time, because of all the people traveling on vacation and
boarding their cats. By late fall, unfortunately, I could expect
less money coming in.

I gathered up the day's dirty towels from the grooming
studio and carried the armful down to the basement. The ag-
ing washer and dryer also came with the place, and keeping
them on the lower level turned out to be fairly convenient; at
least as much of my laundry came from my business as from
my household needs. While down there, I opened the back
of the noisy furnace and stole a quick peek. But the criss-
crossing maze of rusty wires, cables, ducts, and pumps soon
daunted me. I hadn't the first idea of how to solve the unit's
problems, and any efforts of mine would probably only make
them worse. I'd just have to live with the racket until I got up
my nerve to call a professional.

Back upstairs in the shop, I tried to ignore the growing
chill while I made one more round to check on all my boarders. Of the baker's dozen of cat condos, nine were currently
occupied, including the supersized "quarantine" enclosure
that now held Quentin. My lighthearted conversation with
Sarah about horror movies inspired me to take another look
at the massive Maine Coon.

Sprawled contentedly in his plush scarlet bed, he blinked
up at me with those calm but still strangely hypnotic eyes.
One could easily believe he was privy to the kind of dark
secrets Man Was Not Meant to Know.

"Sarah was right," I told him, at the risk of getting on his bad side. "You don't exactly look like a *wolf*. What you look like is a *werewolf!*"

I'm not the superstitious type, so it never occurred to me that it might be bad luck to welcome such a creature into my shop, just a couple of weeks before Halloween.

Chapter 2

Before the movie, Mark and I just had time for a quick dinner at our favorite pizza place, Slice of Heaven. With a cool, minimalist décor—white subway tile on the walls, black pendant lights, glossy red tabletops, and a central brick pizza oven—the place usually attracted a good crowd, even on a weeknight. At the same time, the takeout counter did a brisk business, too.

For October, they were offering two Halloween pizzas. The Jack-o'-Lantern featured triangles of pepper for the eyes, nose, and teeth, while the Spiderweb was drizzled with mozzarella cheese and garnished with a few black-olive spiders. Our jobs have inoculated both Mark and me against most kinds of squeamishness, so we happily ordered the Arachnopizza. Neither of us drank alcohol on weeknights, at least not when we were hoping to stay awake, so he ordered a cola, and I just went for water.

Tonight Mark wore a plum-colored pullover that electrified his deep blue eyes. He grumbled about not having had time lately for a haircut, but I found his dark locks even sexier when a little overgrown. We'd been together more than two years, and sometimes I still could hardly believe my luck, to have paired up with Chadwick's tall, dark, and handsome veterinarian. Not that I was so bad, myself, but when Mark walked into a crowded place like this, a couple of female heads usually swiveled to track him across the room. He didn't try for this attention, and I honestly don't think he even noticed it. But I did, and it tended to keep me on my toes!

While we divided up our spooky pizza, he asked about Mango, one of my own three cats. Mark had pretty much saved the orange tabby's life a month earlier by removing a tricky thyroid tumor.

"He's doing great," I said. "Seems fully recovered and has started putting the pounds back on."

"Well, he needed to," Mark reminded me. "Poor little guy was burning them off too fast, before. We'll keep an eye on him, but he should still have a lot of good years ahead."

We also made plans to attend an opening at the town's art gallery, Eye of the Beholder, the following week. Keith Garrett, longtime significant other of my friend Dawn Tischler, had built himself a decent career over the years as a freelance commercial illustrator. But for a while now he'd also been trying his hand at acrylic paintings on canvas, in an updated Pop Art style, and had amassed a nice body of work. The gallery had accepted some of his pieces to be included in a three-person exhibit, running through mid-November.

"I guess you've never seen the big portrait he did of Dawn that's hanging in her dining room," I told Mark. "It's outstanding! I'm really looking forward to seeing more of his art."

"I am, too." He took the time to devour another olive spider before he continued. "About all I've seen of his commercial work is the cat cartoon he did for the side of your van, and a couple of other ads he did for people around town.

But I'm sure there's a difference between creating a design for some corporate client and doing his own thing. Keith's a great guy, so it's nice to see him get a break like this."

"Well, it's not SoHo, but Nidra does run a nice gallery. She's got adventurous taste, too, which is a shot in the arm for this town."

I took a special interest because I'd minored in art in college while majoring in psychology. (This very practical combination is probably why I ended up grooming and boarding cats for a living—not that I have any complaints.) I'd even gotten pretty good at creating my own work on the computer, and had produced a few rather surrealistic compositions. They'd been exhibited in one student show, but never anywhere else, which was as it should be.

Mark and I made short work of the pizza, paid our bill promptly, and set off for the movie theater. He left his cobalt blue RAV4 on the street near the restaurant, and we walked the three blocks to the Paragon, savoring the light October breeze.

The theater dated back to 1939, but by the 1990s, it had ceased showing movies. It served various other purposes since then, until Avery Lathrop decided a couple of years ago to revive it in period style.

Lathrop didn't reside in Chadwick per se, from what I'd heard, but had a large Victorian home on the outskirts. He made his fortune as a developer, with major projects around the U.S. But in his later years, he had grown tired of constructing bland, new communities, and began to invest his millions in rehabbing picturesque, older structures for updated purposes.

The man either had wonderful taste himself or hired excellent designers. As Sarah had mentioned, Lathrop turned the town's original brick firehouse, too small to accommodate modern hook-and-ladder trucks, into a very cool, pub-type restaurant. It tended toward a spicy menu and even hosted live music a few times a week.

The Paragon was another retro masterpiece. Lathrop had kept the original façade of brown brick with art deco limestone trim, and commissioned a new vertical neon sign that spelled out the theater's name in green letters outlined with gold. That color scheme continued in the dark green front doors with their brass handles, and the diamond-patterned carpeting that ran through the lobby and down the aisles.

Also indoors, fabric in a green-and-gold vine motif climbed the walls between vertical rows of brass deco sconces. The seats were spruce-green velour and, while comfy, did not recline as far as in most contemporary theaters—Lathrop drew the line at too much modernity. He also didn't believe in requiring his audiences to reserve particular spots in advance online, so seating was first-come, first-served. Mark and I had learned to arrive a little early if we didn't want to be stuck too close to the screen.

So soon after dinner, neither of us had room for popcorn, but we did opt for some of the classic candies sold at the concession stand. That night, Mark went for the licorice whips and I for a box of Junior Mints. As we found seats, the place was already filling up more than usual, and in addition to the over-fifty set who usually turned up on oldies nights, I spotted a fair number of families with kids. *The Haunting*, from 1963, was black-and-white, which might not impress today's preteens. But it also was rated G by modern standards, and aside from Disney flicks, how many family-friendly movies could parents find these days?

Another perk of oldies nights that Mark and I appreciated— we had to sit through very few on-screen promotions before the movie actually got underway.

Sarah's verbal review had captured the essence of *The Haunting*. It was more psychological thriller than bloody "horror," and a tour de force for the actress playing the lead. The special effects were minimal by modern standards, but still effective.

I could tell Mark enjoyed it, too, and on our way back to the lobby, I asked him, "So, what do you think? Was Hill House really haunted, or was Eleanor insane?"

He laughed. "Can I pick both? I might have blamed it all on Eleanor, if the others hadn't seen and heard things, too."

"Ah, but don't forget, when she was just a kid, she caused poltergeist activity at her family's house. So she might have been responsible for all of the phenomena!" I pointed out. "In the book, it's more ambiguous. I think the movie nudges you more toward blaming the house and its ghosts."

"Seems scarier that way, I guess."

In the lobby, we disposed of our empty candy boxes and greeted Dave Sheply, one of the theater's frequent ushers on oldies nights. We knew from past conversations with Dave that he studied communications at the County College of Morris and belonged to its Student Film Association. He worked at the theater a few evenings a week for extra cash, and his field of study made him an entertaining source of background information on the movies.

Tonight his lean frame was bolstered somewhat by a well-tailored vest in a deep green that went with the theater's décor. He wore his short blond hair combed forward and stylishly rumpled, but the collar of his long-sleeved white shirt was anchored by a formal black bow tie that matched his trousers. He also sported a big grin, probably because *The Haunting* had drawn such a large and age-diverse turnout.

When Mark and I enthused about the movie and praised

the acting, Dave noted that the camerawork also contributed a lot to the film's ambience. "For instance, you often see the characters, especially Eleanor, from above," he said. "As if something overhead, or maybe even the house itself, is looking down at them."

Mark recalled this with a nod. "What I liked best was the scene with the door."

"That's the scariest part in the book, too," I told him, then turned back to Dave. "Was it a special effect?"

The usher chuckled. "Not the kind you probably mean. Even though the door looks like it's carved of solid oak, they made it out of a material with some 'give.' Then they just had someone ram it from the other side with a piece of wood."

While Mark looked impressed by this, I asked Dave, "What's coming up next?"

"This Thursday we have *Rosemary's Baby*, and next Tuesday it's *Dracula Has Risen from the Grave*. Of course, the whole week before Halloween we'll have the werewolf marathon."

"Why did you pick werewolves?" asked Mark. "Or I should say, why did Mr. Lathrop?"

Dave shrugged. "He figures vampires have had their day in the sun, so to speak, and thought the shapeshifters should have a turn." He led us a little farther down the lobby wall and pointed to a montage of lurid posters with titles like *I Was a Teenage Werewolf*, *An American Werewolf in London*, *Wolfen*, and *The Howling*. "Like with our regular movies, the newer and more 'adult' films will be up Monday, Wednesday, Friday, and Saturday, and the older and tamer ones on Tuesday and Thursday. But we'll have two a day, that week, afternoons and evenings."

His use of the word *tamer* made me smile, and I told him, "I have a cat in my shop right now who could have posed for one of these posters." I explained to him and Mark about Quentin. "I told the woman who's boarding him that she should enter him in the Halloween pet parade, but she doesn't want to chance it with all of the dogs."

Dave played along. "Hey, maybe we could use him for a mascot. Lathrop's been trying to think of ways to drum up more publicity for the marathon. He wants to lure in some new people, along with our regulars. He actually wondered about coordinating with the pet parade somehow, but couldn't think of a logical way to do that."

We stood just inside the front entrance now. Through the center glass panels of its multiple doors, we saw a police cruiser speed down the town's main street, lights whirling. Dave muttered dryly about "some excitement somewhere," and we all shrugged it off.

Mark went back to brainstorming with him. "Maybe you could have a werewolf look-alike contest for pets?"

The young usher cocked his head. "That could be fun . . . but we'd probably just get a bunch of dressed-up German shepherds and huskies."

"Don't allow any dogs!" I proposed. "After all, they've got the park contest. Say it's for non-canines only."

"And you could judge from photos," Mark added, "so the animals wouldn't have to parade around or be stressed out. That way, people can enter everything from cats to ferrets to monkeys. Post the photos in your lobby, and let your patrons vote."

I gave him the side-eye. "Monkeys and ferrets that look like werewolves?"

"Hey, you should see some of the crazy critters that pass through our clinic! We have one client with a pretty ferocious African grey parrot."

Dave's face, meanwhile, lit up brighter than one of the art

deco sconces. "I like that idea! It's a little wacky, but just the kind of thing Lathrop might go for. I'll suggest it to him."

"If he thinks it's ridiculous, we don't want you getting fired," I cautioned. "Feel free to blame us."

He laughed. "You signed our membership list, right? So we know where to find you!"

Now an ambulance streaked down the main drag in the same direction as the police cruiser, howling past the front doors. This time, we all wondered aloud what was up, and Mark and I almost hesitated to leave the safety of the theater.

When his cell phone rang, he pulled it out and looked at the screen. "Maggie, at this hour? That can't be good." He stepped aside to take the call from Dr. Margaret Reed, his partner at the Chadwick Veterinary Clinic.

In the meantime, another frequent patron buttonholed Dave to discuss the evening's movie.

I went back to scanning the montage of werewolf-movie posters. They interpreted the legendary monster in a variety of ways, from the Lon Chaney type with a flat, manlike face, to the more animalistic variety with long snout, daggerlike fangs, and lolling tongue. I realized, with some disappointment, that none of these really looked like the purebred cat boarding at my shop. Yet both Sarah and I had made the comparison instantly when we'd met Quentin, and from what Nancy said, other people had, too. We must have seen his type of lycanthropic creature someplace!

From idle curiosity, and because I'd never seen *Dark Shadows*, I used my phone to search for *Quentin Collins . . . werewolf*. A few pictures popped up immediately, but still no match for Nancy's cat. Just a variation on the Lon Chaney makeup—fangs jutting up from an undershot lower jaw, but the same humanoid visage. Pointy ears, but still on the sides of his head, like a man's.

A strong hand dropped onto my shoulder, and I spun around. Mark's face had turned grim, even pale. "I need to get over to the clinic. We had some trouble tonight."

"Oh, darn. Did one of the animals . . ."

"No, there was a robbery."

That confused me for a second. The Chadwick Veterinary Clinic had a modern security system, plus a vet tech always stayed there overnight, in case a sick animal might need attention. "But wasn't Sam . . ."

"The thief forced his way in. Sounds like Sam got hurt." Mark started for the door, and I kept pace with him.

As we hurried the three blocks back to Mark's RAV4, I also remembered that the clinic usually didn't keep any cash around after closing. "They were after money?"

He shook his head, still with a tight, pained expression. "Drugs."

Both of the vehicles we'd heard speed by—a Chadwick police car and an ambulance from St. Catherine's Medical Center—stood in the parking lot when we pulled up at the veterinary clinic. The rambling white colonial, formerly a private home, looked too sedate to be the setting for any type of violent crime. But Sam Urbano, a fortyish but sturdy-looking tech who often worked nights, reclined on a gurney while a female EMT checked his vitals. I took it as a good sign that the head of the wheeled cot was raised so Sam could sit up a little, and he seemed able to answer the questions of a young, blond cop whom I recognized as Officer Steve Jacoby.

Near the clinic's side door, Lieutenant Wayne Bassey stood talking with Dr. Reed. I hadn't seen him lately but remembered Bassey well—when I'd first moved to Chadwick, and before his recent promotion, the heavyset older cop with the military brush haircut had helped investigate a break-in at my shop.

Jeans and sneakers peeked from below the hem of Maggie's long, khaki trench coat. No doubt she'd been relaxing at home, with her husband, when she'd gotten a call.

Mark hesitated, as if he wanted to talk to Sam but didn't feel he could interrupt Jacoby. Meanwhile, Bassey wound up his conversation with Maggie. She spotted Mark and me and walked over to join us. Her curly brown hair, graying at the temples, frizzed back from her high forehead, and her large eyes behind their dark-rimmed glasses looked stunned.

I laid a hand on her arm, and Mark asked quietly, "What happened?"

She clutched the front of her coat together more tightly against the evening's chill. "From what Sam says, he got here about an hour ago to start his shift, parked in the lot, and didn't see anybody else around. But as soon as he punched the door's keypad, someone stuck a gun in his back—at least, that's what he thought it felt like. The guy told him to keep quiet, do as he was told, and he wouldn't get hurt. He walked Sam back into the clinic that way."

"Oh my God." So far, despite my sideline of sleuthing and a couple of close calls, I've never actually felt the muzzle of a gun between my shoulder blades. I figured Sam must have been terrified.

Maggie reached beneath her glasses to knuckle away a tear. "He says the guy marched him straight down the first-floor hallway to the anesthesia storage closet. That door isn't even marked!" She glanced at Mark for corroboration. "We have several other storage areas that *are* labeled, for prescription food and other kinds of medications and supplies. But Sam said this guy seemed to know right where to go. He made Sam unlock the door, and of course, he was afraid for his life!"

Mark cursed the thief under his breath.

"We keep the narcotics in a special steel cabinet, bolted to the wall," Maggie explained, for my benefit. "You need two keys to open it. Sam explained this and claimed he didn't have access to the cabinet, but the robber didn't believe it and threatened again to shoot him." She sighed deeply. "Luckily for Sam, I guess, he did know where we kept spare keys. Finally he got them and unlocked the cabinet. As soon as he'd done that, the thief put him in some kind of a chokehold until Sam passed out."

"Yow!" I glanced toward the strongly built man on the gurney. "Is he going to be okay?"

"The EMTs think so, thank God. He said he woke up in the same storage room, in total darkness, but managed to find the light switch. He saw the steel cabinet had been cleaned out. He ran outside in time to hear a motorcycle pulling away down the street, but he can't be sure it belonged to the thief. He dialed nine-one-one, and the police called me."

A pleasant-looking, balding man in a hooded jacket sidled up to Maggie, and she introduced him as her husband, Paul Reed. He wrapped an arm around her and said, "You must be cold. Do you have to stay here much longer?"

"I really don't know." She sounded worried. "Sam is in good hands, I guess. But I should stay at least until the police have finished, and make sure the place is locked up."

"I can do that," Mark volunteered. "Go home, Maggie. I can see you're upset."

She shook her head, tears welling again. "I've heard of things like this happening in urban clinics, but I never expected it out here. Guess no place is really safe anymore, is it?"

Lt. Bassey gave Dr. Reed and her husband the okay to

leave the scene. Officer Jacoby had finished questioning Sam, so the EMTs packed him into the ambulance and cruised off, without sirens, to the Medical Center.

Mark told Bassey he was going to drive me home, and then would come back to answer any more questions the police might have and close up the clinic.

Overhearing, I protested, "It's only a few blocks, Mark. I can walk."

"In the dark, with a violent mugger on the loose? Forget it!"

"Then I'll wait with you . . ."

"No point, Cassie, really. I could be here a while—there's going to be stuff to sort out. On the one hand, this place is a crime scene now, so the cops will be looking for evidence. On the other hand, we've got a bunch of sick animals in there that don't need to be stressed out anymore. And while we might be able to reschedule some of tomorrow's appointments, we won't be able to close completely."

I saw Mark's point and accepted the ride. On our way back to my place, I added, "Poor Sam! At least he wasn't shot, but I hope he doesn't have any aftereffects from that chokehold."

"I hope not, too." Mark fell quiet for a couple of minutes.

"Something's bothering you," I guessed.

"What Maggie said, about the thief steering Sam directly to the anesthesia storage room. We purposely leave that area unmarked, so only employees know it's for narcotics. A total stranger probably would have tried at least a couple of the other doors marked for 'storage' before getting around to that one."

I could see what Mark found troubling about this. Could the robber have had an accomplice . . . someone on the inside?

Chapter 3

Mark had little more to say about the incident during the four-block drive back to my shop. He walked me to my front door and waited while I unlocked it and checked that my shop alarm had not been triggered. Before he left, I kissed him good night and wished him luck in straightening things out.

I knew Mark and Maggie both took pride in their clinic's excellent reputation. They seemed scrupulous about their procedures and about the people they hired, even to staff the front desk. Mark hadn't mentioned taking on anyone new lately, or anyone on the staff he didn't completely trust.

But who can tell? Maybe that's why he was so quiet just before he let me off tonight. Mark does tend to clam up, not wanting to "burden" me, when he's really worried.

At least I found nothing awry when I entered my shop around eleven. These days, I habitually set the alarm system before I went out in the evening, and nothing had triggered it. Feeling both jittery and fatigued after the stress of the clinic robbery, I quickly checked on the boarders. All seemed to be sleeping, though Quentin sprang to his feet and chirruped at my approach. Probably he was used to having his freedom at night and maybe hoped for a late play session. I poured him just a little more dry food instead.

"Sorry, pal, I'm beat," I said. "Sarah and I will take you into the playroom tomorrow and wear you out, I promise."

A rattle from the basement made my heart jump, until I remembered my geriatric furnace. *With a mugger/thief running around town, I'm going to have even less patience for weird noises in the night!*

Upstairs in my apartment, I also gave a small bedtime snack to my own three cats: black Cole, calico Matisse, and orange tabby Mango. I was delighted to see that, although Mango scarfed up his food as enthusiastically as the others, he didn't immediately whine for more. During the summer, his weight loss despite a voracious appetite had moved me to take him to the clinic, and Mark had found the thyroid tumor. I'd tried to manage Mango's hyperthyroidism for a while with medication, but he had fought the pills so strenuously that in the end I'd opted for surgery.

Mark had removed the benign tumor, and after a few weeks of recovery, the tabby now seemed as good as new. Because he was my eldest cat, though, I knew the thyroid problem could recur, so I kept a close eye on him.

I finally hit the hay around midnight, almost too tired to let worry disturb my sleep. I knew Sarah would arrive at nine sharp the next morning, ready for work. Depending on whether the clinic robbery made the online news, she still might know nothing about it.

I had to assume she didn't, because when my African American assistant showed up that morning, she had a big smile on her face and a lilt to her voice. "How are you today, Cassie? And how are our furry charges?"

"We're all fine," I assured her. "You sure seem cheerful! Something good happen?"

"I don't know if you'd call it *good* so much as amusing."
Sarah hung up her coat in the shop's rear closet but kept her
purse handy. "You remember my son Jay."

It wasn't really a question, but I assured her, "Of course,
how could I forget him?" In his early thirties, Jay Wilcox
had followed in his mother's footsteps by teaching high school
math. He'd also helped me staff a table promoting my business
at the Chadwick Day street fair, my first summer in town,
when Sarah had been hobbled by a sprained ankle.

"Well, I was talking with him last night, about this new
cat we got in the clinic, and he reminded me about something. So, I went digging through one of our family scrap-
books. Remember those? The kind people kept when they
still took actual photographs, and had them developed on
glossy paper?"

"Gee, I don't know." I pretended to think hard. "I did
read about that once, maybe in a history book . . ."

With a mock scowl, Sarah peered at me over her wire-
rimmed glasses. "C'mon. You're young, but not that young!
Anyhow, I found this."

She reached into her satchel-sized purse and handed me
a color photo of Quentin. Except he wore an ugly snarl that
bared long fangs, and lunged toward the camera with furry
gray hands that sprouted nasty claws. He also wore jeans and a
red-and-gold baseball jacket, and had the body of a small boy.

"Ooookay . . ." I said.

"Believe it or not," continued Sarah, "that's Jay on Halloween, 1984. You remember Michael Jackson's *Thriller* video?
His werewolf costume was still really big that year, and Jay
insisted on wearing something like it to trick-or-treat. So,
my husband and I found vampire fangs, paws, and a wig that
had the pointed ears. Then I just copied a photo to do the
makeup."

"Great job." I marveled over the little boy's transformation. Though I'd been even younger than Jay when the *Thriller* video came out, I'd seen it since then. It certainly could have made enough of an impression that I remembered it when I'd first set eyes on Quentin. Of course, on the body of a grade schooler, the monstrous face and paws seemed cute and funny.

"He really wanted the authentic, full-head mask," Sarah added, scrolling on her phone. "It was expensive, and would have been too big for Jay at that age, anyhow. You can still buy them online, though, see?"

She passed me her cell. The small screen showed a truly scary, snarling animal face framed by a lush, flowing, gray-and-black mane. With its tall, pointed ears, yellow eyes with slit pupils, short muzzle, and bushy white whiskers, this creature looked more like a cat/dog mashup than any of the others I'd seen.

"Wow, that *is* Quentin, isn't it?" I said. "I mean, thank God it isn't him, but it's sure his evil twin!"

Sarah laughed, taking the phone back. "Silly of me, I know. But once I remembered that photo of Jay, I just had to find it and show you."

"Actually, it's not so silly." I told her about my conversation at the theater the night before with Dave-the-usher. "If Lathrop decides to hold a photo contest for pets that look like werewolves, Nancy definitely should enter Quentin. They don't have to appear in person unless they win, so she won't even have to worry about him being hassled by a lot of other animals."

"That would be ideal, wouldn't it?" agreed Sarah.

She checked the day's schedule to see which of our boarders would be turned out first, so I didn't immediately have a chance to tell her what had taken place at the clinic the night before. Meanwhile, Mark called me on my cell, which got my attention. He didn't usually do that during the workday.

I stepped into our grooming studio to take the call and kept my voice low as I asked him, "How is everyone doing over there? Are you still able to see patients today?"

"We canceled some appointments." He sounded rueful. "Anything routine that could wait. We're just dealing with the most urgent cases. And we had to get some emergency supplies sent over from a clinic in Morristown. Not easy to operate on patients with no anesthesia."

"I'm sure it isn't! Were you able to figure out what all was taken from the storage safe?"

"Oh, yeah. We keep a strict inventory, of those drugs in particular. The thief got morphine, diazepam—which is basically Valium—phenobarbital, and ketamine. All sedatives or painkillers of one kind or another."

I shivered at the thought that some drug dealer had singled out Mark's clinic and made off with such dangerous substances. "Can those be sold on the street? I mean, if they are, won't the cops find out?"

"I don't think we'll see dope peddlers standing on street corners in downtown Chadwick, hawking vials of morphine." I heard the irony in his voice. "Most likely, this ring has connections in more urban areas. Though they'd probably find takers for the Valium around here. And maybe for the ketamine, too—that sometimes shows up at dance clubs and parties, even in the suburbs."

"Well, I'm sure Chadwick's finest will be on the lookout, anyway. Be nice if they also found the guy who choked Sam. How is he?"

"He says he feels better, but we gave him a couple of days off. We're leaving two staffers on night duty for the rest of this week, and the PD will have a patrol car sitting at the end of our block. We're going to beef up our electronic security, too. Though I really doubt there'll be any more robbery attempts here, at least not soon. They'll know that we haven't even had a chance to restock, and that we'll be on our guard after this."

"Sounds like everybody there is under a lot of stress. I'm so sorry."

"Yeah, it's getting messy now." He lowered his voice, as if to keep any of his co-workers from overhearing. "The cops seriously suspect that someone here at the clinic abetted the robbery. From what Sam told them, the guy seemed to know just when Sam's shift started and that he'd be on duty alone. Of course, that's something anyone could have learned by just watching the building for a couple of nights in a row. The fact that the robber also knew which storage room had the anesthetics, though, is really suspicious."

"But you and Maggie vet your hires—no pun intended—very carefully, don't you? I'm sure you screen for any sort of criminal background."

"We do, but I guess the staffer himself, or herself, wouldn't necessarily have any record. They might have been manipulated by a friend or a family member. Heck, they might just have bragged to someone, in a casual conversation, about how secure our storage was, and that we kept those drugs behind an unmarked door. The cops have questioned all of us about whether we talked to anyone about stuff like that. So far, though, no one's admitted to it."

It was true, I thought, that someone could have leaked the information innocently. Maybe at a party or a bar after one drink too many. That made me feel just a little better. I didn't like the Chadwick PD suspecting employees at Mark's clinic of being complicit in the robbery. Not to mention either Mark or Maggie!

On the other hand, the clinic's vet techs and receptionists

came and went, some even being part-time. A lot easier to suspect one of them of "loose lips."

So far, it looked as if Detective Angela Bonelli hadn't gotten involved in this case, which surprised me. She usually dealt not only with suspicious deaths, but with any other serious crimes in Chadwick. Maybe the chief was trying to give Lt. Bassey more authority. Still, I'd been surprised not to see Bonelli's trim, soberly tailored figure at the scene the night of the robbery. Certainly she could vouch for Mark's character, and probably Maggie's, as well.

"Anyway," Mark went on, "I just wanted to give you a heads-up that my hours here might be unpredictable for a while."

"Sure, I understand." I remembered the only firm date he and I had made together for the coming week. "Do you think you'll still be able to get to that art gallery opening on Thursday night? I wouldn't even mention it, but it is Keith's big debut as a serious artist . . ." When Mark hesitated, I reminded him, "It's six to seven-thirty. Think you'll be free by then?"

He sighed, and I knew it wasn't from lack of desire to support Keith. "I hope so, but I can't promise anything. Sorry to say, you might end up going by yourself."

"Oh well, if I do, I'll still have Dawn and Keith to talk to. And Nidra, of course, unless she's too busy." Exotic, sophisticated Nidra Balin owned and operated the gallery, in business for almost two years now.

"That's right. And if I do miss the opening, I'll pop into the gallery and check out the show another time." Someone in the background called Mark's name, and he groaned. "See what I mean? We're all hopping today! Anyhow, talk to you later, babe."

I rejoined Sarah in the shop's playroom, where she had turned out a lovely Burmese boarder. The chocolate-brown cat's formal name was Godiva, but most often she answered to "Diva." With expert technique, Sarah flipped a feather "bird" at the end of a long fishing pole to give the cat some exercise.

I knew my assistant must have noticed my secretiveness over the phone call. I also knew she wouldn't ask me about it, respecting my privacy. But the story would soon be all over town anyway, so I explained about the robbery of the clinic.

Sarah paused in her play session with Diva and looked suitably horrified. "Oh, no! Never had that kind of trouble before, did they? Is the vet tech okay?"

"He's resting up at home today, but yes, he should be." For the time being, I didn't mention that everyone at the clinic was under suspicion, or why.

She shook her head of short, salt-and-pepper curls. "I've heard of that kind of thing at city clinics—veterinary and human—but you like to think it wouldn't happen in a town like Chadwick."

"I guess no place is immune," I philosophized.

"What did our friend Angela Bonelli have to say about it?"

"She wasn't there last night. Maybe she was busy elsewhere, or maybe Chief Hardy likes to save her for murder cases and other serious stuff."

Sarah sniffed. "Drug theft seems pretty serious to me. If they don't solve it right away, bet you anything she gets involved."

I smiled. Very likely—the toughest cases always ended up on Bonelli's desk.

Soon after, Sarah returned Diva to her condo. Because Quentin had begun strumming the wire-mesh door of his enclosure, we turned him out next. I picked him up and, even with his full cooperation, staggered my way into the playroom.

Seeing this, Sarah laughed. "That is one big cat!"

"He sure is." I set him down in the recreational space. "But it didn't seem worth putting a harness and leash on him, just to walk ten feet."

We both played with Quentin for a few minutes until we got the hang of which toys he preferred. He liked chasing balls more than most of our boarders, and even skittered them back in our direction to be thrown again, his version of fetch. We guided him onto the sturdiest cat trees and wall shelves, and away from any that might wobble under his bulk.

My front door sounded, and a well-known voice called out, "Hello? Any humans in the house?"

Sarah also recognized Dawn's greeting and smiled at me. "You go. I can entertain this guy by myself. Though when it's time for him to go back in the condo . . ."

"Don't worry," I promised her, "I'll gladly do the heavy lifting."

Chapter 4

Tall, striking Dawn Tischler waited beyond the sales counter, dressed in yet another traffic-stopping outfit.

Much of the time, she favored long, hippie skirts and dresses, some authentically from the 1970s and picked up at vintage shops. Today, though, she wore a more modern combo of a sage-green, tunic-length sweater over leggings. But Dawn always had to give any ensemble a different twist, so her sweater had an artistically unraveled hem, and the leggings were a paisley print of assorted autumn colors.

"My, don't you look . . . seasonal!" I commented.

She grinned and tossed back her wavy, auburn mane. "Thanks. Keith hates these pants, though I don't know why. He's got his own collection of Hawaiian flowered shirts!"

"Let's just say, you're the only person I know who could carry them off so well," I told her. "You don't usually drop by in the middle of the day. I guess your helper is working out okay?"

"Seems to be, so I thought I'd trust her to fly solo for an hour or so."

I'd met Dawn's new assistant, Tanith, just once so far. If

Dawn embodied the Summer of Love, Tanith suggested the Twilight of Goth. On the day I'd visited, she'd been decked out in black activewear, including a low-backed leotard; it revealed a colorful dragon tattoo spreading its wings between her shoulder blades. Not *too* many piercings, just three studs in each ear and one in her left nostril. Her ragged hair looked too black for her pale complexion, though, and her eye makeup a little too ghoulish for the ambience of Dawn's health-food store.

I needled my friend, "Have you suggested that maybe your customers would feel more at ease with someone who didn't look ready to drink their blood?"

"Hey, far be it from me to criticize anyone else's fashion choices. Besides, Tanith actually had a fine résumé for the job. Not only has she worked as a stock clerk and cashier at a couple of convenience stores, but also as both a nurse's aide and an attendant at a fitness center."

Now that I thought of it, despite her pallid makeup and spooky style, the young woman had looked rather toned and healthy. "Well, that's good."

"And even though I didn't say a thing to her, after the first few days she did ditch the skull earring and purple eye shadow. She's even covering up Clyde more often, and he's her pride and joy."

"Clyde?"

My friend pointed to her own back. "The dragon."

"Ah. Yes, keeping him under wraps should help."

Dawn perched on one of the two stools in front of my sales counter, and meanwhile glanced over her shoulder toward the rear of the shop. "Do you hear, like, a rattling sound?"

I explained about the issues with my furnace. "It came with this place, and I know it's really old."

"You should junk it and get the high-efficiency kind,"

she suggested. "That's what I did. I wanted something more environmentally friendly, but my heating and AC bills went way down, too."

"That's an idea." Lower monthly bills did sound attractive, though I worried about the up-front cost of a whole new unit. "First I'm going to call Nick. With so much going on, I haven't found the time yet."

"I'm sure you haven't." She lowered her voice. "I heard about the clinic break-in. Poor Mark and Maggie—that's so awful! Was the guy on night duty hurt?"

"Not too seriously; mostly shaken up. I guess he'd come to think he was pretty safe from anything like that happening in Chadwick."

"As a business owner, I like to think so, too. Guess you can never be sure. I know you've had a couple of incidents at your place, Cassie, but those were different. They involved people who knew you personally, and were after something specific."

"The guy who mugged Sam was after something very specific—the anesthesia drugs."

"Is that what he took? The newspaper didn't say what kind, but those would probably be the only drugs worth stealing, wouldn't they?"

I slid onto my usual seat behind the counter, across from Dawn. "It's thrown the clinic into a tailspin. The vets are limited in the procedures they can do until they re-stock. But even worse, the thief seems to have had some kind of inside knowledge about the setup of the place. So, there's a cloud of suspicion over everybody who works there, even Mark and Maggie."

"Oh, c'mon. Why would they do anything to sabotage their own clinic?"

"It might not have been deliberate. If either of them confided in the wrong person about their security measures . . ."

"But they're adults and highly trained professionals. It wouldn't be like them, would it, to go boasting about how their clinic stored the narcotics?" She tilted her head in thought. "Now, the other employees, the vet techs and receptionists . . . some of them are young, and they come and go more often, don't they? Easier to imagine one of them blabbing about it, to impress their friends."

"That's what I think, too. But until someone is arrested, everyone there is suspect. And it's wearing on Mark's nerves already, I can tell." I warned her that if the clinic was still in turmoil, he might have to miss the opening reception for Keith's art show.

"Oh, that would be a shame. I think Keith needs all the moral support he can get!" She smiled in sympathy. "He's trying to stay cool, but I can tell he's nervous. He said it's one thing for a corporate client to turn down a design, because that's work for hire—he can always re-do it. But these paintings are all very personal to him."

"Well, I'm still going to be there," I promised. "I can't wait to see them!"

During the lull in our conversation, we could hear Sarah talking in a chirpy voice, back in the playroom, to our newest boarder. I hopped down from my stool and grabbed Dawn's hand. "Before you leave, you've gotta meet Quentin!"

She circled the counter and let me tug her toward the door in the screen. "I gather that's a cat?"

"Like none you've ever seen before."

By the time the two of us joined Sarah in the playroom, the feline Lord of Darkness had grown tired of chasing his feather toy and stretched out on one of the wall shelves, about four feet from the floor. He narrowed his golden eyes at Dawn and me—actually a friendly cat greeting, though in poor

Quentin's case, even the most innocent expression took on a menacing cast.

Dawn was as astonished as Sarah and I had been, and when I used my phone to show her an image of the *Thriller* mask, she laughed out loud at the resemblance. I told her Mark and I had suggested a "werewolf look-alike" contest to drum up attendance at the Paragon for Halloween, and she supported that idea.

"I'm going to try something special for Halloween at Nature's Way, too," she told us, while tentatively stroking Quentin's thick ruff. "When I attended that holistic expo this past spring, I went to a great program by a psychic, Ripley Van Eyck."

Sarah raised one eyebrow, and I asked, "C'mon, that can't be someone's real name!"

Dawn waved a long, graceful hand. "I don't know if it's real, and I don't care. The important thing is, he was terrific! Not one of those con men who make really broad statements that could be true of anybody. He told people in the audience very specific things about themselves that he couldn't possibly have known."

My assistant listened with one hand on her hip, a pose that expressed her skepticism. "Unless they were working with him, and planted in the audience."

"He told *me* that my mother has a very unusual job, and most people would think she couldn't make a good living at such a thing, but she does very well."

Sarah and I exchanged startled glances. Dawn's mother is a professional fiber artist, has been for decades. Her abstract tapestries hang in museums and sell for big bucks to collectors. She's frequently asked to curate fiber-art shows or write catalogue copy on the subject, also for decent pay.

"Okay," I admitted, "that is pretty good."

"He told a chiropractor friend of mine that one of her clients who was having lower back pain should be checked for kidney problems. Sue said Ripley couldn't possibly have known what she did for a living, and his description did fit one of her clients. I haven't talked to her since, so I don't know if Ripley's diagnosis was right, but still—!" Dawn pulled out her phone and searched briefly. "Here's his site."

She passed it to me. I expected to see a Mr. Manifesto type with a top hat, satin cape, and curling black mustache. But Van Eyck's headshot showed a rather sweet, elfin face with wire-rimmed glasses, a high forehead ringed with fluffy gray hair, and a red bow tie. He looked like an absentminded but genial old guy who would be great at reading bedtime stories to his grandkids.

"He lives in upstate New York, and has a weekly cable TV show there," my friend continued. "It's also on YouTube, and I think people from this area know him mostly that way."

I handed Sarah the phone, so she also could see, and admitted to Dawn, "He looks normal enough. What did you plan to have him do, though, at your shop? Not give medical advice, I hope!"

"Oh, I'm sure he wouldn't prescribe for anybody, or give them any kind of dire prognoses," she said. "But if he nudged one or two people to take better care of themselves, that wouldn't be so bad, would it? I invited him by email, but we're supposed to talk on the phone tonight to settle on the details. I can ask more specifically what sort of program he'd be comfortable doing."

"It's just two weeks until Halloween," Sarah observed dryly. "I'm surprised he's not already booked solid."

If Dawn picked up on the gentle dig, she chose to ignore it. "I know. If I'd acted sooner, I might have been able to get him for that weekend, but I'll probably have to settle for a weekday appearance." While the three of us ambled back to the front of the shop, she asked me, "So, you think it's a good idea?"

"No reason why you shouldn't try something different to bring in customers," I said. "And I think you have the good sense not to get taken in, if this Ripley guy seems off the rails in some way. Just find out how much he'll charge and get a written contract."

"Well, of course." She tucked her phone away with an excited grin. "I'm still following the advice you gave me this summer, Cassie, when my business was in a slump. You said I should do more mail order, maybe get an assistant, and work harder on promotion. I've been trying to do all those things, and they do seem to be helping. So, thanks!"

After Dawn left the shop, Sarah met my gaze with a shrug.

"I don't remember telling her to hire Marco the Magnificent to read people's palms," I said. "But I suppose as a gimmick to get people into her store, it's harmless enough."

"As long as he doesn't advise somebody with a heart condition to enter the New York Marathon," my assistant said.

Imagining that, we both winced.

Later on, just after Sarah left for the day, I got a short text from Dave Sheply, the theater usher. He told me Avery Lathrop loved the idea of the photo contest and might be in touch with me to ask about local pet owners who might participate. As Dave had reminded me, they did have my contact information from the theater's list of supporting members.

I texted back that I'd be glad to help. I felt a tingle of curiosity at the prospect of finally meeting the mysterious real estate tycoon and developer.

While tidying up the front counter, I glimpsed the stack of flyers for the pet costume parade that would benefit FOCA.

I hoped a photo contest wouldn't lure entries away from that event. The last thing I'd want to do was sabotage the shelter's fundraiser.

Maybe I should give Becky a heads-up about the contest, before it's set in stone. She probably wouldn't object, but it seems only fair.

I called her cell. When there was no answer, I figured the question was a little too complicated to explain in a message. I told her it was nothing urgent, but to give me a call when she had time to talk.

Becky didn't get back to me until the next morning, when I'd just finished breakfast and was headed for the shower. Her greeting of "Hi, Cassie" did not have its usual perky ring.

"Hi," I said back. "Anything wrong?"

"I guess you haven't heard yet, but Chris and I just got some really bad news."

"Oh, dear." That could mean anything. Becky's parents lived nearby, and though they couldn't be very old, I knew nothing about their health situations. Or, since she and her boyfriend, Chris Eberhart, both worked at the shelter, there also might have been some animal-related tragedy. "What happened?"

"Someone we knew, who used to be a good friend, died suddenly last night. She was at a party up at Starlight Lake, with a bunch of people. Nobody seems to know what happened. I mean, she was only twenty-two, my age!"

"What a shame! She had no unusual ailments?"

Becky hesitated. "She once mentioned that high blood pressure ran in her family, but I don't know if she actually had it, herself. I didn't see a lot of her after college. Karin ran with a pretty fast crowd, and that's never been my style."

True, as far as I knew. Despite her youth, her platinum-bleached cap of hair, her boyishly casual clothes, and her streetwise air, my on-the-road assistant seemed to lead a pretty clean, responsible lifestyle.

"So maybe at the party—"

"That's what I think, that she took something she shouldn't have." I heard a sniffle on the line. "The police were called, but by the time they got to her, it was too late. Chris says it was already on the morning news."

"I'm so sorry, Becky." I felt glad that at least he was there to console her.

She seemed to pull herself together. "Anyway, you called me about something else, I'm sure."

"Nothing crucial; it'll keep until tomorrow. Are you working at FOCA today?"

"Yeah." She sighed. "The animals are always so sweet, they help to take my mind off any human craziness. I'll be in touch, okay?"

After I showered and dressed for work, I still had a few minutes to spare. I sat at my kitchen table and booted up my laptop to search for the local news. It didn't take me long to find the headline:

ROCKAWAY WOMAN DIES AFTER WEEKNIGHT PARTY

Police responding to a 911 call at a Starlight Lake house party found twenty-two-year-old Karin Weaver unresponsive. In spite of lifesaving efforts, she died en route to St. Catherine's Medical Center. The cause of death is still to be determined, though police said signs point to a drug overdose.

Chapter 5

Just before opening for work, I sent Becky an email explaining about the Paragon's planned photo contest and asking her if it would infringe on FOCA's costume parade. I figured she could respond after she'd recovered a bit from the shock of her former friend's death. When Sarah arrived for work, she also had heard about the overdose at the party, but was surprised to learn that the victim had any connection to Becky.

While donning her apron and gloves for our first grooming session—sprucing up Taffy, a Turkish Van cat and repeat boarder—Sarah mused, "The news story was short, and very vague about the 'overdose.' Did Becky say what kind of drugs were involved?"

Her question brought me up short. "No, and I didn't think to ask, especially since she sounded so upset."

"Of course not," Sarah conceded.

"You're not thinking . . ."

"Probably no connection. Lord knows, there must be party drugs going around from a lot of sources."

For most people of Sarah's age, that might have sounded like a strangely jaded observation. But she had taught high school math for decades, in tougher areas than Chadwick. Her son Jay still did, and I was sure he shared plenty of stories with his mother about what he saw in and around the schools these days.

The possibility that someone might actually have died after taking narcotics stolen from Mark's clinic, though, made my stomach turn over. As Sarah said, I had no reason to assume that yet. Still, I felt the urge to give Bonelli a call. Any suspicious death in town would surely fall under her jurisdiction. Maybe I'd do it after we finished grooming Taffy.

Before I had a chance to even take the cat out of her condo, though, an intriguing character walked in our front door. Over six feet tall, he had dressed for the brisk, fall day like an English country gentleman: brown tweed jacket; checked, button-down shirt; olive-green tie; and camel-colored, corduroy pants. In an especially striking touch for a casual, small town like ours, he topped all of this with a natty brown fedora.

I suddenly felt even shabbier than usual in my CCC apron and latex gloves. While grooming, to stay cleaner, I normally wore no makeup and pulled my shoulder-length brown hair back into a low ponytail.

When I approached the sales counter to greet our visitor, he removed his hat, demonstrating manners as old-school as his attire. He was nearly bald, and his remaining gray hair and beard were neatly trimmed. He smiled and asked in a deep, resonant voice, "Are you Ms. McGlone? The eponymous 'Cassie'?"

I quickly reviewed my college-English vocabulary. That just meant, the one whose name was on the front of the store. I smiled back, peeled off my gloves, and offered my hand. "I am, indeed. What can I do for you?"

He was not toting a cat, but many customers dropped by first to scope the place out before bringing their animals to me. Usually, they do call ahead to make sure the visit will be convenient, but not always. And this fellow looked wealthy enough to own purebreds, or maybe even to breed them.

"My name is Avery Lathrop. I'm involved with the Paragon theater, down the road?"

His tone seemed to ask if I'd heard of him, but of course I had—the developer/renovator with the passion for old movies! No wonder he seemed dressed like a character out of the 1940s. "Involved with" the theater, though? He was being modest, since he owned the place outright.

Shaking his hand, I gushed, "I'm so glad to meet you! My . . . friend Mark and I go to the Paragon at least once a month, and usually on oldies night. We've really enjoyed catching up on classics that our parents and other people always raved about."

I stopped myself, worried that I was making him feel old, but Lathrop just responded with a hearty laugh.

"That's great to hear. I like to think I'm entertaining not only people of my generation, who are nostalgic for those films, but also younger folks who might never have been exposed to them."

I heard Sarah come through the screen door behind me, trying to be discreet, and waved her over. "Come meet the legendary Mr. Lathrop!"

She joined us, also glad to make the man's acquaintance. "I have to admit, I've never been to your movie theater yet, but I've eaten at The Firehouse. The way you kept that industrial look, while still making it so cozy, is just wonderful!"

He thanked her with a gracious nod. "I haven't yet seen all the high spots of Chadwick, myself. Yours is one of the few downtown businesses I've never visited, so I thought I should get around to it. Ms. McGlone, our usher David told me about the idea you and Dr. Coccia came up with, for the pet photo contest."

"Please, call me Cassie," I said. "And if Mark were here, I'm sure he'd also want to dispense with the formalities." Good grief, now Lathrop had me using fancy language, too!

"All right, Cassie. I wanted to talk to you a little more about that, and see if you thought there would be enough real contenders in the area to make a contest worthwhile." He hesitated and glanced over our shoulders toward the back. "But I probably shouldn't have dropped in like this, unannounced. You two probably have a full schedule of tasks to perform."

"Actually, you came at a good time," I told him. "As long as you're not allergic to cats, c'mon in back. You can meet the purebred gentleman who sparked the whole idea."

As soon as I lifted Quentin out of his condo, and Lathrop caught sight of that leonine visage, the man's mouth fell open. Then he gave a "Ho-ho-ho!" that reminded me he had dressed as Santa Claus to greet Paragon patrons last Christmas.

"Very impressive!" he admitted. "What on earth is he? What breed, I mean?"

I explained that Maine Coons were the largest domestic cat. "His color is called *smoke*, which is a mix of black and gray."

"He certainly has the right look." Lathrop dared to peer closer. "His fur is like a wolf's, but his face is almost more . . . human."

On her phone, Sarah found the *Thriller* mask again and showed it to him. Our guest hooted once more in delight.

I explained that Quentin was staying temporarily with a friend of his owner, and the two women would have to decide whether to enter his photo in any contest.

"Of course, the decision would be entirely theirs," Lathrop said. "Though I suspect he'd trounce the competition."

"I've also thought of someone else you should contact." I searched on my own phone for a site I'd discovered the day before, a cattery called Children of the Night. "A couple in the next county breeds Lykois. They're actually known as 'werewolf cats.'"

Over my shoulder, Lathrop studied the photos of several normal-sized cats with wiry-looking hair that grew sparsely in certain areas, such as around their faces. It almost made them look as if they were transforming from animal to human.

"These are very cute," he said, "and their fur does have a more doglike quality. But they're nowhere near as scary as our big friend here."

"Still, if you want entries, you might want to contact these breeders. They'd probably love the publicity."

"Good idea." When he searched his pockets, as if for a pen and paper, I offered to just email him the link. He gave me his business card, printed in an antique font, that fortunately did include a modern email address.

As we all returned to the front of the shop, Lathrop added, "Dave said your veterinarian friend talked about other types of pets we could feature."

I hoped Mark hadn't oversold this idea; his patients might not appreciate being told that their beloved furry or feathered friends resembled scary monsters. "Mark did mention some that he thought had potential. I'll check back with him. Again, there's no guarantee their owners will go for the idea, but . . ."

"I understand. Right now, I'm just testing the waters. If enough people seem interested, I'll personally invite them to participate. There will be no cost or risk to enter. They only have to send in their pet's photograph, to be displayed for a week or so in our lobby. We'll number the pictures, giving no names or other information. The owners can costume the animals in some way, if they want to, but they don't have to."

I could see Sarah behind him, smiling at the prospect, and I thought it sounded like fun, too. "I'll ask Mark if he has any recommendations and get back to you in a day or so, one way or the other."

"Can't ask for more than that!" He buttoned his tweed jacket and popped the fedora onto his head again. "Thank you for your time, Cassie. I'll leave you and Ms. Wilcox to minister to your feline charges."

After Lathrop left, Sarah met my eyes. "Why do I feel like we just had a visit from royalty?"

"Really. If I knew he was coming, I'd have worn my tiara!"

We finally got around to grooming Taffy. Although she was a semi-longhair, and pure white except for touches of rust around her ears and in her tail, her coat didn't pose that much of a challenge. Elegant and silky, it didn't mat too badly. She mostly cooperated, only balking when we got around to clipping her claws. But most cats resisted that at least a little, so Sarah and I had learned to work quickly and efficiently, before they had a chance to get too riled up.

With Taffy done, I finally got a chance to check my email. Becky had responded, and luckily, she saw no problem with the idea of a photo contest for non-canines at the Paragon. She conceded that the pet parade in the park attracted mostly dogs, so FOCA should still benefit from a good number of entry fees.

I passed this information along to Sarah.

"Looks like Chadwick will be howlin' this Halloween," she said, "with two contests for animals!"

"I just hope the werewolf look-alike thing attracts enough entries. Mark and I *will* have to find more pet owners for Lathrop to contact."

I hadn't heard from Mark lately and wondered how he was making out, his first day back at work since the robbery. By the time he finished, he would probably be dog tired, no pun intended.

Should I pick up some takeout and invite him to have dinner at my place? It would save him driving across town to his condo complex, and if necessary, he could get back to the clinic extra early tomorrow morning. I knew he tended to keep a change of clothes in his locker at work, because he wore scrubs much of the time on the job.

Around five, after I closed the shop and Sarah went home, I called his cell phone to make my offer. I got voice mail, which was common; Mark couldn't answer if he was dealing with a patient.

About ten minutes later, though, he got back to me. His voice sounded tired but warm. "Dinner at your place sounds great, especially since we had to cut our date short last night."

"I was thinking that, too. How did things go today?"

"Hectic. I had to operate on a cat who swallowed a sewing needle—luckily, it hadn't done much damage before I got it out of her. We also had a couple of other procedures that couldn't wait any longer. And as if that wasn't exciting enough, around lunchtime we got a visit from your friend Angela Bonelli."

"You did?" I had wondered if the resident detective of the Chadwick PD would ever get involved in the clinic's case. "I thought she might pass on this one, since it was just a robbery."

"It's a little more than that now. Did you happen to hear about the woman who died up at Starlight Lake last night?"

"Becky mentioned it, because they were friends in college. She wasn't there, but she heard it happened at a party, and that the cops thought it was a drug overdose."

"Yes and no. The cops questioned other people at the house, and they think someone 'slipped her a mickey,' as they used to say in the old days. It might have just knocked her out, but because she'd been drinking so much beforehand, the combination turned out to be fatal."

"Wow." I remembered what Becky had said about Karin's reckless lifestyle and possible high blood pressure. "But how does that lead back to you guys? Does Bonelli think the drug came from your clinic?"

"She has reason to make the connection. They'll do an autopsy, of course, but from the post-mortem exam, the M.E. thinks the victim died from a mixture of alcohol and some type of anesthetic. The most likely suspect would be the ketamine."

I called Hunan House, a new restaurant on the highway that already had become a favorite of Mark's and mine. I ordered Szechuan shrimp for him and tofu with steamed vegetables for me, since lately I'd been watching my waistline. The delivery guy brought it to the front door of my shop about five minutes before Mark arrived.

We kissed, and I commiserated with him about his stressful day. Upstairs in my apartment, we got mobbed by my three cats. Maybe they'd been lonely, but the way their noses twitched suggested that they also coveted the shrimp. We did notice, happily, that Mango showed Mark more affection than he had in quite a while. For about a month after his thyroid surgery that summer, the orange tabby had given his veterinarian a wide berth whenever Mark came to the apartment.

The distant rattling from the furnace soon caught Mark's

attention, and his dark eyebrows lowered over those baby blues. "Cassie . . . do you hear that noise?"

"Relax. No one's breaking in, it's just my wonky furnace. I've *really* got to call Nick to come and look at it."

Mark looked relieved. I could imagine that strange banging sounds in the night also set his nerves on edge since the clinic break-in. "I'd offer to help you, but I'm pretty hopeless with stuff like that. I know my way around the insides of a Labrador retriever, but not machinery. The few times I've tried to fix a large appliance, or a car, I've only screwed things up more."

I set the takeout containers on my 1950s yellow Formica-topped kitchen table, which came with four coordinating chrome-and-vinyl chairs. I gave the felines a little extra canned food to distract them while I got out two of my turquoise Fiestaware plates. I poured a small glass of white wine for myself, but Mark opted for a beer from the refrigerator. He obviously was hungry, as I was, and for several minutes we concentrated on spooning the food onto the colorful plates and wolfing it down.

Thinking he probably needed to hear some happy talk, I told him about Lathrop's visit to the shop. Mark seemed amused by my description of the man's attire and courtly manners, and optimistic that he would be able to suggest some pet owners to take part in the Paragon's photo contest.

"Meanwhile, we had some good news at the clinic," he said. "Sam's coming back to work tomorrow, though we're not putting him on the graveyard shift again any time soon."

"No, I'm sure he wants a break from that!" I said.

"I talked to him right before I left work tonight. He never really saw the guy who accosted him, but he feels sure it was a man—probably about Sam's own height, and at least as strong, judging from the chokehold," Mark said. "He remembered two other things that he told Bonelli. The robber had a low-pitched voice that also sounded muffled, as if he might have had a mask or a scarf over his lower face. And when they passed an office door that had a window, Sam caught a quick reflection of the two of them, from the side. He thought the guy had collar-length, dark hair."

"It's good that he was so observant," I said. "At least that should give the cops something to go on."

"Sam and Bonelli both figure the thief brought some kind of bag with him and carried it while he was using the gun, but set it down to use the chokehold. When Sam passed out, it gave the thief a few minutes to dump all the drugs he wanted into the bag, then take off before Sam came to."

"It's lucky that he didn't just shoot Sam," I reflected, "but also surprising that the thief took such a chance. He sounds pretty sure of himself."

"I was thinking that, too. Though, if he covered part of his face, was he worried someone would recognize him? Sam also had a wallet with some cash and a credit card, but I guess the robber didn't even check for that. Just went straight for the heavy drugs."

Mark's look of intense concentration made me smile. "You always warn me about getting mixed up in police investigations, but you see how hard it is to resist? I think you've got a bit of detective in you, too!"

He shrugged. "Maybe. Medicine is part detective work—trying to diagnose what's wrong, and the best way to fix it. But no one can say *I'm* poking my nose into a case that's none of my business. Our clinic's reputation, and even my own, is at stake here! If people think someone on our staff is providing narcotics to a drug ring . . ."

I put a hand on his arm. "I'm sure no one thinks that."

"I hope not. Lieutenant Bassey did say some other vet

clinics in nearby states also have been hit recently. If that's the case, it must be a pretty big operation."

I shuddered to think some large, well-organized ring would have targeted Mark and Maggie's business in our fairly sleepy little town. "Let's just hope they can track down the thief this time. It might help them round up the whole gang."

"That's a nice thought. The guy didn't leave behind much evidence. But now," Mark pointed out brightly, "we do have Bonelli on the case!"

"If anyone can crack it, she can," I agreed.

Though Mark didn't utter any of his customary warnings to me, this time I felt little temptation to get personally involved. A tristate ring dealing in narcotics sounded way beyond my level of expertise. This time, I silently vowed, I really would leave all of the "detecting" to the police!

Chapter 6

I knew it was only a matter of time before my mother, who lived about forty-five minutes away in Morristown, would read or hear about the robbery at the veterinary clinic. She left me a phone message Thursday night that I didn't answer—Mark and I having better things to do—but I got back to her the next morning during a break at the shop.

Mom's a serious worrywart, so as soon as I told her that Mark was okay, she jumped to fretting over whether Cassie's Comfy Cats would be the next business targeted.

"Not very likely, Mom," I reassured her. "You might have noticed in the news story that the thief stole drugs. He wasn't after money. He didn't even take the cash or credit cards from Sam's wallet. So unless he also has a fetish for organic pet shampoos or carpeted cat furniture, we should be pretty safe."

"But he might think that you keep drugs around, too, for calming the cats!"

Right now, I wished I had something to calm *her.* "You know I've got an alarm system these days and keep pepper spray behind the counter. I really think we're good." I had hoped that after Mom started up with her new boyfriend,

Harry Bock, she'd be kept too busy to fuss about my well-being all the time. That suggested a change of subject. "How's Harry doing? The two of you got any plans for Halloween?"

A dry laugh, as if she couldn't imagine what a couple in their late fifties would be up to on that particular holiday. "Oh, no. These days, I'm not even sure what we're doing from one week to the next. He's gotten an important commission to design a new pharmaceutical company headquarters in Basking Ridge, so lately he's out there half the time."

Ah, no wonder her disaster meter has gone back into full swing. Too much time on her hands! Harry was an architect of some repute in the state, but this probably was the first time in a long while that he'd landed such a big job. "Sounds great for him, but pretty boring for you."

Never liking anyone to feel sorry for her, Mom rallied. "Well, we do have tickets for a symphony concert at the Morristown Arts Center this weekend, and I can't imagine he'll miss that. But Halloween?" She chuckled again. "I don't think people our age make plans for that, anymore."

"Never say never," I encouraged her. "I don't suppose the two of you would be up for a werewolf movie marathon . . . ?"

Unfortunately, true to his prediction, Mark could not make time to get to the opening of the art exhibit on Friday night. He and Maggie were still catching up with urgent cases that had been postponed while the police had been going through the clinic and questioning the staff. Bonelli had even paid them another visit after the ketamine-related death at the Starlight Lake party.

I still intended to show up at the reception in support of Keith and Dawn. Since it started at six, I let Sarah go and closed the shop promptly at five. I needed that hour to clean up, before I could mingle with polite company.

Upstairs, my apartment once again felt colder than it should have. At least I could hear that the furnace was running, but even on the second floor, it sounded as if a large truck was revving its engine down there. If someone ever did break into my shop, with that racket, how would I ever know? I'd have to at least call Nick Janos to ask his advice, and soon!

Once I'd showered and done my makeup, I set about picking an outfit for both the occasion and the cool temperature. I started with narrow-wale, brown corduroy pants that had a velvety sheen. Lacking Dawn's height, vivid coloring, or strong features, I couldn't carry off the kind of artsy outfits she favored, so I did much less shopping in vintage and boho stores. But a gallery opening called for something unusual, and I did have one piece that I figured might work.

I pulled out a cardigan sweater from the 1950s that I had picked up at one of our local haunts, Towne Antiques. It was a buttery yellow wool, beaded down the front placket with abstract white leaves. The design didn't look *too* summery, and the sweater's long sleeves and lining suited the season well enough. After I got to the gallery, I could push up the sleeves and undo the first few buttons to make it less "proper."

Searching for earrings that wouldn't clash with the beading, I noticed a pair Mark had given me about a year ago, almost as a joke. The size of nickels, they resembled iridescent yellow cat's eyes. Because they always drew teasing comments, I didn't wear them often, but this seemed like the perfect occasion. I popped them onto my lobes and had to grin at the offbeat effect.

Last, I stepped into the tall, espresso-colored boots I wore for most cool-weather, semi-dressy occasions. The heels were high enough to have some style, but comfortable enough to walk the five blocks to the gallery.

Suddenly, in spite of the boots, I got cold feet. Normally

I walked around downtown Chadwick all the time. It gave me a chance to check out what was new and provided some good exercise. Tonight, for the first time in a long while, I had second thoughts.

In my head, I heard Mom's cautionary voice asking, *What if the thief is still out there? What if he's decided he* does *want money, after all? Or what if he thinks you know something more than you do about the robbery?*

And I remembered Mark saying Tuesday night that he wouldn't let me walk home from the theater "in the dark, with a violent mugger on the loose."

C'mon, Cassie. It's five blocks, straight down the main street. You've walked that far a hundred times. And it's not even dark yet.

But my trek home would be after the reception was over. And I'd walked that distance before Sam Urbano, a strong and fairly streetwise guy, got taken by surprise and choked unconscious, right at the clinic where he worked.

I'd always assumed Chadwick was safe, even after dark. I couldn't anymore.

Heck, it's kind of cold out, anyway.

I shrugged into my chocolate-brown faux-leather jacket, slung my purse strap over my shoulder, shut the door to my apartment, and trotted down the stairs. Passing through the shop, I did a last, quick check on the boarders.

I didn't leave by the front door, though. Instead, I went out the back way to the small parking lot, clutching my car keys.

I had to park on the street, half a block down from Eye of the Beholder, because its own lot was full. *Good going, Nidra!*

The gallery's large front windows showcased medium-sized works in three distinct media, representing the trio of artists. The theme of the show was "New Talent," so I guessed that the others, like Keith, also might be exhibiting for the first time. I admired a close-up photo of water cascading over rocks, its hues probably enhanced by special color filters. Also intriguing was a life-sized wire sculpture of a man's head that resembled an unfinished drawing in 3-D, the lines unraveling to one side.

An acrylic painting on canvas about two feet square represented Keith. Although I had seen only two examples of his Pop-influenced works before, both in Dawn's apartment, I couldn't mistake his style . . . or his subject. As if viewed through a fish-eye lens, a big-eyed brown tabby cat nosed its way curiously toward the viewer. The witty piece perfectly captured the mischievous personality of Dawn's pet, Tigger.

Through the window, I could see that the brightly lit, white-walled gallery was jammed with people. They probably included not only friends of Keith and Dawn, but of the other two artists, and maybe also folks who'd just been strolling by and decided to drop in. I had expected it to be a more casual gathering, and suddenly felt awkward, as if I were crashing some upper crust Manhattan event.

Squaring my shoulders, I gave myself a pep talk. I had minored in art in college and did computer montages of my own back then. I probably knew as much about the subject as most people here. Maybe more!

I pushed open the door and slipped in, unnoticed at first, and that was fine with me. Taking my time, I made a circuit of the whole show. The rest of the photographer's stuff struck me as a bit repetitive, though it all was attractive enough to appeal to buyers. The wire sculptor's pieces interested me more; he pushed his illusionary technique a bit further each time, for a "dissolving" man's torso, an ethereal female figure, and a disembodied running leg that left streaks in its wake.

In all, Keith had seven pieces on view, some of them fairly large. It impressed me that he'd been able to produce so many and of such high quality. I knew his regular work as a free-lance graphic designer and illustrator kept him pretty busy.

The largest, and in my opinion the most striking, was his offbeat portrait of Dawn, which I'd seen before in her dining room. It zoomed in on just the left half of her face, her one eye shut and her rosy lips smiling. A string of hippie beads dipped across her forehead, and her wavy, russet hair floated off to the side.

Keith also offered a couple of medium-sized views of Chadwick's own Riverside Park—in one, I recognized the central gazebo. Another, more woodsy landscape included Dawn, in cargo shorts and rugged footwear, posing near a large boulder among dark fir trees. I imagined that depicted one of their summer hikes to nearby Rattlesnake Ridge.

A tight cluster of people surrounded Keith and Dawn, so I took my time working my way in their direction. I passed Nidra Balin, owner of the gallery, chic as always in a slim, long-sleeved black dress. She seemed deep in conversation with a tall and very good-looking blond man who had dressed up his jeans with a striped, button-down shirt and a navy sports jacket. I heard him toss off the comment, "Pop Art can get kind of kitschy sometimes, but these have a lot of heart. And his use of color is terrific."

Could this stranger be an art critic? Our local paper, the *Chadwick Courier,* sure didn't have one on staff, but occa-sionally I saw a freelance critique in the *Daily Record* out of Morristown.

Dawn finally spotted me and waved me over. Tonight she wore a chamois-colored suede skirt and a pullover sweater that seemed patched together from several different, coordinating patterns. She had wound her thick, coppery tresses into a knot at the back of her head, with just a few wavy tendrils hanging loose. I never could figure out how she managed such tricks, though probably she'd inherited her mother's talent for weaving fibers!

Keith, her slim, brown-bearded significant other, affected his own masculine version of Bohemian. He topped his pleated wool pants with a vintage-looking, collarless shirt and an olive-green vest.

As I approached, Dawn hoisted her glass of white wine in my direction. "Cassie, we have you to thank for this, y'know."

"Me?"

She announced to the rest of their circle, "Cassie was the one who first suggested Keith should talk to Nidra about showing his work. He was too modest, kept saying he wasn't ready yet. But eventually he got up his nerve, and of course Nidra loved everything!"

"Well, I knew Keith was a terrific commercial artist," I told them, "but I had no idea he also was painting until I saw this in Dawn's apartment." I gestured toward the supersized half-portrait of her on the wall to our left.

"It's nice, isn't it?" A pudgy pal of Keith's squinted at the piece and scratched his head. "That woman looks strangely familiar . . ."

Dawn swatted him on the arm, and the rest of them laughed. Even Keith quipped, "Oh, that's just some redhead I had a fling with, a while back."

A few minutes later, Dawn pulled me aside and lowered her voice. "I talked to that psychic on the phone last night. You remember, the one I'm trying to book at the shop for Halloween?"

I nodded. How could I forget anyone who looked like a Keebler elf and bore the name of Ripley Van Eyck?

"He's coming the Wednesday before; isn't that great? I

scheduled him for the early evening, around this time, because I think after business hours he'll get the best audience."

"Sounds smart," I agreed. Well, the timing, anyway.

"You'll never believe, though, what he told me on the phone. He said someone close to me was just starting a new venture, and he asked if it had to do with sales." Dawn gave me a canny smile. "You'd have been proud of me. I said that was true, but I didn't give any other details. And Ripley said this person should do very well and would get off to a good start—that he'd make a big sale very soon."

I hoped the prediction wouldn't raise my friend's expectations too much. "Be great if that came true, right?"

"I think it will." She looked around at the packed gallery. "It could be my imagination, but I hear people talking more about Keith's work than about either of the others."

That had been my impression, also. My mind immediately went to the largest canvas in the show. "What will you do if somebody wants to buy your portrait?"

The question made Dawn pause, but only for a second. "It's not for sale, though if somebody really loves it, they can get a lithograph. Keith is having prints made of his larger works." She leaned closer to confide, "From what I've heard, people especially love the daylilies. I'll bet that's going to be his 'big sale.'"

The five-foot-tall piece *was* spectacular. Against their plain, charcoal-gray background, the giant flowers seemed to glow, their orange, yellow, and green hues vibrating with life. To me, they even suggested the idea of "day" triumphing over "night"—hope in the darkness—and I wondered if Keith had intended that message.

An art lover would need lots of wall space, though, to showcase a piece like that. I couldn't think of many folks around Chadwick with such roomy accommodations. I once knew a retired Wall Street exec who'd had a McMansion on the edge of town and collected fine art—I'd visited there to groom his cat. Unfortunately, that gentleman had come to a bad end. His cat had been luckier, and now lived with Sarah.

Noncommittally, I told Dawn, "I hope you're right."

At that point, Nidra broke into our circle, apologizing for the interruption, though of course none of us minded. She introduced us to the handsome blond guy, Dez Mitchelson.

"Mr. Mitchelson is new in the area, but he's an art lover and made a special trip here tonight to see the show," Nidra added, with pride.

"Well, I'm very glad you did," said Keith, shaking the other man's hand.

"I'm glad, too," Dez told him, with a brilliant smile. "I really like your work, Garrett. Reminds me of early Alex Katz. I guess he was one of your influences?"

I thought Keith's bearded cheek flushed a little, as if he thought Mitchelson was accusing him of copying that famous artist. "He was."

"You've definitely got your own style, though. It's a little warmer, I'd say. More down-to-earth."

Keith's chest expanded, and he smiled. "Thanks. That *is* what I was going for."

Dawn sidled away from her boyfriend, cueing the rest of us to do the same. If there was a chance of Keith making a sale, he didn't need us distracting the potential customer.

I roamed nearer to a small table, where Nidra was setting out more glasses of wine. In a whisper, I asked her, "That guy Mitchelson . . . is he writing something about the show?"

"I don't know, Cassie," she answered, also in a low tone. "He does seem very astute, doesn't he? If he is planning to do a review, he didn't say anything about it to me. Of course, that's not unusual. Critics sometimes keep a low profile, because they don't want people trying to influence them."

"I guess that makes sense," I said.

"He told me he saw my ad in the *Courier* online, and was surprised that Chadwick even had an art gallery. I guess he just dropped by out of curiosity, but apparently he's impressed by the caliber of the work."

"He should be," I told her. "You did a great job, as usual. All three artists have really distinct styles, but they also complement one another."

"He's had the highest praise for Keith's stuff," Nidra said, "so I wanted them to meet."

As if she'd overheard this, even from several feet away, Dawn threw me a sideways *told-you-so* glance. No doubt she was thinking again of the psychic's prediction.

Meanwhile, Dez and Keith appeared to be discussing her supersized portrait, and finally, Keith waved Dawn back over. "Yes, she's my muse. Actually, that was my first painting in the new series. I took that photo of her, in the park, and it inspired me."

"But then he cut my face in half!" She feigned outrage.

"I just didn't know if the world could handle your beauty, full-strength," Keith teased in return.

"Showing just half her face gives it a nice sense of mystery," Dez told him. "And the off-balance composition is unexpected."

I nodded at his interpretation. "It also really captures her personality. Dawn is such a free spirit!"

Dez swiveled in my direction, and the sudden weight of his full attention threw me. Had I said something incredibly gauche or naïve?

Keith jumped in to explain, "Cassie's kind of a connoisseur, herself. You studied art in college, right?"

"My minor." I felt more self-conscious by the second. "And I did some surrealistic computer-art prints in school. Nothing of the caliber that Nidra ever would consider showing!"

"You gave it up?" Dez asked. I finally realized his intense focus on me was not from scorn, but . . . interest. "So, are you a commercial artist now, like Keith?"

My friends smiled in sympathy, probably guessing that I'd feel odd about revealing my profession. "Not exactly." I explained about Cassie's Comfy Cats.

The gorgeous man grinned again, as if he found this refreshing. "How about that! This town has all sorts of hidden surprises I never would have expected." He glanced over his shoulder in Nidra's direction. "Well, before I leave, I've got some business to transact with Ms. Balin. It was great meeting you all!"

Once he'd gone out of earshot, Dawn repeated slyly, "Business to transact, eh?"

"Now, don't lead our chickens to water before they're hatched," Keith warned her. "Or . . . something like that."

"Whether or not Mitchelson buys one of your paintings, I'll make Ripley's prophecy come true," I told him. "I want that adorable portrait of Tigger."

"Oh, Cassie, I'd gladly *give* you that," he said.

"Yes, really," Dawn chimed in. "You need to save up for that furnace repair, remember?"

Although she had a point, I protested with a laugh. "No, no." I'd already checked the show's price list and figured I could afford the small piece; maybe the wine also put me in an expansive mood. "I had a pretty good summer at the shop this year, and I like to support our local artists and this gallery.

So when Dez is finished with her, I'll be the next one talking to Nidra."

Keith met my eyes with a sincere look. "Thanks, Cassie, I appreciate that."

I picked up a complimentary glass of wine and sipped it while I waited for the gallery owner to be free. Meanwhile, I wondered whether Mitchelson actually *was* buying something of Keith's. For some reason, he struck me as a guy who played things close to the vest, who might imply one thing and do another. But maybe I was judging him unfairly because he was so damned good-looking.

And *polished*. That was the word.

He concluded his chat with Nidra and turned away so abruptly that he bumped into me. The wine in my glass sloshed, and a few drops hit my sweater.

"Oh, gosh, I'm sorry!" Dez rested a hand on my shoulder to steady me. "Did I spill your drink?"

"No, it's okay." I felt a jolt at his touch, and my face warmed. "There wasn't much of it left."

"You sneaked up on me!" He removed his hand but dazzled me with another white grin.

"Bad habit of mine. I actually want to buy one of the paintings, too."

"Ah, a fellow collector."

"I'm not sure I qualify as that, but I do have one other piece from this gallery." I hadn't paid for that one, though. It had been a joint gift from Mark and Dawn.

Dez bent his head nearer, as if to share a secret. "I'll bet you're buying the cat picture in the front window."

"Damn, am I that predictable?"

"I just took a guess, because of your line of work." He was near enough for me to catch a whiff of his spicy aftershave. "But are you always predictable? I doubt that."

Crap, this guy really was coming on to me. And the worst part was, I liked it.

"Hey, I don't know many people around here yet, and definitely not many fellow art lovers," he went on. "Would you like to get together for coffee some time, to talk about such things?" His clear, green eyes had become high beams.

Never, since I'd first met Mark, had I felt so tempted. And Mark had never been such a slick operator! That notion helped me put the brakes on.

"Thanks for the invitation," I said demurely, "but I'm in a relationship." When Dez glanced around, as if to emphasize that I'd come to the reception alone, I added, "He had to work late tonight."

The art-loving Adonis accepted my explanation with grace. After another quick word with Nidra, he said good night to both of us and left.

Alone with the gallery owner, I told her I wanted the tabby cat picture.

"Isn't that one sweet?" She made a notation on her laptop and asked for a twenty-five-percent deposit. "All the pictures stay here until the end of the show, but I'll notify you when you can pick it up. Your friend did very well tonight!"

"I'm so glad," I said. "The guy right before me—the one we thought might be a critic—did he buy one of Keith's, too?"

"Yes." Her dark eyes twinkled.

"Can you tell me which one?"

She hesitated a second, but maybe because I was a fellow shopkeeper and a repeat customer, she confided in me. "The daylilies."

Wow, one of the biggest in the show! I knew it was priced at almost a thousand dollars. And Mitchelson had just popped into the gallery, decided he liked it, and bought it . . . on a whim.

I could have had a date with a guy who was handsome, smooth, *and* rich. If I wasn't already committed to a handsome, workaholic veterinarian. The thought just amused me . . . at least now that Dez and his charisma had left the building.

When I rejoined Keith and Dawn, I intended to keep my mouth shut. But because Dawn kept speculating about whether Keith had sold anything major, I finally broke down and told them about the daylilies painting.

"I think Nidra wants to keep it quiet," I warned her.

That at least prevented Dawn from shrieking with glee, but she still looked about to burst. "You see?" she taunted Keith. "It's just like Ripley predicted."

Shaking his head, he glanced at me. "She's on a first-name basis with this psychic, and she hasn't even met him yet."

"Well, speaking of mysterious strangers," Dawn said, "Cassie was getting pretty friendly over there with Mr. Mitchelson! I saw him with his hand on your shoulder."

"That was just because he backed up into me, by accident."

"You didn't have any influence on him buying my painting?" Keith teased.

"Of course not! He'd already made the purchase, by that time." But I felt myself reddening again.

"I was getting worried, for a minute." Dawn sounded more serious. "Mark shouldn't leave you on your own so much. He might be sorry!"

"He has no reason to be concerned," I assured her. "I told Mitchelson that I'm in a relationship."

Dawn raised an eyebrow when she heard that our conversation actually had gone that far.

"Good girl," Keith said, with an approving nod. "But if you *do* ever want to lead him on a little, just to sell another of my paintings . . . I can keep a secret."

Dawn elbowed him. "You're terrible! Don't let him give you any ideas, Cassie."

I chuckled along with them. "I won't."

Unfortunately, I could come up with way too many ideas about Dez Mitchelson all on my own.

Chapter 7

The next day at work, Sarah wanted to know how Keith's art opening went. I told her I bought one of his paintings, and he had sold at least one other, larger piece to a newcomer who claimed to be a collector.

"That's exciting," she commented, while we tidied up the boarders' condos from the night before. "An older man, I guess, like Lathrop?"

"No, this guy was pretty young—early thirties, I'd say. Must have the bucks, though."

"Maybe he's from a wealthy family, or else he's one of those tech entrepreneurs."

"Probably."

I tried not to display any undue interest in the newcomer, and Sarah didn't appear to suspect that I had any. I turned up the wall thermostat, and the resulting racket from the furnace below finally spurred me to action. *No more stalling, Cassie!*

Once the boarders had been taken care of, and the first one turned out in the playroom, I phoned Nick. I got his voice mail and left him a message describing the unit's symptoms.

Even as I recited them, an imaginary cash register racked up the dollar signs in my mind.

Half an hour later, the handyman got back to me. "That rattle is probably just a loose bearing in the blower, which I can fix," he said, "but those other noises could be more serious. You got any idea how old your unit is?"

"I might have paperwork on it somewhere," I said, though after almost three years in the building, I had no idea where to put my hands on it.

"Could be time to replace the whole thing," he warned. "Anyhow, I'm all tied up today. I'll swing by there Monday, while you're open for business, okay? I'll give you a call before I come."

"That would be great," I said, and thanked him. I trusted the furnace would at least go on functioning for the rest of the weekend.

Sarah and I then got started on our main project of the day, grooming Quentin.

Of all the breeds that came through my shop, a few always presented challenges for strictly physical reasons. Sphynx cats needed special handling, because they had so little fur; Rexes and some other types, because their hair was so thin and fragile. Typical longhairs like Persians were our bread and butter, because their fur often matted beyond what their owners could cope with; however, except for the rare one with a cranky temperament, they usually were easy to handle.

Ah, but an adult Maine Coon was always good for a solid hour, or more, of intense labor. There was just so much real estate to cover! Good thing most of them, like the Persians, came with fairly laid-back personalities.

Sarah helped me lift Quentin onto the grooming table. Even though he didn't seem poised to give us a hard time, we put a lightweight harness on him just to be safe. If he did suddenly try to leave the table while I was combing, my rather petite assistant might not have the brawn to stop him by herself.

Nancy had kept up with his brushing, but I went over him with a de-matting tool to break up any remaining tangles in his coat. After that, I used a shedding comb to get rid of any loose hair; since it was fall, this wasn't the problem that it would have been a few weeks earlier. I checked his belly and hindquarters, where dirt tended to accumulate, and decided they could use a light trim with a shaver. Sarah moved him around with practiced skill to give me access to these areas.

Quentin made no complaint. About six years old, he had been shown for most of his life. By now, he knew the drill.

I combed out the thick tufts between his toes, then clipped his claws—which amounted to talons on a beast his size. Most cats loathed this procedure, but although the fluffy Lord of Darkness muttered a little, he didn't fight me. The last step was to give him a bath, and here again, Quentin did not behave like the average cat. As Sarah filled our raised, metal tub, his long ears flicked toward it with interest, and we lifted him into a few inches of lukewarm water with no battle. Like most Maine Coons, he actually liked the stuff. He was less enthusiastic about me wetting him down from above with a gentle spray and massaging shampoo into his fur. At one point, he let out a low-pitched moan.

"Sarah, get him a treat, wouldja?" I suggested.

She came back with a few, and when she started hand-feeding them to Quentin, he soon cheered up.

I heard my ringtone, "Stray Cat Strut," play from my back pocket. I doubted the call was anything important. Sarah and I would be taking a break soon, so I'd check my phone messages then.

We rinsed Quentin for about ten minutes, because it was crucial to get rid of all the soap residue, then drained the water from the tub and blotted him with a thick towel. Usually I put shorthaired cats in a dryer cage afterward, but this guy had so much fur that I opted for blow-drying him. Most of our feline customers were too skittish for that, but I had a hunch that Big Q would take it in stride . . . which he did.

"His coat has so many layers," Sarah marveled, ruffling them with her gloved hand. "They just go on and on."

I laughed. "Yeah, these guys invented the shag hairdo. Guess it helps keep them warm." Combing out his mostly dry coat, I appreciated its many shades of gray—there really might have been fifty. "That's one reason why I don't want to trim him too much."

Sarah, who never missed a nuance, asked me, "Is there also another reason?"

"There is. If Nancy does get the go-ahead to enter him in the Paragon contest, he shouldn't look *too* civilized, should he? That wild lion's mane ought to make him a shoo-in to win."

"Good thinking. I guess we'll find out what she's decided when she comes to pick him up."

Nancy wasn't due until mid-afternoon, so we tucked Quentin back in his condo, with a few more treats for being such a gentleman.

When I finally checked my phone message, it was from Mark.

"Just wanted to find out how the reception went last night, and to apologize for not being there," he said. "We stayed busy all day yesterday and closed up late. We had to deal not just with our patients, but with the cops . . . again. There may or may not have been some breakthroughs in terms of the burglary." He paused. "Anyhow, my schedule's still pretty full for the rest of today, but I'll try to reach you again later and give you the updates."

His weary tone made me feel almost guilty about having spent the previous evening at an art reception. I'd been drinking wine and socializing while Mark was patching up sick or injured animals and being grilled yet again by the police. Of course, I would have felt even guiltier if I'd said or done anything to encourage Dez Mitchelson's interest in me.

During my lunch break, though, I did something almost as naughty. I sat in a side chair in the playroom and, while keeping our Burmese boarder company, used my laptop to search the web for info about Mitchelson.

I found only a couple of men in the U.S. with that name, and none listed in New Jersey. Well, he had said that he only moved here recently. One "Dez" in upstate New York had a website with photos of him racing cars, but his hair was gray, and he bore little resemblance to the hunky young guy at the reception.

Finally, I did turn up something promising, a byline in an art webzine. Dez Mitchelson had posted a detailed, rather caustic review of a "post-apocalyptic" installation at a Delaware art museum. It had to be the same guy—the writing even sounded like the way he'd spoken at the reception, though he was much harder on this conceptual artist than he had been on Keith. Poking around further, I found a second review from two months earlier on a different art blog. It praised a photography show that featured rather disturbing close-ups of children's battered toys, at a small gallery in lower Manhattan.

It looked as if Dez Mitchelson really got around the metro area. And he did write about art, a least part-time. But I did not find him listed on the masthead of any major print publication.

Not likely that anyone could make a living, I thought, by just writing a freelance review now and then. Those online magazines probably paid peanuts, if they paid at all. Yet Dez put down a deposit on a high-priced canvas by a little-known artist, just because it appealed to him. Besides, he gave off an air of authority and professional confidence.

Sarah had speculated that he might come from a wealthy family. If that were true, I couldn't see him as a shiftless playboy—he'd have a hand in the family business. Or, as she'd also said, he could be some kind of entrepreneur. That, I could envision more easily.

Someone who worked for himself, had just a few people under him, and made things happen.

But in either case, wouldn't his name also show up in connection with some other line of work, somewhere?

Another possible explanation struck me. "Dez Mitchelson" could be a pen name, used for his critiques and also when he visited art galleries. Nidra had said that reviewers often liked to keep a low profile when they attended shows, but maybe Dez figured no one in the boonies of Chadwick would have read any of his articles.

I was still puzzling about all of this when Sarah called me to the front of the shop to answer a question for a visitor. I flinched as if I'd been researching something illegal.

"Be right there!" I told her.

Get a grip, Cassie. You're committed to Mark, whom you love, and who is an all-around great guy. What do you care about some man who flirted with you at a party? You'll probably never even see him again, so why give him any more thought at all?

I powered down and closed the laptop before Sarah could come back to the playroom and ask what had me so absorbed. I wouldn't be able to come up with a good answer.

Except that I'd never been able to resist a mystery, and now Dez Mitchelson loomed more mysterious to me than ever.

"I got a personal phone call from Mr. Lathrop," Nancy Whyte told us, when she came for Quentin. "At first, I thought it was some kind of solicitation, until he dropped your name, Cassie. He said you and Mark came up with an idea for a contest, and that there was no entry fee, because it was just to attract people to the theater during the Halloween season."

"All absolutely true," I guaranteed. "And you don't even have to bring him there until Halloween Eve . . . assuming you win."

"Yes, Lathrop said even then he'll probably just invite the top three pets, the winners in each category. Guests can attend, the animals and their owners will pose for pictures, and that will be it. I checked with Angie—poor dear, she's not doing so well this week. She said whatever I decide is fine with her, and she trusts my judgment."

Nancy stated all of this in such a positive tone that I got my hopes up.

Just then, Sarah emerged through the playroom door, walking Quentin on his leash. We gave him a boost onto one of the high stools so Nancy could admire our handiwork. Including his tail, the cat measured almost a yard long, and when sitting erect at least eighteen inches tall, from his tufted paws to the tips of his long, devilish ears.

His clean coat now showed off its full array of smoky hues. He seemed to thrust out his bushy chest with pride, while riveting us with those uncanny golden eyes. I could see why he'd done well in the show ring, with so much presence.

Sarah broke down first. "Oh, come on," she goaded Nancy. "You *have* to enter him. He'll be the star of the whole event!"

The blond woman smiled. "You two have certainly made him even more gorgeous than he was before. Oh, all right, how can I say no? Even though I don't know very much about this theater. Lathrop told me a little, but . . ."

While Sarah tallied up Nancy's bill, I told her more about the Paragon's restoration and its dedication to showing classic films. "On your way out of town, at least drive by. It's just five blocks south, across from the diner, on the right. You can't miss the marquee."

"I'll do that," she promised, while loading her supersized cat into his rolling carrier.

Sarah held the front door open for her. "Gee, we should have taken a picture, for the contest, before you put him away."

"Oh, don't worry." Nancy smiled again, mysteriously. "I've done publicity shots of my own cats over the years, and have gotten pretty good at it. Now that I've made up my mind to enter Quentin, I'm already getting a few creative ideas."

I helped her lift the carrier into the back seat of her sedan. "Going to dress him up?" Privately, I worried that might be like gilding the lily.

"Not too much. Maybe just a little something befitting . . . a gentleman of his stature."

Mark and I usually had dinner together on Saturday nights, and I was glad he managed to keep our date that week, even if we pushed it a little later than usual. We went to Chad's, the local retro diner that stayed open until the wee hours.

With its turquoise-and-chrome décor, miniature juke-boxes in the booths, and waitresses in fifties garb, Chad's always existed slightly in the world of make-believe and didn't have to adjust much for Halloween. The glass-block vestibule had been decorated with a few expected cardboard images of skeletons, ghosts, and witches riding brooms. Over the main entrance hung a framed headshot of actor Chad Everett from his 1960s heartthrob days, a standard fixture; someone had even defiled that with a stick-on, furry black mustache.

The dessert showcase, just inside, offered an array of spooky cake designs for any upcoming parties, and plastic models of Frankenstein's monster and Dracula flanked the cash register. But the mature hostess who showed us to our booth had not bothered to upgrade from her usual white blouse and black pants, though her teased-out Jersey hair did add some extra drama. I wondered if she might don full witch regalia for the big day.

Used to eating earlier, both Mark and I were famished and ordered promptly. He went for the turkey chili, while I couldn't resist the vegetarian potpie, its crust carved to resemble the creepy, smiling face of Jack Skellington from *The Nightmare Before Christmas*.

While we waited for our orders, I told Mark as much about the gallery reception as I'd shared with Sarah. I mentioned Keith's big sale, and my suspicion that the buyer might also be an art reviewer. I added that Dawn believed Keith's success had been predicted by a psychic, whom she'd lined up for a pre-Halloween appearance at her shop.

"Most likely just a tribute to Keith's talent," Mark said, "but I have to give Dawn credit for trying to drum up business." He sounded as if, after a long, grueling day, he didn't even have the energy left to make fun of her gullibility.

"Anyway, you've got me in suspense," I told him. "Did the cops make any more progress on the burglary investigation?"

"Only a little. Some good news, some not so good." He drew a deep breath. "They found tire tracks from a motorcycle in the far corner of the clinic's parking lot. No one on our staff rides one, and hidden back there, it might not have been visible to Sam when he came to work. Also, you know that big screen we have around the trash bins?"

I did. Because the clinic disposed of several kinds of waste, some requiring special handling, they separated it into three large bins. They corralled these behind a white, prefab barrier about four feet tall and six feet long, anchored with screws to the side of the building.

"Bonelli thinks whoever arrived on the bike could have hidden behind there and waited for the night-shift guy to show up," Mark went on. "That means he knew that the door opened with an electronic passkey, that he'd have to force someone to let him in, and even about what time Sam would be coming."

More information that suggested an inside job, I thought. Unless . . . "He could have figured that out just by surveilling the clinic, over a couple of days, and staying hidden."

"I thought of that, too," Mark said. "The other bit of good news is an eyewitness saw someone riding a dark-colored motorcycle down Center Street around ten-thirty or eleven that night. She even remembered there was a saddlebag of some kind on the back. She told Bonelli the driver looked like a man, medium height and with a strong build, which jibes with what Sam thought. She also said the guy had longish hair, down to his collar, that showed under his helmet." A chuckle stole into Mark's voice. "And even though she got just a quick glimpse as he rode by, in the dark, she said he was 'really ugly'."

I laughed, too. "I hope the Chadwick PD doesn't question every homely guy in town who happens to have that build and hairstyle. Talk about adding insult to injury!"

"I'm sure they won't, but I guess the witness was too

distracted by his looks to notice anything more useful, like a license plate. Of course, she didn't know at the time that someone had committed a crime."

As our dinners arrived, we broke off this dicey conversation and spent a few minutes appreciating the food, always top quality at Chad's.

Meanwhile, I reflected on the updates Mark had shared with me. "Doesn't all of this new information at least take suspicion off the staffers at the clinic?"

"To some degree, I guess," he said. "It doesn't sound like any of our employees actually committed the theft, but we never really suspected that. It's still possible that someone from the clinic leaked too much information to the wrong person. Which is the other piece of bad news."

"Oh?"

"One of our techs, Susan, admitted to Bonelli that she told her younger sister about the anesthetics storage system. I guess Susan was warning the girl about drug abuse and what some of this stuff can do to you. But apparently the sister is a little wild, and there's a chance she let the info slip to someone she shouldn't have. So now Bonelli's going to question *her*."

"Oh, dear. I guess your tech never thought there was any harm, telling someone in her own family."

Mark paused to douse the fire of his chili with a long drink of water. "It puts us in a rough position, though," he explained. "On the one hand, we don't make our employees sign an agreement, or take an oath, not to mention where we store the serious drugs. We just expect them to use good judgment. And it seems like too small a mistake to fire someone over. Except that . . . we did get robbed, we had to replace all of those medications, and that stuff is out there now on the street!"

"It is a tough call, all right."

"And now that Sam's off the night shift, at least for a while, we're having a hard time getting anyone else to take it over. Many of our techs are female, and though they want to do their fair share, I can see why they'd be especially worried about staying at the clinic alone at night."

Mark sounded as if he'd been brooding about these problems all day, and there didn't seem to be any easy solutions on the horizon. I decided to lighten the tone a bit and told him Nancy Whyte had agreed to enter Quentin in the werewolf look-alike contest.

"Glad you reminded me," he said, more brightly. "I reached out to four of our clients about the contest. The two I connected with so far also thought it sounded like fun. I'm going to pass their names on to Avery so he can invite them himself."

I wondered how those invitations would be worded, especially with Lathrop's penchant for formality. *"Congratulations, Madame! We have been informed that you are the owner of an exceptionally terrifying gerbil . . ."*

"You already gave him the name of that breeder in Warren County, didn't you?" Mark asked.

"With the Lykois, yes. I'd be surprised if they didn't enter a cat, if only for the publicity."

"Sounds like this contest may actually happen." His face and tone relaxed a bit. "Be nice to have something fun to look forward to. So far, this Halloween has been shaping up as way *too* scary."

Chapter 8

By the time Mark headed home to his condo on Sunday afternoon, he seemed in a slightly better frame of mind about the issues affecting the clinic. At least I'd managed to convince him that things would work themselves out, and in the meantime, there probably wouldn't be any more break-ins. I hoped I was right about that.

I made my usual midday check of the boarders and turned Godiva out in the playroom for a while. As I took a seat to keep an eye on her, I pulled out my cell phone. I stared at it for a few minutes, undecided, then dialed Dawn's number.

She sounded a bit out of breath when she answered. "Oh, hi! I wondered who would be calling on a Sunday."

Was Keith visiting? I hoped I hadn't caught them during a romantic moment! "I'm not interrupting anything, am I?"

"Just my yoga session, but I can take a break."

"I thought yoga was supposed to be relaxing."

"Some of what I do is pretty strenuous, and I've been bad—I got away from it for a couple of months. So, I'm taking advantage of my day off to make up for that. Anyhow,

Cassie, thanks again for coming to the opening Friday! Keith told me it meant a lot to him, having friends there to support him."

"I was glad to do it, and really enjoyed myself. I haven't been to a gallery opening in years. I have a question, though, and I hope it won't unnerve Keith or blow anyone's cover. Did you know that Dez Mitchelson writes art reviews?"

"What? You're kidding! Did he tell you that?"

"No, but Nidra also wondered about it, so I did an online search." I told Dawn about the articles I'd found with that byline. "Not likely there would be two people with such an unusual name. So, maybe that's how he ended up coming to the opening."

"Well," said Dawn, "he also came because Keith invited him."

"Oh?"

"Mitchelson lives in Keith's building. Y'know, Public Storage?"

That four-story warehouse near the railroad tracks was another of the area's cool restoration projects, completed shortly before I'd moved to town. The architects had preserved and cleaned up the original red brick façade, but gave it new windows with snazzy black trim. The first two floors consisted of loft-style, two-bedroom apartments, while supposedly the top floor offered some more luxurious units. Though the building did have a street number, a limestone arch above the double front doors still branded it as "Public Storage, 1881," and most people referred to it that way.

"I guess Dez is new there, but Keith has run into him a couple of times," Dawn explained. "He told me that one day last week Dez was walking his dog in the parking lot, while Keith was loading the paintings into his van to take them to the gallery. Dez admired them and said he'd dabbled in art himself when he was younger. Keith told him about the opening, and Dez said he'd try to make it."

That made sense. Thinking back, I *had* gotten the impression, when the two men were talking at the reception, that they already knew each other.

"But Mitchelson didn't even say that he collected art, much less that he wrote about it," Dawn continued, with mounting excitement. "Do you think he'll do a write-up for the *Courier*? Or maybe even the Morristown paper? If Keith could get a review for his first show ever, that would be awesome!"

"Like I said, I just saw a couple of posts on some fairly obscure art blog sites. Maybe Dez could freelance something to one of the papers, but who knows what their rules are about such things." I remembered something else. "Funny, though . . . he told Nidra he came to the opening because he saw an ad she ran in the *Courier*."

"That is odd," Dawn agreed. "Maybe he didn't want to let on that he was friendly with any particular artist. I mean, if he does intend to do a review . . ."

"Yeah, it could be something like that. Nidra did say that some critics like to play it cool when they come to galleries, so people don't try to influence their opinions."

"Do you think I should tell Keith? Or maybe I shouldn't, huh? I wouldn't want to get his hopes up for nothing."

"Yeah, might be best to just wait and see what happens. No matter what else comes of it, at least he did sell Dez a painting!"

"You're right. That's a big deal, in itself—if a *critic* liked his work well enough to buy it."

I let my friend go to resume her intensive yoga session. I put Godiva back in her condo, then went upstairs to give my own cats their lunch and grab something for myself. While we all were finishing up, I got a call on my cell from Avery Lathrop.

He apologized for disturbing me on my "day of rest," but wanted to keep me posted concerning the pet photo contest. He said he already had received a dozen entries, most electronically.

"The owners have outdone themselves, I must say," he told me. "If we blow these pictures up and print them out, it should make a great display for the lobby."

"So glad it's working out!" I said.

"I gave a deadline of this Wednesday, because I want to leave the photos on view as long as possible, for people to vote. I do think, though, that we need to screen out a few that just don't make the cut, and I'd like to delegate that job to someone other than myself. Would you and Mark be willing to do the pre-judging? Maybe Wednesday evening?"

I told him I'd be free, but I would have to check with Mark. "Things are a little crazy at his clinic these days. You may have heard about the break-in last Tuesday."

"Yes, that sounded awful! I did read about it, and Dave, our usher, said the police car went by while the three of you were still in the lobby discussing the movie."

"It did, and right after that, Mark got a call telling him what had happened. It was an upsetting end, I'm afraid, to a fun evening."

"The clinic is in a converted home, isn't it? That white colonial on Laurel Street? Nice building, but I suppose it's a challenge to make really secure. Lord knows, I had enough problems with the Paragon and The Firehouse. Not easy to retrofit older architecture with modern electronic security."

"Well, they thought the clinic had a pretty good system, but I guess now they've got to boost it even more." I held back from sharing further details. "Anyway, I'll talk to Mark today and ask if he can make time on Wednesday evening. I am looking forward to seeing those entries!"

"You won't be disappointed, Cassie. Some are very cute, some are *howlingly* funny, and a few will really chill your blood—*brrr*!"

I hung up with a smile. Lathrop did have a flair for the dramatic! No doubt Quentin's portrait fell into the "chilling" category. I wondered what Nancy might have done to enhance his natural, sinister charm.

By Monday, I had a real-life reason to shiver—my furnace was not even putting out as much heat as usual. I had to crank it way up to keep my boarder cats comfortable, not to mention me and Sarah. Our spirits lifted when we saw the JANOS HOME REPAIR truck pull up in front, and stocky, gray-haired Nick knock on our glass door.

I practically considered Nick a kind of uncle these days, because we've been through a couple of scrapes together over the past few years. Shortly after I started my business in Chadwick, I even helped prove his innocence when he was framed for a murder! Maybe because of that, he usually does repairs for me at very reasonable rates.

We caught up on the latest town news, including the clinic break-in, and I passed along what little information the cops had shared with Mark. In the background, Nick had a chance to hear for himself the bizarre noises that emanated from my heating system.

He made a face. "Yeah, I can see why that's driving you crazy, Cassie. Sounds like a bearing and maybe the belt. Furnace is in the basement, right? You got an outside entrance for that?"

"That door next to the back stairs," I said.

"I'll pull my truck into the lot, then, so I can work without disturbing you folks up here."

While Nick did this, I went down to the basement by an inside flight of stairs to unlock the door for him.

Why is it that whenever someone comes to work in your cellar, you tend to feel self-conscious, even embarrassed? Well, maybe not everyone feels that way. Maybe *your* basement is spotless, neatly organized, and well-lit, with everything in good shape; the repairman comes only for annual maintenance, which you carefully note every year on your calendar. (If that's the case, I'm not sure I want to know you.)

Anyhow, aside from hauling loads to and from the washer and dryer, I only used my basement to store a couple of extra cat trees and some bargain-sized bags of dry food and litter—anything too large to fit on the shelves of my restroom-cum-storage closet on the main floor. When I did go down, I mostly ignored the aged fieldstone walls with their crumbling mortar, the cement floor that also was deteriorating back to sand in spots, and the mysterious network of pipes, cables, and wiring that served to keep my house and shop going. I'd had all of that stuff checked out when I moved in, and anything that wasn't up to code had been corrected by Nick, so I shouldn't have to worry about any real disasters. And since he knew its history, I didn't feel I had to apologize to him about its shabbiness . . . at least, not too much.

While Sarah kept a casual eye on the sales counter, I hung by Nick's side as he opened the back of the furnace and revealed its mysterious—to me—insides. Before too long, he had found the loose blower bearing and spotted various other signs of wear and tear.

"You ever clean or change these filters?" he asked, with a bemused expression. When I shrugged, he just shook his head. "I'll replace them for you, and fix the bearing, but for the other stuff you really should get an HVAC guy. I'd say this unit's about fifteen years old, which means it hasn't got much life left, anyway."

I nodded glumly. "Dawn told me I ought to get a high-efficiency model."

"You really should. It'll burn cleaner and last longer. Cost you more up front, but you'll save money in the long run. I'm sure you can get financing for one."

"I'll have to think about it. Meanwhile, can you at least make this thing run a little better than it has been?"

"I'll do my best, and I'll give you the number of a good HVAC pro. He can check out your ducts, too."

"Hey, don't get personal!" I joked.

I left Nick alone for the next half hour while he tinkered with the furnace. By the time he knocked again, this time at my back door, the rattling had stopped, and the unit did seem to be rumbling more quietly. As usual, he charged me only a very modest fee for his services. Before leaving, he again recommended that I have it checked by a pro and handed me a scrap of paper with the name of a local HVAC company.

"And don't wait too long," he told me in parting. "It's supposed to get real cold this winter."

Even my friends kept telling me things I really didn't want to hear.

We had no more visitors for the rest of the morning, and Sarah and I agreed that we kind of missed the Maine Coon's presence in the VIP cat condo. Once we'd finished with our usual duties, I took some time to call the police station and leave a message for Bonelli.

Overhearing, my assistant asked, "Anything wrong?"

"Nothing new," I told her, "but Mark says the vet clinic is

really in turmoil, with the whole staff under suspicion. I just want to find out if there's anything I can do to help."

Sarah tilted her head sympathetically. "You know Bonelli. She's liable to say the best thing you can do is stay out of it, and let her guys do their job."

I shrugged. "If that's the way she feels, she can tell me over the phone. But if she's open to it, I'd like to stop down and talk with her in person."

I had just taken off my grooming apron and headscarf when my cell phone rang.

"I've got a few minutes now," Bonelli said, terse and businesslike as always.

"Be there in a jiff!" I told her.

Watching me pull on my pleather jacket, Sarah laughed. "Bet they don't get many people so eager to go to the police station."

These days, Angela Bonelli usually welcomed me with a cup of some aromatic brew from her burgundy Keurig coffeemaker. It was the sole luxury in her glass-walled office, which gave her a partial view of the "perps" coming and going to the cells at the back of the station. We both indulged in mugs of seasonal Pumpkin Spice coffee as she settled back behind her gray metal L-shaped desk, and I lowered myself—gingerly—into the hard-seated wooden guest chair that faced it.

Maybe because of her role as a female police detective in a small town, Bonelli, in her mid-forties, always maintained a professional air. She kept her dark hair in a short, businesslike bob, used minimal makeup, and usually wore pants and a coordinating blazer in some dark, neutral color. Gradually, she'd been livening things up, though, and today had combined a navy herringbone jacket with a burgundy turtleneck. When

I complimented her on the pieces, she admitted that her husband, Lou, had given her the sweater for her birthday, and she'd bought the blazer with a gift card from one of her sons.

"They told me I've got enough credibility in this town by now," she added with a smile, "that I can afford to loosen up a little."

"Well, they're right." Still, I knew better than to waste Bonelli's time, so I plunged ahead. "I hope I'm not overstepping, but I'm worried that the break-in at the veterinary clinic is affecting morale there. Mark tells me they all suspect each other of leaking information about the anesthetics storeroom, and some of their regular customers have canceled appointments, as if they've decided the clinic isn't reliable."

The detective clasped her hands on the desk blotter, and her dark, world-weary gaze met mine. "That is a shame, Cassie, but you must realize we had to question everyone. It seems as if the robber had inside information, and if we can find out who provided it, we might be able to catch him. We're following up on a few leads at the moment, and I'm hoping at least one may pay off."

"Mark told me about the guy on the motorcycle," I said.

"Yeah . . . Sorry to say, that's the least promising lead. We can narrow down some details by the tread tracks in the parking lot. It was a medium-weight bike, probably a cruiser, and we've got the specs of the tires. But the witness who saw the man riding through town couldn't tell us the make, so we have no idea if it was even the same model that was parked at the clinic."

I could see where that might be a dead end. Still, I resolved to keep my eyes peeled for anyone cruising around on a motorcycle. *Especially someone really unattractive?*

"Mark said one of the techs admitted to telling her sister about the storage system for the anesthetics."

Bonelli stayed quiet for a beat. Was she unhappy that he'd shared this news with me? But since both Mark and I had helped the cops with cases before, she must have expected it.

"Yes, we questioned the sister," the detective said. "She swears she didn't repeat the information to anybody. Whether she did let it slip during a weak moment, and doesn't want to admit that, I can't be sure. Or maybe she told someone and just doesn't want to make him a suspect. We grilled her for a bit, but in the end had to let her go."

Another idea occurred to me. "How long ago was the special storage room set up? Could someone who worked on it have a connection with the drug ring?"

"The clinic's been in business for about four years, and they installed that system early. It was specially adapted to the existing building, which used to be a private home."

I remembered what Lathrop had said about the challenges of adapting a modern security system to an older structure.

"We met with guys from the security company, which is a highly reputable chain. They seem very concerned and conscientious about dealing with the problem," Bonelli continued. "Did someone who was on their staff years ago, and helped with the installation, later fall in with a bad crowd? Maybe, but that might be hard to verify."

I could see that. "This also has happened at other East Coast clinics, too, right? Did they use the same security company?"

"No, different ones. But you're right, in that someone who'd set up a top-security storage room in one clinic would understand how to defeat a similar system in another." Bonelli made a trip to the Keurig and poured more coffee for both of us. "We're liaising with the police departments in those areas, hoping to come up with some common threads."

"How about the girl who overdosed at the party last week?"

"Did Mark tell you about that, too?"

"Actually, I heard about it first from Becky Newmeyer, my on-the-road assistant. She went to college with the dead woman, Karin."

"Yes, we've spoken to Becky."

"Do you think her friend was drugged with something from our clinic?"

"She definitely ingested ketamine. Not a good mix with all the alcohol she'd been drinking, or with her heart condition. But assuming she would have known better, and not taken it deliberately, anyone who dosed her drink could be guilty of manslaughter."

"No suspects there, either?"

"Again, no one's admitting to the act, and no one's ratting out the culprit." Settling behind her desk again with her coffee, Bonelli frowned. "That might be our best shot, though. Chances are, whoever used the drug on her was just the buyer. If we can find out where he got it—finger a dealer—we'd be closer to busting the whole operation."

"Any ideas on how to do that?"

"Maybe. You know that place up on the mountain, The Roost?"

I nodded. I'd heard it mentioned often, ever since I'd moved to Chadwick. It was mainly a roadhouse, known for its picturesque, mountainside setting and somewhat rowdy nightlife.

"You've been there?" Bonelli prodded me.

"Never to eat. Mark and I stopped by once, but the music was so loud and the crowd inside was so raucous . . . it wasn't our kind of place. We just left and came back downtown for dinner."

The detective smiled. "No, it's not really geared toward

couples. Fridays and Saturdays, they do get a more sedate crowd, with some older people. But during the week, it's a real singles' hookup joint. They have specials on certain drinks, karaoke nights, sometimes speed-dating events. They've never gone as far as wet T-shirt contests, but you get the idea."

I did, and felt grateful again to have Mark in my life.

"They've also had some serious problems, lately, with men spiking the ladies' drinks. One woman got assaulted in her date's car, in the parking lot, and another was barely rescued by a friend before the same kind of thing happened to her. The place has its own security guard, but either he's lazy or deliberately looks the other way. We recently assigned a couple of our guys, Jacoby and Waller, to go undercover on different nights, mingle with the crowds, and see what they could find out."

I tried to picture this and smiled. Both officers were youngish and good-looking, but they also had that straight-arrow demeanor typical of small-town cops.

"Neither turned up much, and I'm afraid they were 'made,' as we say, pretty quickly. Could be that if any drug nonsense had been planned, it was shut down the minute our man walked in."

"Could be," I agreed. "Plus, any bad guys from the Chadwick area probably know all the faces in your department."

Bonelli shook her head. "I wish Haley Lorenger was still here. She left the department right before you moved to town. Very pretty, but she could take care of herself—not only on the street, but even around her fellow officers! She got married, moved to Hillside with her husband, and joined their PD. She would have been perfect for this job, though. That's what we need, really—a young woman to infiltrate the Roost crowd and study the action."

In the weighted silence that followed, I wondered if she was intentionally dangling the bait in my direction. "Okay," I said. "Just tell me what I need to do."

The detective threw me a shocked look. "Oh . . . no, Cassie. I didn't mean you! Although after I talked to Becky, I did make the suggestion to her."

Becky might be willing, I thought, if only to help solve the death of her former friend. "And?"

"Apparently she once did some waitressing at The Roost and knows people there. But that's not such a good thing. They're aware that she's dating Chris now, so if she showed up without him, it might raise their suspicions." Bonelli shrugged. "Just as well. I don't like to ask any civilian to take such a risk."

"Doesn't sound so risky to me. Go to The Roost for an evening, hang out at the bar, look for any suspicious activity. Unless, of course, I'd have to arrest somebody."

I must have sounded all too ready, because Bonelli laughed. "No, I'd still have one of our guys lurking around, in case there was any arresting to be done. We do have a new hire, Eddie MacDonald, who wouldn't be familiar to the Roost crowd. But you . . . or whoever does this . . . would have to go on one of these singles' nights."

"I figured."

She cocked her head, as if surprised I'd be willing to venture out without Mark. "You'd probably get a lot of jerks trying to pick you up."

"Isn't that the idea? To sift through the harmless jerks and spot the psychos?"

"True. But unlike a female officer, you might not have the resources to protect yourself," she cautioned me.

"Angela, remember whom you're talking to. I've done okay so far, haven't I?"

My confidence, gained over several past encounters with bad guys, seemed to surprise her, and she smiled again. "You have. But if you try to pull this off, you absolutely should not go alone."

My mind had already been running along that line. "No respectable lady would, would she? I'll check with my favorite partner in crime, though, and see if she's also up for a girls' night out."

Chapter 9

I dropped over to Dawn's on Tuesday night for a very informal supper. She made a hearty vegetable soup, and we ate downstairs in her shop by the central, wood-burning stove. The antique appliance had come with the building, and in warmer months served as just a quaint conversation piece. At this time of year, though, Dawn actually lit the stove once in a while and fed it logs she kept in a basket nearby. An old barrel set on end, with a round piece of wood nailed to the top, served as our table, and we sat in armchairs draped with Indian-patterned bedspreads.

Nature's Way had started life as a feed store, and Dawn preserved much of that atmosphere. She had refinished the wide, rugged planks of the floors and modified the equally rustic walls with just a wash of pale green paint. Rows of wooden shelving, divided into departments, held baking mixes; packaged cookies, crackers, nuts, and dried fruits; canned goods, jams, and spreads; and other types of ready-to-eat foods.

A large freezer across the back wall offered all-natural frozen meals, many of them vegetarian; some free-range, organic meats; various types of cheeses, milks, and yogurts;

and bottled smoothies and soft drinks. A central produce display showcased locally grown organic fruits and vegetables according to the season. Right now, these included apples, pumpkins, squash, sweet potatoes, and colorful kales and cabbages.

Dawn maintained such high standards for her merchandise that many customers traveled from several towns away to buy from her. That was one of the reasons she recently had expanded her mail-order business.

While she ladled our soup into bowls from her collection of hand-thrown pottery, her irrepressible tabby cat, Tigger—the same one captured in Keith's painting—frolicked around her feet. I worried that he'd trip her and spill everything, though Dawn seemed used to maneuvering around him by now. I jangled my car keys to lure him out of her way. That worked, probably because the soup included no fish, chicken, or beef to really hold the cat's interest.

Meanwhile, Dawn enthused about the responses she'd gotten so far to her announcement of Ripley Van Eyck's appearance. "I'd planned to run an ad online, but I don't think I'll even need to, Cassie! I just put out the word among my customers, and Sue Brookings from the *Courier* also ran a short item in her Lifestyle column. Since then, people have been signing up like crazy."

That might be the word for it, I thought, but kept my cynicism to myself. Glancing around, I asked, "How many can you safely pack in here?"

"I was thinking at least twenty, though I probably can go a little over. Move a few displays out of this central area, and there should be plenty of room. I'll have to rent some folding chairs, though. Ripley said his program sometimes runs a couple of hours, and people won't want to stand for that length of time."

Another disparaging quip started to form in my mind, but I bit it back. "Where is *he* going to stand . . . or sit?"

"I was thinking, right near the big display case." She nodded toward the antique, glass-fronted, carved oak piece near the front of her store. "That way, everybody should be able to see and hear him. Gee, I wonder if I should rent a microphone, too!"

"You probably don't need to. Can't he project his thoughts into their minds?"

Oops, I actually said that one aloud!

Dawn acknowledged the shot with a tolerant smile. "C'mon. You have to admit, he predicted Keith would make a big sale at his first art show, and it came true."

"Well, he didn't predict that, specifically, Dawn. Ridley didn't even know Keith was having an art show."

"I didn't tell him, no. Which is all the more amazing! And even Keith and I were surprised by that sale. I mean, we just hoped some of our friends might buy a few smaller pieces, like you did . . . Thanks, by the way."

"Glad to. That study of Tigger is adorable."

"But we didn't really think anyone would go for the bigger, more expensive canvases. Nidra told me that Mitchelson asked about my portrait first, but when he heard it wasn't for sale, he opted for the daylilies."

"Sounds as if he came prepared to spend some serious cash. Of course, I don't suppose he paid in cash . . ."

Dawn shrugged. "He only needed to leave a deposit, so far. He probably either charged that or wrote a check. Why?"

I hesitated. "I'm *not* saying this because I don't think Keith's art is terrific, and certainly should impress a serious collector. It's just that I'm . . . curious about Dez Mitchelson."

She grinned and wagged a finger at me. "I thought you and he were having a pretty intense discussion at the reception.

Just because poor Mark couldn't come, though, I wouldn't expect you to ditch him for some flashy stranger!"

"I have no intention of doing that," I swore, though I felt myself color a bit. "I only said I'm curious. Didn't he impress you as the successful type? He must do more for a living than just write the occasional freelance art review. But I tried to find some more information about him online, and there's no website for another business, no personal Facebook page, nothing."

"So? Maybe he's got family money and doesn't have to work. And even today, not everybody posts their whole life on social media. Some people think it's in bad taste, and they only give out their personal information to close friends, relatives, or business contacts."

"You're probably right," I said. "I'm thinking like a hard-working, self-employed business owner, who constantly has to promote and advertise. I guess the really successful folks can get new customers just by word of mouth. I was just worried that Dez might be not-quite-legit, and might end up stiffing Nidra—and Keith—when it came time to pay for the painting."

"Oh, I doubt that." My friend eyed me more critically. "You've been mixed up in so many police investigations the past couple of years, Cassie, I think it's making you suspicious of everybody."

"Could be." Was this the right time to broach my real reason for visiting her this evening? Might as well try. "Speaking of which . . ."

I told her about my discussion with Bonelli that morning, how she wanted to send a woman undercover at The Roost to report on possible drug activity, and how I'd volunteered.

"Gee, Cassie, are you sure? That's such a hookup joint these days, especially on the weeknights."

"Exactly the point," I reminded her. "Have you ever had a bad experience there?"

"Nothing serious, but . . . a few years back, before you moved here and before I made any commitment to Keith, I did drop in to The Roost one night with a girlfriend. Her idea—she just wanted to grab a beer and some bar food. It was early, about seven, and we were in our normal work clothes. But random guys kept cruising us, and one jerk who was already pretty wasted just wouldn't leave us alone, until we left. It's that kind of place."

"I had the same impression, from the one time I stopped in with Mark," I admitted.

"The crowd tends to be kind of young and crazy." With a wink, Dawn added, "Not settled old millennials, like us."

"Bonelli also mentioned that." I paused, significantly. "So, you want to come with me?"

She grinned. "Wouldn't miss it for the world! When do you plan to go?"

"Well, Mark and I are supposed to pre-judge the Paragon's pet photo contest tomorrow night." I explained to her what that involved. "So why don't you and I hit The Roost on Thursday?"

"Sounds fine." She cocked her head at me. "You're going to tell Mark about our plans?"

"I guess I'll have to."

"You know he'll try to talk you out of it."

"Hey, I've officially been recruited by the Chadwick PD," I reminded her. "I'm just informing him, not asking his permission."

Wednesday, I left Sarah in charge of the shop for most of the afternoon, while I went out on a mobile-grooming call with Becky. We now visited a few customers on a rotating schedule of every two months. Some owners preferred to have their cats groomed at home, because it was more convenient than bringing them back and forth to our shop. Others made the arrangement to suit their cat's physical or temperamental needs.

Today's call fell into the second category. We were dealing with Cloud, a seventeen-year-old white Persian mix with arthritis. Because bending and stretching had become difficult for her, Cloud could no longer keep herself totally clean and free of mats. Her owner, middle-aged bachelor Richard Braff, originally brought her to Cassie's Comfy Cats, but the strangeness of the surroundings, plus her discomfort, had stressed her out—something extra dangerous for an elderly animal. She also had a harder-than-average time negotiating the three levels of our condos. So, all of the humans involved decided it was best if Cassie's Comfy Cats came to her.

Becky and I took off at about ten o'clock in the grooming van, upgraded almost a year ago from a battle-scarred black panel truck that I'd gotten for a steal. Now it was bright white, with a raised roof, its own generator and water tank, and a large cartoon of a smug, prancing Persian on each side, designed by Keith. It drew a lot of attention on the road, which also had proven good for my business.

I did not intend to bring up the death of Karin Weaver during our drive, but Becky did that on her own. She told me the young woman's family held a private funeral, so she hadn't gotten a chance to speak to Karin's parents.

"I did talk to a couple of friends we still had in common, from the old days, though," Becky said. "They admitted she was still drinking a lot, mainly at clubs and parties. But a year ago her doctor had warned her about messing with any recreational drugs, because of her heart condition, so she gave up all of that."

I mulled this news. "In other words, she may not have taken the stuff that killed her intentionally."

"Exactly." Becky's pixie face darkened in a scowl. "I'll bet some lowlife spiked her drink. If that's true, I don't know how the cops will ever catch him. Nobody from the party is talking, of course."

"Of course."

"The Weavers swear that Karin had mended her ways, and they're looking everywhere for someone to blame. I hear they want to sue the owners of the house where it happened. It was a brother and sister my age who threw the party, and their parents were away at the time. But I guess they figure that, whoever spiked Karin's drink, someone must have invited him, and the parents should have been more aware." Becky's pert features twisted in annoyance. "Really, it's not like anyone sends out engraved invitations to a party like that! Word gets around. The son and daughter asked their friends, who brought friends of their own, and other people might just have dropped by."

I could envision that scenario. "So, even if the cops can manage to question half the guests, they'll still probably never track down who was to blame."

"That's right." Becky paused. "I should warn you, Cassie, that the Weavers also mentioned suing the veterinary clinic. Talk about blaming the victims! But I guess they're saying the clinic should have had better security, or maybe the night-duty guy was in on the heist."

My hands gripped the van's steering wheel more tightly in anger. "That's outrageous. Poor Sam was injured and taken to the medical center! Mark and Maggie are still doing everything they can to help the police find the thief."

"You and I know that, but Sharon and Archie Weaver aren't too rational right now. And if they want to sue, they've got the bucks to hire a real pit bull of a lawyer. So I thought I'd better give you, and Mark, a heads-up."

Depressed by this news, I wondered if my paralegal mother could help the clinic connect with a good attorney of their own. Maybe someone with her Morristown firm, McCabe, Preston & Rueda?

Eyes still trained on the road, I thought I could risk some inside information of my own. "I had a talk with Angela Bonelli yesterday. She says there have been a couple of incidents similar to Karin's up at The Roost. None fatal, fortunately, but the Chadwick cops are keeping an eye on that place. Maybe they can nab the guy who was responsible for her death, or at least his supplier."

Becky responded with a grim chuckle. "She mentioned that to me, too, but I dunno. I waitressed up there for a while, and whenever there was a cop on the premises, everyone always knew about it. Our Chadwick boys aren't real good on undercover work—they're too stiff, or something."

Although the detective had approached Becky first to go undercover at the roadhouse, she might not want me to reveal that Dawn and I had agreed to a similar plan. So I only said, "From what she told me, she's got some new tricks up her sleeve. So don't give up hope, Becky. She may clear your friend's reputation, yet."

We pulled up in front of Richard Braff's tidy Cape Cod home, which was shaded by a vast maple tree. Although the tree had shed some of its fall color by now, the lawn looked freshly raked, and three brown sacks overflowing with leaves stood by the curb to be collected.

Braff, a cheerful, round-faced man of about forty, already had Cloud in her carrier and brought her out to us. We showed him all around the van's interior and explained our process. He asked to stay and watch, but I explained that we didn't permit that because the quarters were so tight. I didn't add that some owners tended to micromanage, and if their cat made the slightest peep, they'd accuse us of mistreatment. Braff reluctantly gave up control to me and Becky for the next hour or so.

The arthritic Persian did require careful handling, and while she probably still felt a few twinges, we made every effort to keep her comfortable. Most of her complaints sounded the same as those of any feline who didn't like being handled by strangers, or held still while we carefully loosened the mats in her coat. Because she couldn't keep herself clean as well as a young, healthy cat, we trimmed the fur extra short under her tail and down the "britches" of her hind legs.

By the time we handed her back to Richard, both her snowy coat and her disposition had brightened considerably.

"She looks great!" He hugged his fluffy pet without any concern for his nubby, navy-blue pullover. He paid us, even adding a tip, and made an appointment on the spot for Cloud's next session.

On our drive back to downtown Chadwick, I mentioned to Becky that the Paragon's pet photo contest had attracted a good number of entries, and Mark and I were going to pre-judge them that evening. In turn, she enthused about the upcoming costume parade in the park.

"We've got our two judges," she told me. "A syndicated pet columnist and blogger who's based in Morristown, and a guy who runs a theatrical costume shop out in Sparta. We figured, one animal expert, one costume expert. Terry, our boss from FOCA, will oversee the whole thing, to make sure the entries follow our rules and all the people and animals stay safe."

This chitchat kept us both occupied until I pulled up in

front of the single-story FOCA shelter, where Becky had left her car. Even though she might have been interested in the surveillance Dawn and I planned to do at The Roost on Thursday, I decided again to keep that information to myself. I knew Bonelli would not want me sharing it with too many people, especially beforehand.

Unfortunately, I saw no way to avoid telling Mark.

"I don't believe it," he ranted. "I'm going to strangle Bonelli. She has no right to get you mixed up in a situation like this!"

Anticipating his reaction, I'd braced myself. Still, I hadn't expected him to lay all of the blame on our hardworking police detective. "Mark, if you don't want to be considered a suspect, you probably shouldn't go around threatening an officer of the law."

"She can't send you undercover with no training, no backup . . ."

"Please calm down. First, I'm not officially 'undercover.' I certainly can't arrest anyone. There will be a real plainclothes cop at the restaurant, and we can tip him off if we do see any suspicious activity."

He snorted. "And Dawn! Might have known she'd egg you on. Don't forget how much trouble the two of you got into when—"

"You're putting the blame on everyone but the real guilty party. When Bonelli commented that it would be helpful to put a young woman on the scene at The Roost, I volunteered."

"Sure, like she probably knew you would."

"And *I* recruited Dawn to come along, because if there is any risk, we can look out for each other. But there shouldn't be, really. We're going to mingle a little, ask a few questions, listen to the answers, and observe what goes on. Just like anyone else who's there to have a good time."

Mark frowned again. "Is *that* image supposed to make me feel better?"

I grinned at his jealousy. "C'mon. You know I'm not interested in picking up anyone, and neither is Dawn. But we're not regulars at The Roost, so people will probably assume we're both single. That's what makes it so perfect. We can just play it cool and take in whatever is happening around us."

"I still don't like it," he grumbled, but his vocal pitch had come down a notch or two.

I got up, crossed behind his chair, and draped both my arms over his shoulders. "Would it help if I reminded you that I'm doing this for you, and your clinic? If we do uncover any more leads, they may point the cops away from your people and toward the real bad guys."

"How about I come along with you?" Mark suggested.

Though I appreciated the concern, I bent my head to give him a sideways look. "That would kind of defeat the purpose, wouldn't it? Most likely, a bunch of guys are behind this drug ring, so we'll be trying to talk to the *male* patrons. They're not going to chat us up if you're hovering nearby."

He raised both hands in surrender. "Okay, you're right. I know you're doing this for all the right reasons, Cassie, and I can't stop you. But if you and Dawn go through all this tomorrow night, and it doesn't turn up anything new . . . you're not going to keep doing it, are you?"

I hadn't even considered that, but gave him a prompt, definite answer. "No, I promise. It will be one and done. Okay?" Circling back to my place at the table, I caught sight of my squarish, retro wall clock, yellow-rimmed to match the kitchenette set. "Yikes, it's seven-thirty already. We'd better get over to the Paragon."

That evening, Mark met Lathrop for the first time. I gave him a sense of what to expect, so he didn't blink an eye when the developer showed up in pleated pants and a rust-and-brown vest that would have suited a dad in a 1960s sitcom. Avery's height and theatrical way of speaking lent the getup a certain dignity, though.

He thanked us for making time to help him with the contest and commiserated for a few minutes with Mark about the clinic break-in. He suggested a couple of measures they could try for extra security. Wisely, I felt, Mark just nodded and did not let on what improvements were actually under consideration.

Those pleasantries out of the way, Lathrop escorted us over to the concession stand. He had set up stools for the two of us in back of it—nothing like a desk being available—and opened a laptop computer on the counter to show us the contest entries.

"Most people sent their pictures electronically," he explained, "but I did get a few glossy photos. I scanned those so you could view them along with the rest. Since I didn't want old pictures of animals that died years ago, I made the owners sign a pledge that if their pet won, they would bring it in person to the theater on Halloween Eve."

"Good thinking," Mark said.

Lathrop started the slideshow, and the first pet portrait made us both whoop with laughter. It was a close-up of perhaps the world's most ferocious-looking ferret, wearing a doll-sized buffalo plaid shirt. Held by an almost invisible human hand, he glowered with beady black eyes, bared nasty little fangs, and reached toward the camera with long claws. The fur of his face was pale gray, and long, white whiskers framed his snarl.

"There's one horror movie that never made it to the big screen," Mark quipped. "Ferret-man!"

"Ah, but if he were the size of a man, he'd be pretty scary, right?" I threw back.

Lathrop smiled. "Just remember, we're offering three prizes—Scariest, Cutest, and Funniest."

Many of the entrants had used the gimmick of dressing their pet in some type of human clothing. We saw an intimidating gray cockatiel with a huge white crest, shot from the side to capture his sly expression; with his little black cape and his raised wing, though, he looked more like Count Dracula. I think the ripped-workshirt-and-jeans combination paid homage to Lon Chaney in *The Wolfman,* and variations of that costume appeared on one disgruntled black Persian, a wiry male Lykoi, and a bearlike Maine Coon kitten.

Mark and I ruled out a capuchin monkey in a similar getup, after he pointed out that they were illegal to keep as pets in New Jersey. We vetoed a few shots that were out of focus, or too cheesy, or ones where the photographer had made no real effort to make the animal look scary or spooky. Ditto, a portrait of a sweet-looking husky, whose owner had completely ignored the "no dogs" rule. We also eliminated any picture where it looked like the pet had been tormented to act "wild" for the camera.

After we'd been at it a while, one image popped onto the screen that made me gasp and Mark whistle.

"Is that another Lykoi?" he asked.

I nodded. "Isn't she amazing?"

The female cat sported the breed's classic wiry-looking gray coat, which I'd heard was actually very soft. It grew sparsely around the nose, mouth, and eyes, giving her a half-human appearance. Her owner had draped her in a miniature silver lamé cloak and hung a silver crescent moon on a thin chain around her delicate neck. The upward tilt of her wrinkled little face completed her persona of an exotic werewolf princess.

Mark and I agreed that she was bound to win at least one category.

Guessing we had to be near the end, I started to wonder about an entry that seemed conspicuously absent.

"Almost done," Lathrop told us. "I think I've saved the best for last."

He scrolled the laptop's screen one more time. I giggled in recognition, and Mark said, "Wow!"

He had never seen Quentin before, even in a photo, and Nancy had posed and lighted her dark prince to make the most of his natural charisma. As she'd promised, he wore only a minimal costume, but it was effective—a Victorian, white wing-tip collar tied with a burgundy satin ascot. The end of the puffy tie disappeared into the thick silver fur of the cat's chest, as if into a ruffled shirtfront.

"That collar looks great," Mark said. "But is it really a werewolf thing?"

"Quentin Collins from *Dark Shadows*," Lathrop told him. "He was a werewolf in both the present-day storyline and the 1890s flashback." The theater owner glanced at me. "And that's actually the cat's name, right?"

"It is."

The theater owner smiled broadly. "Very clever."

Figured, I thought, that Lathrop would also be familiar with the eerie vintage soap opera. He was the right age to have watched the show on TV as a teen.

By a little after nine, we had narrowed down the entries

to Lathrop's satisfaction. He said he would create a montage, identifying the contestants only by number, and have it up in the lobby by the time the audience arrived for the next evening's movie.

"It's *Dracula Has Risen from the Grave*," he reminded us. "Free passes for you both, if you want to come."

I smiled and told him, "Thanks, but I'm going to be busy."

Mark made no comment until we had left the theater and started back to his car. "That's right, you and Dawn will be fending off plenty of real wolves tomorrow night. Bonelli should at least give you a gun with silver bullets."

Chapter 10

Ned Cooperman, of Cooperman Heating & Cooling, represented his company well with his trim head of graying brown hair, heroic jawline, and crisp navy-blue jumpsuit. The jumpsuit hardly looked mussed, even after he'd spent an hour tinkering with my aged furnace, and he called me to the basement to give me his diagnosis.

"I replaced that faulty blower bearing and put in a new drive belt," he said, "but according to the serial number, this model is about seventeen years old. Your heat exchanger is out of warranty, so if that goes, you're looking at an expensive repair. And with winter coming . . ."

He didn't need to finish the sentence. Any repairs later on might have to be made under emergency circumstances, which meant I'd have to come up with the cash fast.

Packing up his tools, Cooperman continued, "At this point, you're probably getting less than seventy-five-percent AFUE. That's annualized fuel utilization efficiency, the amount of fuel you're burning for heat versus the amount that's lost to combustion. A new, high-efficiency furnace will give you an AFUE of ninety percent or more. So, in spite of the up-front cost, you'll see lower gas bills from day one. In a cool climate like we've got around here, that can pay for itself pretty quickly."

Sounded good, I thought, if one could easily cover the "up-front cost."

"At the very least, you'll need to replace that heat exchanger before winter," he said. "The longer you put that off, with your unit running so high, the greater the chance it will start leaking carbon monoxide." He straightened up, looked me square in the eye, and delivered the zinger. "You board a bunch of cats on the first floor of this building, right? If any CO leaks into the air, they'll be the first ones to get sick. Kind of like canaries in a coal mine."

That broke through my sales resistance with a sledgehammer. I swallowed hard and asked, "How much would the replacement part run?"

When he gave me a quote of four figures, not including labor, I blanched. Cooperman must have noticed.

"You see why I say that it probably makes more sense to replace the whole unit." He handed me his card. "Whichever you decide, we'll be glad to work out a financing plan for you. And we have several nice new models that would heat your whole place more safely and efficiently, if you choose to go that route."

After he left, I passed along the grim news to Sarah. She commiserated and shared some home-appliance horror stories of her own.

Though it was Thursday, I did not say anything to her about my plans for the evening. Normally, I kept Sarah abreast of my sleuthing adventures, but Bonelli had told me not to share the information with any more people than necessary. I also spoke with my mom on the phone for a few minutes, and you can be sure I didn't tell her about my plans, either.

Her meltdown probably would have surpassed Mark's, if only because she could shriek at a higher pitch.

Around four, Dawn called to coordinate our movements, and I took my phone into the grooming studio for privacy. We decided we would drive to The Roost in my modest silver-blue CR-V. She owned a lime-colored Jeep Wrangler that was fun for promoting her "green" business but could draw too much attention to us if we were supposed to be undercover. After hanging up, I realized I hadn't asked what Dawn planned to wear that night. I did wonder, since my friend was no more into barhopping and the wild singles scene than I was.

Dawn always tucked a surprise or two up her sleeve, though. When I parked in front of her shop at seven, she stepped out the back door in what looked like a cream crocheted, mid-calf dress and high-heeled boots. For warmth, she had wrapped herself in a long, beige knit shawl.

"We don't quite look like we're going to the same place," I noted. Not really trolling for a date, I'd worn my favorite black skinny pants, a long-sleeved coral blouse with small black polka dots, and my trusty brown jacket. The outfit would have worked just as well for an office job, except that I had tied the neck bow of the blouse lower than usual.

Dawn dismissed any concerns with a wave of her hand. "I think we both look great, and it's not like we're really trying to pick anyone up. We're just out for a night of fun . . . and espionage."

"Well, since you put it that way."

She folded her tall frame into my passenger seat. "Do you think we need aliases?"

While pulling out of my shop's small parking lot, I considered this question. "Don't know what good that would do.

Both of our significant others know we're going to this place tonight, and why. And if anybody else we know does recognize us, we won't be able to fool them."

"I mean for the people we don't know. If some guy hits on you and you're not interested, which you won't be, it's better if he has no idea how to track you down again. Especially since your name is prominently displayed on the front window of your shop."

"Good point," I agreed. "But let's not go too far afield, so we won't forget to answer to our new names. I'll be Cathy, and you can be Donna."

She assented with a nod.

I headed down Center Street; in a couple of miles, I'd turn off onto a less-traveled road that wound up into the wooded hills. Meanwhile, I admitted to Dawn, "I've spent so little time around the club and bar scene, I don't even know how good I'll be at spotting illicit drug activity. I learned a little about ketamine while I was studying to be a vet tech, but not really its effect on a person. Even if someone was dosed with one of these anesthetics, how would we know she wasn't just drunk?"

"*I'd* probably be able to tell. Remember, it's a sedative. Did you ever get what they call 'twilight anesthesia'?"

I thought back. "Yeah, once, for some tricky dental work."

"From what I hear, it's like that. You feel slowed down and removed from your own body. You might be aware of what's happening around you, and to you, but you don't really *care*. Someone on ketamine might stumble or slur their words, but not like a drunk—more like somebody coming out of surgery. If it's a bad trip, they might also hallucinate, like with LSD."

This didn't sound like much of a "party" drug to me. "Holy crap. I can't imagine why anyone would take something like that for fun!"

"Some kids are just thrill-seekers. It's popular at big concerts and raves, where they want to get lost in the music. The real problem is if somebody slips you a strong dose without your knowing. Makes it a lot easier to assault someone when they're almost unconscious."

I switched on my headlights against the deepening twilight, then glanced across at Dawn. "I hope you don't speak from experience."

"Thank God, no. But it happened to a cousin of mine, a few years back. They caught the guy and put him away, but she's had mental problems ever since." Dawn's jaw took on a determined thrust. "So I admit, I'm not coming with you tonight just for a lark. If we do spot any nasty stuff going on, and report it, I might be able to get a little justice for Marianne."

Arriving around seven-thirty, we found The Roost's large parking lot pretty full. I finally found a spot toward the back, where the roadhouse offered a wraparound deck for outdoor dining. Not many people had braved the autumn weather to sit at any of those tables, but a few in jackets and sweaters leaned on the wooden railing to take in the view.

I remembered that vista from the one time Mark and I had come to The Roost. It had been early summer, when we could appreciate the green mountains sloping dramatically from both sides toward the river far below—an offshoot of the mighty Delaware, which lay to our west. Tonight, in the clear twilight beneath a waxing moon, the vista remained spectacular, though I could just barely make out its autumn hues. Some foreground trees had begun to shed their leaves, and beyond them, the terrain seemed to drop even more sharply downward than I remembered. At the distant bottom, a silvery patch of moonlight reflected on the river.

Partway down this slope, and maybe forty feet out from

the deck, a semicircle paved with flagstones dared the restaurant's guests to venture even closer to nature. Only a low,
picturesque edging of boulders stood between any sightseers
and the sheer drop. At the moment, just one couple cuddled
there on an Adirondack-style recliner, maybe to take advantage of the privacy.

They probably also found the stone patio's atmosphere
more romantic than the ambience of The Roost itself. Before
Dawn and I even stepped indoors, we could hear the relent-
less pounding of the techno-pop dance music. We exchanged
looks, and she rolled her eyes.

I laughed. "What we won't do to preserve and protect our
fellow citizens, right?"

"You said it, 'Cathy.' Guess we'd better get in there and
try to look desperate."

Beyond the deck's tall glass doors, we found a large interior space that had been cleared in the middle to create a
medium-sized dance floor. Colored lights blinked erratically
from the high, beamed ceiling, and dark leather banquettes
along two walls invited people to mingle in groups.

Dawn and I agreed that neither of those locations would
give us the vantage point we needed to scan the activity
around the room. The barstools were all taken when we first
walked in, but we hovered nearby until one couple got up to
dance, then stole their seats.

As I've said, Dawn was tall and striking, but I thought
at first that she'd dressed a bit conservatively for our mission
tonight—she certainly didn't "look desperate." But when she
shrugged off her knit shawl and draped it over the back of
her barstool, I appreciated her strategy. Though her crocheted
dress definitely covered all the body parts it needed to, and
probably was fully lined, lacy holes at the sleeves and waist
gave it a peekaboo look. When she crossed her long legs in

their high boots, a slit appeared on one side that reached to mid-thigh.

My timid attempt at cleavage couldn't compete with that effect, but it didn't need to. Dawn could reel the guys in, and I'd try to subtly pump them for information.

A mocha-skinned bartender in a natty red vest asked what we were having. Dawn, my passenger, ordered a white-wine spritzer. Because I was not only driving but trying to stay alert to my surroundings, I didn't want to drink any alcohol. But I also feared that a teetotaler drink would blow my cover.

Quietly, I asked Dawn, "What can I order that's non-alcoholic, but will look cool?"

She squinted for a minute in thought, then inquired of the bartender, "Know how to make a Cinderella?"

He paused. "Hmm, I think so. Club soda, orange juice, pineapple juice . . ."

". . . With a little lemon and a dash of grenadine. You got it," Dawn commended him.

"In a cocktail glass, please," I added.

We both nursed our drinks while we scanned the couples gyrating on the dance floor and congregating near the bar. No one would find our behavior suspicious, because they'd think we were just sizing up prospective dates. I saw so many women younger than Dawn and me, and more provocatively dressed, that after a while I figured no one was going to approach us. Which would have been fine, actually, for our purposes; we really just wanted to blend in with the crowd.

Before too long, though, a couple of guys who looked to be in their thirties sidled up next to us and ordered beers. After they'd been served, the one with tortoiseshell eyeglasses, receding sandy hair, and an intentional-looking shadow of beard, pivoted toward me.

"Hi, I'm Joe," he said, and offered his free hand.

I shook it and told him, "I'm Cathy."

The taller guy introduced himself to Dawn—or "Donna"—as Gary. He had a rather narrow, mournful face framed by longish brown locks, and it occurred to me that she and I had attracted parallel types. My dude wore a button-front, pale green shirt with the sleeves rolled up to make it more relaxed, but like me, he looked as if he'd stopped off on his way home from some office. Gary, with his hippie hair and T-shirt with the logo of some band I'd never heard of, probably thought he'd found his match in my friend, the leggy boho princess.

We spent a few minutes on the usual getting-to-know-you chitchat . . . except that Dawn and I didn't really *want* anyone here to get to know us. "Donna" said she worked as a sales assistant at a chain furniture store, out on the highway, and I said I was a hair stylist (not that much of a stretch). Joe told us he was a medical-supply sales rep, and Gary described himself as a "barista and blogger." Because they seemed like such different types, I asked how they knew each other. Joe said they'd met in a self-help group for people trying to reinvent their careers.

Dawn and I reinvented ours the easy way, I thought, with an inner smile. *We just lied!*

Gary tilted his head at Dawn and told her, "You look familiar. I don't think we've ever met before, but I think I saw you somewhere."

My heart rate speeded up a bit, and I could imagine the statement rattled Dawn, too. She kept her composure well, though. "Maybe you stopped by the furniture store?"

"No, don't think so. That stuff's out of my price range. Maybe you stopped into Best Beans sometime? It's not far from where you work."

She snapped her fingers. "That must have been it."

Nice save, Dawn, I thought, and let out a breath of relief.

Paired up with Joe for the moment, I tried to act interested and attentive while still scanning the bar area behind
him. After a while, he caught onto this and asked if I was
waiting for somebody else.

"No, not at all." I raised my voice to be heard over the
music. "It's just that this is my first time here, and I'm kind of
amazed that they get so many people on a weeknight."

"They're pretty smart about their marketing." Joe warmed
to the subject of his expertise. "They have their singles mixers
on certain nights, Happy Hour specials on other nights, and
free bar food on Wednesdays between four and five."

"You come here a lot?" I asked.

He creased his nose. "Not that much. I do know some
people who stop here almost every night after work, but
they're bigger drinkers than I am." He caught me stealing
another glance across the room and asked, "Would you like
to dance?"

Not only would I have felt odd dancing with someone besides Mark, but again, it wouldn't help my surveillance. I tried
to look apologetic. "Oh, thanks, but . . . I've been on my feet
all day, y'know?" At least that was no lie.

"Oh, right, at the salon."

Meanwhile, Gary asked Dawn, "This your first time here,
too?"

"Second. I was here once for dinner, during the summer.
We ate out back on the deck, which was beautiful. But my
ex-boyfriend never wanted to come at night. He told me the
place gets too wild after dark."

"Oh, I don't know about that. It's a younger crowd at
night, that's all. More singles, and they like to party."

Dawn leaned closer to him and lowered her voice a bit. "I
heard that the security here tends to look the other way, too,
even in terms of drugs."

Gary looked a little put off by her implication and shrugged. "I never saw anything really bad going on. People smoke weed sometimes. Y'know that lookout platform, right over the ravine? They sneak out there, and the breeze usually blows the smoke away from the restaurant."

"Maybe that's what my ex was talking about. He's kind of straightedge." She winked. "One reason we're not seeing each other anymore."

I had to hand it to "Donna" for her vivid imagination. She was conjuring up a whole new persona for herself, complete with a recently jilted boyfriend.

To do my part, I tossed back the last of my Cinderella and searched with my eyes for the bartender.

"I'll get the next one," Joe offered gallantly.

I accepted, but didn't want him to know it was a virgin drink. When the scarlet-vested bartender approached, I just said sweetly, "Same again, please!"

The bar offered pretzels and chips to help keep the drinkers somewhat sober. I'd already had a light dinner and was also getting filled up on fruit juice, so I only nibbled at those. I asked Joe a few more questions about his work, and we both bemoaned the difficulties of meeting people through the singles scene. While he came across as a pretty decent guy, in my eyes he posed no competition for Mark, even if I hadn't come to The Roost tonight for a much different reason.

I tried to nurse my second Cinderella as if it actually contained alcohol, and to survey the bar crowd without arousing Joe's suspicions. Still, I was beginning to think the evening would be wasted time, in every sense, until a scenario several seats down from us caught my attention.

A young brunette in a low-cut pink dress had been talking for about twenty minutes with a slick-looking guy in tight jeans and a black, open-necked shirt. She sat on a stool with a drink in front of her, and he hovered nearby with a glass in his hand. Another woman came by whom the brunette must have known, because she squealed and slid off her stool to give the newcomer a hug.

While Pink Dress was turned away, gabbing with her friend, Black Shirt made his move. He pulled something out of his jeans pocket, held it over her highball glass, and gave it a quick tap. Then he closed his palm again and tucked whatever it was—far too small for me to see—back into his jeans.

I could hardly believe I'd just seen that happen. Apparently, I was the only person who had.

A jolt of adrenaline shot through me, and I wondered what to do. I could use my phone to call Officer Ed MacDonald, who I knew was staked out tonight at the restaurant, but he might come too late! Already, the lady in pink sat back down at the bar and began to reach for her glass.

"Excuse me," I told Joe, abruptly. "I need to make a trip, you-know-where."

As I slid down off the stool in the semi-dark, my heel caught on the edge of the bar's footrest, and I almost pitched forward. A gentleman, Joe grabbed my arm to steady me.

That gave me an idea. I thanked him and giggled, "Whoa, those pretty drinks can really sneak up on you!"

Frowning, Joe stepped aside, and I pretended to totter off toward the ladies' room. I passed the brunette just as she put her glass to her lips. Helped by the crowded conditions, I bumped her arm, hard. The doctored drink splashed down the front of her nice pink dress.

A shame, but better than the alternative.

She shrieked at me in anger. "Watch where you're going, you— Damn, look at my dress!"

I quickly turned into an embarrassed, remorseful drunk. "Oh God, I'm sooo sorry! I didn't mean to . . . somebody pushed me! I'm *really* sorry."

She'd completely forgotten her date, and, twisted in rage, her face didn't look so lovely. "You should be! Do you know what this dress cost me?"

"It'll be all right." I put a hand on her shoulder. "C'mon in the ladies' room, it'll probably wash off."

"Leave me alone." She tried to squirm free. "You've done enough!"

I took a firm hold of her upper arm. "Really, I'm *sure* we can get it clean. Come with me . . . don't forget your purse."

Pink Dress looked alarmed, maybe because I'd stopped slurring my words, though she did grab her bag. "Why? W-what're you trying to pull?"

When we'd gotten a few steps away from the bar, I whispered in her ear. "I'm not pulling anything, but your date just slipped something in your drink. Be glad I spilled it."

This news intrigued her enough that she accompanied me into the nearest women's room, and no longer glared at me as if I were a random slayer of cute pink dresses. In fact, she formed a much different opinion, and asked in a hushed tone, "You a cop, or something?"

"Or something." I wet a couple of paper towels under the faucet and pumped on a little soap before handing them to her. That should help—polyester crepe wasn't so easily stained. "Who was that guy with you? Your boyfriend?"

She took the towels and started dabbing at her dress. "No, I just met him here tonight. You actually saw him put something in my drink?"

I described what I'd witnessed. "There have been some incidents in town lately, so I was keeping an eye out."

"I heard about that girl at the party who died." Her dress

sufficiently cleaned, the brunette gaped at me in shock. "You don't think he—"

"Not necessarily the same guy. But maybe the same source for the drug."

She pressed a hand to her forehead. "What should I do?"

"Stay in here for a few more minutes." I spotted a worn brocade sofa in the vestibule of the restroom and advised her, "Lie down, like you're not feeling well. I'll make a call, and let you know when he's gone. One way or another."

I waited a minute for one other woman to leave the ladies' room, then seized the chance to phone Officer MacDonald. I told him what I'd seen and gave him a description of the young man in the black shirt. "Right now he's standing just about at the middle of the bar, but he looks nervous. I can't guarantee he'll stay around."

"No problem, I'm right outside," MacDonald said.

A few minutes later, the young, strawberry blond officer made his way through the pulsing crowd of the dance floor. Dressed in a dark sweater and jeans, and with a toned physique, he fit right in. The guy from the bar was heading out when MacDonald blocked him and grabbed his wrist. At first, Black Shirt tried to twist free, but one glimpse of the cop's brass shield took all the fight out of him. MacDonald also used his handkerchief to pick up the tainted cocktail glass.

I stuck my head into the restroom alcove. "All clear."

The woman in pink got up from the sofa. "He's gone?"

"With a police escort."

Still dazed, she accompanied me back toward the bar area. "Thanks so much . . . what's your name?"

"Cathy," I remembered to say.

"I'm Judy." She clasped my hand. "Thanks again!"

I let her go her own way then, hoping no bad guys in the vicinity would remember that Judy and I had taken off for the restroom together. By the time I reached Dawn, she sat alone, though still looking self-possessed and unconventionally elegant.

She peppered me with questions. "What was all that about? Did you bump into that girl on purpose? MacDonald just showed up, in civvies, and hauled off her date. That can't have been a coincidence."

I explained what had happened, and Dawn's jaw dropped.

"You really did it, then. You busted someone!"

"Not personally," I pointed out. "And I could hardly believe it, myself. That woman, Judy, was furious at me until I told her what was up. She'd just met the guy, so she was really grateful I sabotaged his plan."

"Unbelievable." Dawn shook her head. "And I thought I was being so clever, pumping Gary for information on the drug scene. Not that he admitted to knowing much about it."

"At least those two seemed like okay guys." I glanced around the room. "So, where'd they go?"

My friend grinned widely. "I think we scared them off. By now, they probably figure I'm a hopeless stoner and you're a sloppy drunk!"

I slid back onto my stool and finished the rest of my Cinderella, which had remained safe under Dawn's watchful eye. "Just as well, we won't have to break their hearts. I bet they tell all their friends, though, about the totally *trashy* women who come to singles' night at The Roost."

Chapter 11

The next morning at work, I got a phone call from Bonelli. She sounded pleasantly surprised that during my undercover job, I'd not only spotted some criminal activity, but interfered before any damage was done, and in time for MacDonald to apprehend the black-shirt guy.

"Did you find enough evidence to hold him?" I asked.

"Yes, indeed." Her husky voice had an almost cheerful lilt. "An empty ketamine ampoule in his pocket, and residue in the lady's glass."

"Wow. Might as well just have signed his work, eh?" I recalled what Dawn had told me about the effects of ketamine, and felt a chill over how close the brunette, Judy, had come to suffering that fate.

The detective's tone sobered. "But again, Cassie, you need to be careful about taking these risks. We both agreed that you and Dawn were only going there to observe, and would call Eddie if you saw anything suspicious."

"I would have, but Judy picked up the glass and was just about to drink from it—there was no time! I played tipsy, though, so other people would think I bumped her by accident."

"Let's hope they bought your act, especially Pete Nardone. He's the slimeball we picked up. MacDonald told Nardone that *he'd* been surveilling the bar and saw for himself what Pete did."

Relief washed over me. "Great! Thank Eddie for me."

"I will, but Nardone still may suspect you were in on it. Of course, you may be safer if he thinks you're working with the police. Even so, you and Dawn keep your wits about you for the next couple of weeks."

"Do you think Pete was the one who robbed the clinic?" Of medium height with dark hair, he loosely fit the physical description.

"We're holding him for possession of a controlled substance, with intent to commit a felony, but frankly I think he was just a customer. Probably bought the stuff off a local dealer, who may or may not have been the original thief. We leaned on Nardone to tell us who sold him the drug, but now he's lawyered up. Probably smart enough to know that ratting out a dealer could be bad for his health."

"And even that wouldn't be the end of it," I reasoned. "There's probably someone above the dealer, and maybe even someone else above him."

"Exactly. That's the trail we want to follow, but I doubt Pete's willing to help us, even if he has to do jail time. We also talked to the bartender, but he claimed not to have seen Nardone put anything in the woman's drink."

I considered. "If this kind of thing keeps happening at The Roost, the bartenders and the security staff must be aware of it. Why would they just turn a blind eye?"

"Maybe they're told to," Bonelli guessed, her tone ominous. "By someone with some influence, legitimate or ille-gitimate."

"You mean, organized crime? Maybe someone with a stake in the restaurant?"

"Could be. We've been coordinating with PDs in Del-aware and New York State, where other clinics have been robbed. Those areas also have had a few incidents like this, at private parties and dance clubs, so there does seem to be a definite link to restaurants and bars. We even picked up some-body making a drug buy, a couple of months ago, behind The Firehouse."

"You're kidding!" My friends and I loved that place for its cool décor, spicy food, and live soft-rock and jazz acts. The patrons skewed young-professional to middle-aged. I'd never felt unsafe there or thought of it as a hangout for druggies.

"That could have been coincidental," the detective admit-ted. "It wasn't actually inside the building. An opioid bust—fentanyl, I think it was—and too long ago to be related to the clinic robbery. But there might have been a reason why the dealer felt The Firehouse was a safe zone."

"Guess I'm naïve," I said. "After living on a college cam-pus, and then in mostly urban areas, I thought Chadwick was the kind of town where you didn't have to worry about such things. Like a veterinary clinic being robbed, or a woman getting secretly drugged by her date."

"It should be." Bonelli's voice turned steely. "According to Chief Hardy, who's lived here thirty years, it used to be. He's determined to make it that way again, and so am I."

"Good," I told her. "I know your feelings about me taking risks and getting too involved, but still, let me know if there's anything more I can do."

"I appreciate that, Cassie. At least you've helped us get

Nardone into custody. Now you and Dawn should both lay low for a while, all right?"

"You're the boss," I said.

During my phone call, Sarah had gone about her business and didn't pry. But since the bust at The Roost had already made the morning news, I told her about my involvement and how it had gone down. She got a kick out of picturing me and Dawn dolling up to go undercover at a singles' event.

"And Mark was okay with that?" she asked.

"He didn't love it, but he knew I was trying to help nab the lowlife who robbed his clinic. I think he's finally getting used to the idea that I like helping out the cops once in a while."

"Getting resigned to it, you mean!" Sarah shook her head with a rueful smile. "At least the news story didn't say anything about your part in the arrest."

"Nope, just credited it all to the sharp eyes of Officer MacDonald. Which is as it ought to be. No one should suspect that Dawn and I played any role at all."

But had Bonelli also talked with Dawn about being on her guard, I wondered, or was she counting on me to do that? Just to be sure, I used my lunch break to walk over to Nature's Way. I'd ask my friend if she'd had any repercussions from the night before.

Nearing the store's big front window, I could see Tanith finishing up an elaborate Halloween display. Around the base of a dried cornstalk, she'd arranged pumpkins and colorful squashes, a jug of cider, and autumn leaves so crisp and colorful that they had to be fake. To one side, a purple witch's hat studded with silver stars perched on top of a hay bale; next to it, Tanith had parked a straw broom decorated with fake bunches of autumn berries and a big orange bow. She managed to work around Tigger as he burrowed playfully into the pile of leaves, but when he tried to sharpen his claws on the cornstalk, she gently shooed him away.

Tanith could have been part of the scenario herself, in her high-necked black top with cobwebby sleeves, dark red jeans, and black platform boots. Still, the blouse did cover her dragon tattoo, and I thought her goth makeup seemed dialed down a notch from the first time we'd met.

A poster taped to the window from the inside advertised the upcoming appearance by Ripley Van Eyck. It included a black-and-white headshot of the wizard himself and gave the date and time as Wednesday, Oct. 28, from six to eight p.m. The border was embellished with cartoons of ghosts, a Ouija board, a crescent moon, and a crystal ball, all done in Keith's lively commercial-art style.

Tanith finally paused at her work long enough to notice me outside. She grinned and waved with a girlish enthusiasm out of sync with her dead-black hair and ruby nostril stud. She hopped down from the window's inner sill and opened the shop's front door for me.

Tigger also leaped from the window ledge and dashed for the door, but Tanith corrected him sharply. "Tigger, rug!" The adolescent tabby screeched to a halt and eyed her as if to say, *You're not my real mommy!* But then he obediently doubled back and sat on the rag rug a couple of yards inside the door.

Tanith giggled. "Dawn taught me that. I'm always surprised, though, when it actually works."

"I'm so glad it does." As far as anyone knew, Tigger had been born on the street. When Dawn first took him in, as a kitten, he would bolt for the door every time it opened. I gave her a clicker and showed her how to use it, in combination with a treat, to teach the cat to stay inside. We aimed to get him to obey the "rug" command every time, even without the clicker or the reward. Over time, and with much patience on Dawn's part, it had worked.

"Beautiful job on the front window," I told Tanith. "Very professional."

She raised a modest hand to block the compliment. "Dawn came up with most of the ideas, but I'm glad she trusted me to do the work. It was really fun!"

"It's definitely more eye-catching than anything she's done in the past. I guess she's trying hard to drum up interest in Van Eyck's appearance."

"Oh, there's already plenty. People know him from his blog and his call-in cable show. We've had more than twenty people sign up so far, and Dawn thinks we need to cut it off at thirty." The young woman surveyed the more open, central area of the shop. "Some of those might even be standees, because I don't know how many folding chairs we can get in here."

"I'm glad there's been so much response. Dawn might pick up a lot of new business."

A glance around told me that the Halloween theme carried throughout the front of the shop. Amid an array of organic jams on a side table, a ceramic black-cat candlestick stood guard, hissing and arching its back. A pentagram within a circle, braided from grapevines, hung among the usual ferns above the sales counter. The counter's display of New Age jewelry, under glass, included a little placard that read, CRYSTALS OF THE SEASON: OBSIDIAN, CARNELIAN, ONYX, AMBER, HEMATITE, TOURMALINE.

"I'm so glad Dawn got into the whole Samhain spirit," Tanith went on, correctly pronouncing the pagan holiday as *sow-en*. "It's such a totally cool time of year!"

In any other shop, I would have been concerned that all of

the witchy elements might put off customers. But Dawn's clientele was nothing if not liberal-minded, and she'd mentioned that a few were practicing Wiccans. Better than if she'd hung up gory ghosts and skeletons, anyway, which might have run counter to the whole idea of healthy living. The only skulls I spotted were nestled among a few other ceramic Day of the Dead tchotchkes, all decorated with cheery floral patterns, on a shelf above the produce bins.

While I was studying these, Dawn emerged from a rear storeroom. "Do you like them, Cassie?" she asked. "A young guy over in Dalton makes them, so I took some on consignment. We have so many customers these days from Mexican and other Latin backgrounds that I thought it would be nice to recognize their holiday, too. I'm even going to make some Day of the Dead skull cookies to sell."

"With your own hands?" I teased her. "I mean, I know you can bake, but enough to stock the store?"

"I'll put them out just on Saturday, for Halloween. First come, first served." She shrugged. "I'll make a few dozen, and when they're gone, they're gone."

While Tanith fussed with the window a bit more, Dawn and I grabbed a couple of vegetarian wraps from the store's refrigerated section, along with bottles of herbal tea. We took these to the little seating area near her central, wood-burning stove, and sat in the two armchairs she kept covered with exotic cotton throws. Tigger, uninterested in our lunches, wandered over to his dish near the oak display counter and crunched noisily on some leftover dry food.

Keeping my voice low, I told Dawn about my conversation with Bonelli that morning. "So far they haven't got any leads on who sold Nardone the ketamine, and even though MacDonald managed to keep our cover, there's no guarantee that Pete or someone else might not suspect we were working with the cops. So Angela says we should lay low for a while and not take any more chances. Be careful who we trust, I guess, and not tell anybody else what we did . . ."

Dawn choked, as if she had swallowed a mouthful of her wrap the wrong way.

I frowned. "All right, what did you do?"

"Nothing! Nothing that will put us in any more danger, I'm sure. Just . . ."

"Who did you tell?"

She jerked her head in the direction of the picture window.

"Tanith? Are you crazy?"

"I know, I wasn't thinking! But earlier yesterday, she and I got talking about the girl who died at the lake house party. Tanith said she used to do some drugs herself when she was younger, but after a couple of her friends had bad experiences, she'd given up all of that. At the time, I didn't say anything about our plans to go to The Roost. But this morning when I heard the cops had busted a guy, with the evidence still in his pocket, I guess I got a little full of myself. I told Tanith that at least one scumbag had gotten what he deserved. When she wanted to know more, I said you and I were at The Roost when it happened and saw it go down. I didn't tell her we were undercover, though, or that you had anything to do with the guy's arrest!"

I rolled my eyes. "You might as well have. Even if she *says* she doesn't run with a druggy crowd anymore, who knows if that's really true, and who else she might tip off?"

Dawn frowned in doubt. "I don't know, Cassie. She may not have worked here too long, but I trust her. She seemed really glad that a guy who tried to spike a woman's drink got arrested. Maybe we should look at this another way—maybe

Tanith can give us some insights on how the party drugs circulate around here."

While I was mulling this option, Dawn's spooky assistant popped out from behind a nearby row of shelves. "Thought I heard my name. Did you want me for something?"

Dawn tried to cover. "Cassie was just saying, again, what a great job you did on the front window."

I decided to take the plunge. Since the store wasn't busy, I asked Tanith, "Want to join us for a few minutes?"

She pulled up a nearby wooden stepstool and sat on top, like a perky vulture. The narrow seat looked precarious to me, but the slim young woman seemed to balance on it comfortably.

"We were just talking about that drug bust at The Roost last night," I told her. "Dawn and I don't go there very often, and it kind of shocked us. Especially coming so soon after the woman died, up at Starlight Lake."

Tanith shook her head sadly. "I don't know much about The Roost—that's never been my kind of scene. But some crazy stuff does go on up at the lake houses. Those people have money, and some just let their kids run wild."

"We've been wondering if there's any connection with the drugs that were stolen from the veterinary clinic," Dawn told her. "The cops said both incidents involved ketamine, and that's one of the medications that was taken."

"Special K? Yeah, that's definitely around. I never messed with it, but I knew some people who did. In fact, one of my friends was taking it by prescription, for depression. It helped her at first, but if she took too much she would get crazy. Like, seeing-things-that-weren't-there crazy!"

Dawn drew her assistant out on the subject. "It's a little like LSD, right? From what I've heard, sometimes people feel all lovey-dovey and 'at one with the universe.' I guess that's what a guy is hoping for when he drugs somebody's drink. Also, it can kind of paralyze you so you can't escape, which is probably why it's a good anesthetic for animals."

I winced. I'd have to apologize to poor Mango, since he must have gotten a dose of the stuff for his recent thyroid surgery.

The goth girl nodded. "People do talk about having a bad trip, like with acid. They call it 'going down the K-hole' . . . Y'know, like the rabbit hole in *Alice in Wonderland*. They say they feel out of their bodies and lose touch with reality." With a nervous chuckle, she added, "I already can go to lots of weird places in my imagination. I don't need any extra help!"

Unless Tanith was a very good actress, her reactions convinced me that she wasn't part of any local drug ring. Her insights did make me wonder again, though, if some young employee at Mark's clinic could be involved, after all. Maybe someone with money problems, who saw a way to make a little extra on the side? Wouldn't dare to steal the drugs him- or herself, but cleared the way for someone else to do it?

The jangle of the front door announced a customer, and Tanith dutifully went to answer it. Once she'd gone, I confided my suspicions about a rogue clinic staffer to Dawn.

"I don't know about that," she said, "but I just remembered something about one of our dates. Didn't that guy Joe say that he was in 'medical sales'? He might have access to anesthetics. Or maybe that was just a euphemism, and he's the local drug kingpin!"

I laughed. "That's hard to picture. Your guy, Gary, *did* seem a little rough around the edges. But Joe came across as so clean-cut and upright—almost boringly so."

Dawn held up one finger. "Ah, but that would be the perfect cover, wouldn't it? No one would ever suspect him."

"I thought you said he and Gary split because I acted

drunk, and because you asked too many questions about drugs."

"Yeah, but come to think of it . . . they both seemed annoyed that you spilled that woman's drink. And after Ed MacDonald walked over and nailed Nardone, they beat it out of there pretty fast."

Chapter 12

One reason Mark and I generally planned our date nights for Saturdays was because he often got stuck late at the clinic on Fridays. That evening, for example, he sent me a quick text around six-thirty that he had an emergency surgery and didn't know when he'd be finished. *Call U as soon as I can,* he promised.

Resigned to such setbacks, I ate a simple dinner on my own. I played with my own cats for a while, then settled in to watch a mindless sitcom. My calico, Matisse, promptly claimed my lap, while black Cole settled for ramming himself up against my hip as closely as possible. I felt sorry for elderly Mango, who had to balance on the arm of the sofa to get close. Surrounded on all sides, I got the message that they hadn't seen enough of me lately and thought I was spending way too much time fussing over *other* people's cats.

"The shoemaker's children go barefoot, eh?" I asked aloud, while trying to spread my affection evenly among them. In rhythm with their purrs, I started to breathe easily for the first time in days. This low-key evening felt welcome, especially after the stresses of the night before.

Around nine, Mark finally phoned. He explained that

he'd been operating on a cocker spaniel that had gotten loose from someone's yard, was hit by a car, and suffered a broken leg. "It was pretty shattered, but I finally managed to pin everything back together," he said. "I'm going to hang around here, though, until our new night-shift guy comes on. I want to brief him on what to watch out for." After a beat, he added, "With the dog, I mean."

Yes, that needed clarifying, in light of what had happened to Sam, the old night-shift guy. "You're alone over there?"

"The tech who was assisting me is still here, but she's getting ready to split. Someone's got to stay and keep an eye on the cocker. He's still coming out of anesthesia."

"I know, but . . ." Usually Mark was the one warning me not to take chances; now, for a moment, the shoe was on the other foot. If someone could get the drop on a savvy guy like Sam, they might find a way to overpower Mark, too. Especially if they had a gun.

"I'll be fine, Cassie, really," he assured me. "Ever since the robbery, there's been a patrol car cruising past the clinic every hour or so. And all of us stay on the alert, too."

"Please do," I said.

"Speaking of that, someone told me they heard there was a drug bust last night at The Roost. You and Dawn wouldn't have had anything to do with that, would you?"

"As a matter of fact, we did." I gave him a capsule version of the story, though. I just said that I spotted a guy putting something in a woman's drink and called the plainclothes officer on the scene, who had followed up.

"Hey, that's terrific!" For once, my boyfriend sounded simply proud of me, instead of also worried. "And they got enough evidence to make an arrest?"

"The used ampoule was still in the guy's pocket, and they found traces of ketamine in the woman's glass."

Mark groaned over the phone. "I hate to think that it could have come from our clinic. Sounds like a close call for the woman."

"It probably was." I related what Dawn and Tanith had told me about the effects of ketamine. "I learned a little about it when I trained as a vet tech, but nobody ever really explained how it worked. Do you think the animals you sedate go through that kind of thing?"

He considered this only briefly. "No, I really don't. When we administer it for surgery, we give a small amount that's injected slowly. If the animal is nervous, it actually calms them. It does immobilize them during the procedure, but just the same as any anesthetic would."

"That always was my impression, too," I said.

"And one reason why it's considered safe is that it wears off quickly," Mark continued. "You've seen animals waking up afterward. They're a little wobbly on their feet and uncoordinated. You don't want them running around or jumping on things until they've sobered up a little. But they don't act upset or frightened."

"Why would it be so different with humans, then?"

I heard a thoughtful sigh. "If someone's doing it for thrills, they're probably taking a high dose, and in a way that will hit them fast. When you do that, I suppose, all bets are off. Like the young woman at the house party who had the heart attack. Sounds as if she took a big hit after she'd been drinking all night."

"*If* she did it on purpose," I pointed out. "Wonder if Bonelli ever was able to determine that."

"I almost wish she could," he admitted. "It might help get our clinic off the hook. Now Maggie says we might get sued! Karin Weaver's parents are saying the drugs came from our clinic and that we should have had better security. I don't see any way they can shift the blame onto us—the best locks and alarms in the world won't prevent someone from sticking a gun in an employee's back and forcing him to open a door! What was Sam supposed to do, give up his life to keep those drugs from falling into the wrong hands?"

"Of course not, that's absurd," I agreed.

"But even if the Weavers can't win the case, they can tie us up in court for who-knows-how long and drag the clinic's reputation through the dust."

Mark sounded miserable. I offered the only consolation I could, that maybe my mom's firm would take their case. MP&R had some high-powered lawyers, a great success record, and might even cut their fees for a beleaguered veterinary clinic. "Of course, first the Weavers have to find someone to represent *them*," I added. "Their accusation is so flimsy, that might never happen."

Mark and I both agreed to move on to more cheerful and wholesome topics. I told him that I'd stopped by the Paragon earlier and had seen the "werewolf" pet photos on display in the lobby, all numbered. Lathrop was providing notepaper, a tethered pencil, and a locked ballot box, for visitors to cast their ballots. He'd emailed both Mark and me to report that voting by the moviegoers, and even drop-in visitors, appeared hot and heavy.

"Lathrop must be pleased," Mark said. "He wanted more foot traffic into the theater, and it sounds as if he's getting it."

"Speaking of pet-related events," I said, "I'm thinking of going over to the park tomorrow to see the costume parade. Just for a lark . . . or a bark."

He chuckled at my lame joke. "Need a change of pace from felines?"

"More from sleuthing, especially since it doesn't seem to be getting me anywhere. Can you meet me there, maybe when you get off work?"

"I can try, as long as this spaniel gets through the night okay, and there are no more emergencies. The parade's eleven to two, right? I'll see if I can get free by twelve-thirty or one. Meet you near the gazebo?"

"Sounds good." I heard a buzz on the line, and Mark told me, "Oops, that's Maggie."

"Take it, then. Have a good night—love you."

"Love you, too."

Glad that we at least had made plans to get together the next day, I cleaned up the kitchen, gave in to my cats' pleas for a late snack, and started getting ready for bed. I'd gotten so used to the rattling and groaning from my basement by now—worse when the heat came up at night—that it barely made me flinch anymore. Still, even though my shop doors were double-locked and my alarm was set, I also checked all of my second-floor windows, especially the one by the rear fire escape.

I had washed up, brushed my teeth, and donned a long-sleeved tee and PJ bottoms by the time my cell phone rang at ten-thirty.

I saw Mark's name again and worried that some new disaster had struck.

"Hope I didn't wake you," he said.

"I was up. Are you still stuck at the clinic, at this hour?"

"No, the night-duty guy showed up, and the cocker seemed fine, so I'm home."

I didn't think Mark would call again just to share that information. "So, what's wrong?"

"Sorry if I scared you—nothing's wrong at all. I just have

some news, and I thought if I passed it along you might sleep better. The clinic robbery case may be solved . . . and the bad guy may already have gotten his just deserts."

That blew the last wisps of drowsiness from my brain. "What do you mean?"

"Bonelli called Maggie about an hour ago. A motorcycle crashed tonight on Route 94—that kind of lonely stretch just south of here—and the driver was killed. The bike's tire treads match the prints from the clinic parking lot, and the dead guy *could* have been Sam's attacker. He was about the same height, with a strong build. He had short hair, not collar-length, but Sam could have gotten that part wrong. Or the guy might have been smart enough to get a haircut."

If it *was* the thief, I finished silently. "Did they find any drugs on him?"

"No, but they'll do an autopsy to see if he had any in his system. They're also going to check his bike to figure out why he went off the road. Looks like he lost control, Bonelli said, because there were skid marks for about thirty feet before he went into a deep ditch." Mark did not sound particularly sympathetic. "I'm sure Sam will say it couldn't have happened to a nicer guy."

I half-joked, "You don't think Sam spotted him and ran him off the road, do you?"

"Luckily, Sam was home all evening, with his wife and kids, when it happened. Anyhow, once the cops ID the driver, we might know a little more about this whole mess."

Mark and I said our good nights again before disconnecting. I let him enjoy his momentary respite from worry, though I wasn't so sure that the investigation of the theft at the clinic was all wrapped up.

Even if the dead man had been the thief, and even if Sam

did not force him off the road . . . someone else might have. During similar robberies, at clinics in other states, the only witnesses had been killed.

Sam's assailant left him alive, and also left behind evidence of his bike in the parking lot.

Bonelli agreed with me that there was probably someone above the thief—whether or not he also was a dealer—running the show. She thought Pete Nardone was afraid to reveal who had sold him the ketamine. Maybe because he'd heard scary stories about whoever headed up the operation?

Was the top guy ruthless enough to eliminate one of his underlings, just for leaving too many loose ends?

Unexpectedly, the pet costume parade drew a couple of potential new customers to my shop on Saturday morning, animal lovers who were headed to the park out of curiosity. I chatted with them about the services we offered, and reminded them to also check out the photo contest in the Paragon lobby and cast their votes.

Sarah was committed to a family wedding an hour's drive away and had to stop at home first to get ready. So, after we closed the shop at noon, I headed off to the park by myself to check out the parade. I was happy for an excuse to get out in the gorgeous fall weather, despite the slight nip in the air. The brilliant blue sky contrasted nicely with the russet tones of the venerable oaks and maples that abounded in Riverside Park.

There, I soon found myself up to my knees in costumed critters. Most common were dogs of all breeds and sizes dressed as Marvel and DC superheroes in eye masks and capes. Out of several disguised as Star Wars creatures, a pug in a Yoda costume probably pulled it off best. More basic, but amusing, were a golden lab sporting a fake lion's mane and round ears, a black lab sprayed with a white X-ray image of his own skeleton, and a tiny black kitten sporting bat wings.

While some costumes looked handmade, others obviously had been purchased from the highway PetMart. A Chihuahua in a tuxedo-patterned harness looked as if he should have been escorting the King Charles spaniel "princess" in pink satin and a glittering tiara. The funniest, for my money, was a dachshund in a tubular jacket with rows of bent, pipe-cleaner centipede legs sprouting from his sides. A gray pit bull, short-haired like most, sported a matching shark fin. Among the non-canines, an iguana aspired to greatness with a tall, curving dinosaur fin strapped to his back; a guinea pig wore a bumblebee-striped sweater accessorized with delicate fairy wings, plus a headband with tiny antennae.

A FOCA banner draped from the roof of the gazebo marked it as the center of the action. While I made my way in that direction, I spotted Becky and Chris, wading through the crowd, with clipboards. Both wore tattered clothes and zombie makeup, outfits that allowed them to move freely and would not suffer from any contact with the critters. They seemed to be checking in the entries and making sure everyone had followed the rules.

Since the contest benefitted FOCA, the guidelines stipulated that all animals in the competition be leashed or carried securely. The costumes couldn't include any features that the judges deemed too uncomfortable or cruel. Most of the get-ups were based on harnesses or stretchy clothing that the pets seemed to tolerate well. All of the entries got assigned numbers for the judging; the owners who carried the smaller pets wore the numbers on their own sleeves.

Just inside the gazebo entrance, I spotted Terry Elkins, the fiftyish woman who headed FOCA. She had dressed for the occasion as a scarecrow, in a floppy hat, a faded plaid shirt, and overalls that leaked straw at the seams. After tapping her microphone to check the sound, Terry welcomed everybody to the second annual pet costume parade. She went on to introduce the two judges: Vicky Armstrong, who wrote a pet advice column that was syndicated in half a dozen regional papers, and Charlie Griffin, who ran a costume and magic shop in nearby Sparta. Both were young, good-looking folks, at least as far as I could tell that day. Vicky had cloaked herself in black as Maleficent, complete with the horned black headdress and pale green complexion. Dark-haired Charlie showcased both his wares and his toned physique via a satin red devil costume.

I was glad I didn't have a pet in the contest—I wouldn't want to be judged by either of those villainous characters! But both Vicky and Charlie also wore big smiles that counteracted their alter egos.

Neither judge, I noticed, ran a business that would have biased them in favor of any of the entries. Maybe that was why no one from the veterinary clinic had taken part? Or were the docs always just too busy on weekends?

Becky finally glanced up, sighted me in the crowd, and waved. I worked my way closer to the gazebo and congratulated her on the great turnout.

"It's almost twice the number we had last year," she bubbled, a very un-zombielike sparkle in her heavily shadowed eyes. "I'm sure the great weather today didn't hurt."

"So, how do Vicky and Charlie do the judging?" I asked.

She handed me a folded program, but also went on to explain. "There are three categories: Funniest, Most Creative, and Best Non-Canine. A pet can only be entered in one of those. During the parade, the judges will write down their favorites in category, up to six. After that, we'll see how many choices overlap, and let them talk it over if they need to. In the end, we should be able to award a first, second, and third prize for each."

"Sounds like a good number of prizes to go around."

"We are hoping to make as many participants happy as possible." She winked, another gesture at odds with her macabre character. "Besides raising funds, our other goal is to get positive exposure for FOCA."

From the gazebo, Terry called her name.

"Gotta get back to work," Becky said. "Sorry!"

"That's okay," I told my zombified friend. "No rest for the undead, right?"

I threaded my way back to the fringes of the parade, where I could actually view it better, and started to browse through the program.

A smooth, somewhat familiar baritone voice spoke up behind me. "I didn't realize this would be such a big event. Hero and I feel seriously underdressed."

I spun around to face mystery man Dez Mitchelson.

Chapter 13

I knew Dez must be referring to all the people and animals in costume, because he could hardly have been called "underdressed" for an afternoon in the park. A warm-up jacket that looked like suede emphasized his strong shoulders, and its caramel hue played up the golden glints in his breeze-ruffled hair. His shades, dark jeans, and running shoes also looked like designer quality.

Before I could even respond to his comment, I felt a snuffling near my hand. I glanced down and, despite my long experience with animals, shrank back a little. Beside Dez stood one of the biggest dogs I'd ever seen; his shoulder came level with my hip bone, and I'm not that small. He had a brindled coat and a huge, jowly head with cropped ears and hooded, suspicious eyes. His deep-chested, long-legged body wore a padded black, almost military-looking harness.

"I'm sorry, did he scare you?" Dez reeled the beast in a bit, on a leash attached to the harness.

"Startled me, that's all," I said. "Impressive dog. A mastiff of some kind?"

"Presa Canario," Dez responded, with a respectable Spanish pronunciation. "Canary mastiff, bred in the islands for working with livestock. His name's Hero."

"Hi, Hero." I reached out a cautious hand to stroke the dog's blocky head and lingered on one of his ears. I could tell that they'd originally hung as flaps but had been sheared off, pit bull–style, into points.

Dez seemed to read my mind. "He was a rescue. The ears were cropped that way when I got him. Some breeders seem to think it increases the dog's value."

I heard and appreciated the disapproval in his voice. "Are you here for the costume parade? You could have passed off this guy as a pony!"

He responded with a sardonic smile. "Yeah, I've heard that one before. Actually, I didn't know about the parade today. I often walk this guy in the park on Saturdays. As you can imagine, he needs a *lot* of exercise."

Just then, a little girl trotted past us leading the golden "princess" spaniel. The mastiff gave a low huff and strained at his leash, as if eager to give chase.

"Hero, sit!" Dez told him in a sharp tone. Reluctantly, his dog complied.

I remembered that Mitchelson lived in the Public Storage building, according to Dawn. But he might not like the fact that she'd told me, so I played it coy. "Do you have a big property for him to run around?"

"Not at all, unfortunately. My apartment's a good size, but Hero needs to get outside a couple of times a day. Where I live, there are no parks like this close by. I've got to walk him on the sidewalks, or along a railroad track."

"How long have you been there?" I asked.

"About four months. It's a converted warehouse, actually. High ceilings and exposed-brick walls."

"Sounds great! Keith told me you bought his daylilies

painting, so I figured you must have wanted to fill a large space. He was delighted to sell one of his biggest and most labor-intensive pieces."

"It was a steal at the price." Mitchelson favored me with another dazzling grin. "Have to admit, I first was drawn to the other large one, that showed just half of the woman's face. But when I found out it was a portrait of Garrett's girlfriend, and belonged to her, I put a deposit down on the lilies."

The sky had clouded a little, and Dez must have felt he didn't need his sunglasses anymore. He tucked them into the pocket of his jacket, and once again I felt the hypnotic effect of his intense green eyes. Different from Mark's blue ones, though—cooler, more watchful. Maybe because, unlike Mark, Dez didn't know yet where he stood with me?

With a philosophical air, Dez continued, "I admire your friend Keith, and people like him, who follow their passion no matter what. I'm not sure I'd have the patience to do that. Maybe I'm my father's son, after all. I've got too much of a taste for creature comforts, and the good life."

I would have argued that at least he still encouraged artists, not only by collecting their work but also writing about it, but then I'd have to confess that I'd found his articles online. Trying to sound casual, I said, "Keith is hoping that someone might review the show for one of the local papers, but he figures it's a long shot . . ."

I didn't have a chance to pursue this topic any further, though. A motherly little woman walked past us with the black bat-kitten cradled in her arms, and Hero once again snapped to attention. When she paused to let a *Courier* photographer take their picture, the mastiff whimpered softly. I suspected that only the presence of the feline's protective human, plus Dez's firm hand on his leash, discouraged him from making a serious lunge. It seemed kind of reckless, I thought, to bring such a large, high-strung dog to an event with so many other animals, most of them a lot smaller and more vulnerable.

Dez finally got this message, too. "Maybe we should move out of the thick of things." He sidled away from the photographer and tugged Hero across the lawn toward the riverbank.

For the moment, I followed, wondering if he would reveal any more information about himself. "So, did you move here to be near work?"

"Well, I work for myself, but my client base is expanding further into the suburbs around here. I'm a freelance marketing consultant."

If he was the same Dez Mitchelson who'd written those art reviews, he didn't seem ready to admit it. No doubt my instincts were right that he made a good living in a more mainstream line of work. "How did you get interested in art?"

"My father is a collector and used to take me around to the galleries and museums, when I was a kid. One of the few things we ever had in common." He must have heard the bitterness in his own voice, because he softened the comment with a tight smile. "Later on, our tastes grew to be very different. Also, Dad collects mainly for the investment value. I just do it for pleasure—I buy what I like."

"Well, I know Keith is happy that you liked his piece, and we're all glad you decided to move to Chadwick!" I glanced down again at the brindled mastiff, who trotted briskly alongside his master. "And even though Hero looks very healthy, if you ever need a vet, I can recommend the Chadwick Veterinary Clinic. He'll be in the best of hands."

Dez shot me a surprised look, and I wondered if he had heard about the clinic break-in. His cool demeanor quickly returned, though. "Actually, I already brought him there once, for his annual shots."

"Did you? To Dr. Coccia?"

He squinted. "No, I don't think that was the name . . . a Dr. Reed. Nice woman."

"Yes, she is. They're partners."

While his dog paused to check out some fascinating riverbank smell, Mitchelson fixed me with an amused stare. "You're asking a lot of personal questions today, Cassie. You can't be after my business, because I don't have any cats."

Busted, I covered with a laugh. "I suppose I've gotten into the habit of being kind of a goodwill ambassador for our town. I've only lived here a little over two years myself, but I think Chadwick's got a lot to offer. I'm always glad to see other new people discovering it."

"When we talked at the gallery opening, I asked you out for coffee, but you turned me down. Said you were in a relationship. Was that true, or just your way of fending me off?"

I felt my face warm, even though I really did not want to give Dez any evidence of my attraction to him. "No, that was absolutely true. In fact . . ."

By an insane coincidence, I spotted Mark strolling toward us from the direction of the gazebo. Well, it was right about the time he said he'd arrive, and I'm sure he was deliberately searching for me.

". . . In fact, here he is now." I waved an arm to beckon him over.

Mark responded with a smile, which faded slightly when he saw my companion. I guess even to another straight guy, Dez Mitchelson must look like a blond Adonis, the kind of dude who had it all together. And maybe not the sort of stranger you wanted to find chatting in the park with your girlfriend.

When he came near enough, I tried to reassure him—and to discourage Dez—by grabbing Mark's hand affectionately.

"Glad you were finally able to get free. You're still in time for the judging."

"I saw some pretty creative costumes on my way over here," he said. "Even recognized a few patients."

His gaze fell on Hero, and I noticed that even Mark eyed the dog warily. Of course, we pros have learned better than anyone to assess an animal's body language before trying to even pet it. Hero's stance was tense, his ears cocked back and his tail held stiff, not wagging. I would have read those as warning signs, too.

To break the awkwardness, I introduced Mark to Dez. "He was at the art show reception last Saturday and bought one of Keith's largest paintings."

Relaxing at this explanation, Mark held out his hand. "I heard about that—I understand it really made Keith's night! Good to meet you; I'm Mark Coccia."

Mitchelson accepted the handshake with a raised eyebrow. "Coccia . . . Are you—?"

"Yes, he's Dr. Reed's partner," I confirmed. "Dez was telling me that Hero's already a patient."

"Nothing too wrong with him, I hope," Mark said.

"Nothing at all, just needed routine shots." When Hero fired off a thunderous bark at a passing Labrador, Mitchelson once again pulled the dog closer to his side. "I'm afraid bringing him here today might have been a mistake, though. I didn't realize he'd be around so many other animals."

"Dez didn't know about the pet parade," I explained.

"He does seem a little agitated." Though Mark glanced toward the dog, his comment also could have applied to Mitchelson.

"I'd better get him back to the car." Dez pulled his shades out of his pocket and hid his eyes again. "Good to see you again, Cassie, and nice meeting you, Mark."

We both studied the newcomer as he walked away, still struggling a bit with his burly beast. When they reached the parking lot near the riverbank, Mitchelson stopped by a large, expensive-looking, black SUV and used his key fob to remotely open the hatch. Hero obediently jumped inside. Dez took a minute to secure him with the leash, then got behind the wheel and drove away.

Mark finally commented, "Maggie did mention that some new guy came into the clinic with a mastiff, a few weeks ago, but at the time I didn't see him. That's a lot of dog for our sleepy little town."

"Dez said he's a Presa Canario. They used to herd cattle, or something."

"They used to *guard* cattle, against wild animals and rustlers. Dez must have quite an art collection to protect."

I laughed. "Well, he said he got the dog as a rescue, so maybe he didn't realize at the time what he was taking on." We strolled back toward the gazebo, where judging for the parade seemed to have begun. "Dez lives in Public Storage, the same building as Keith. That's how he found out about the gallery show."

Now Mark studied me as carefully as he had the dog. "Sounds like you two had a long talk."

"Actually, he didn't tell me that. Dawn mentioned it the other day." I put my arm through Mark's and smiled. "Don't be jealous. I told him I had a boyfriend, though I don't think he believed me until you actually showed up."

He narrowed his eyes, probably at the idea that Dez had even raised the question. "Think that's why he beat it out of here so fast?"

"I'm sure of it. He must've realized, at a glance, that he was outclassed."

Chapter 14

Porky, the pug dressed as Yoda, took Best in Show. Weenie, the dachshund/centipede, waddled away with Most Creative; and Gus, the guinea pig/bumblebee, scored Best Non-Canine entry. A representative of our local PetMart superstore presented their owners with generous gift cards.

Photos of the three winners, along with their people, appeared in the online edition of the *Chadwick Courier* the next morning. Over breakfast in Mark's condo, he and I enjoyed reading about the contest's results, and how much money the event had raised for FOCA.

Since it was Sunday, with Maggie on call for any emergencies at the clinic, Mark had the leisure to make us both scrumptious Western omelets. His doctor father might be divorced from his mother now, and seeing another woman, but at least the man had taught Mark how to cook . . . very well.

The previous evening, the two of us had managed to forget about most of the drama surrounding the clinic robbery. Mark had been faithfully taking jazz guitar lessons with an older man, Stan Nazarian, who had a local combo. He'd had to set aside all of that, following the recent crisis. But Saturday night, after we'd had some wine, he took out his Ibanez semi-hollowbody and played a few tunes.

He didn't sound as if he'd lost too much ground due to the lack of practice. In spite of some time away from the instrument, his fingerwork had gotten quicker, and his improvisation—something he'd struggled with at first—sounded freer and more playful. I sensed that after sitting in a few times with his instructor's combo, Quintessence, Mark had gained confidence and didn't worry as much anymore about making small mistakes.

He'd added a few oldies to his repertoire, probably due to the influence of his teacher. We had a small nostalgia fest as he strummed and picked his way through "All of Me" and "How High the Moon." I even remembered the lyrics well enough to sing along on a couple of numbers. Luckily, we heard no complaints from his condo neighbors.

We slept a bit late the next morning, past nine. I had already showered, and Mark was taking his turn, when I got a call from my mother.

"We haven't seen each other in a while, Cassie," she pointed out. "I thought you might be free to have lunch today with me and Harry."

Although originally I had not been fond of Harry Bock, I'd grown resigned to the fact that my mother enjoyed his company. I even had to admit that the guy had his good points, including brains, a thriving career as an architect, and a devotion to his Sphynx cat, Looli. But Mom lived in Morristown, about forty-five minutes away, so if they planned to eat somewhere in that area, it would be a drive for me.

"Well," I stalled, "I'm actually at Mark's place now. I'll need to stop home and deal with all of the cats before I can . . ."

"That's fine, dear. We were thinking of coming up your

way and eating at The Firehouse. You've always said good things about it, and though Harry's heard about the renovation, he's never seen it in person."

That plan sounded much more doable. "Yes, I'm sure he'd find it very interesting."

"We'll give you a little time to tend to your shop first. How about meeting us there at one?"

I agreed to that, and Mom let me off the phone to finish dressing. But it turned out to be a busy morning for both Mark and me, in terms of phone calls. He'd emerged from the shower and sat on the side of the bed, still toweling his hair, when his cell played a few bars of the Dave Brubeck standard, "Take Five."

"Oh, hi, Angela," I heard him say. "What's up?"

Like me, he knew the police detective would not call just to shoot the breeze. After he commented with a few *uh-huh*s that told me nothing, he asked Bonelli, "Would you mind if I put you on speaker? Cassie's here with me, and I can tell the curiosity is killing her."

That embarrassed me, but Bonelli must have given the okay, because she let me hear the rest of their conversation.

"We got a name on the guy who crashed on the motorcycle," she said. "Enrique Franco, known as Ricky to his friends . . . and to the cops south of here. We ran his prints. He had a rap sheet for break-ins and a little dealing on the side."

"So, he could have been the guy who attacked Sam." Mark sounded hopeful, and why not? This might sew up the case!

"He certainly could've been, but I wouldn't breathe easy yet. There's some doubt that the roadside crash killed him outright. Franco also sustained a couple of serious blows to the head."

"Was he wearing a helmet?"

"No, and that's why we assumed at first that he died from the collision. He also broke an arm and a couple of ribs. But even though it's kind of lonely farmland out there, he didn't hit a tree or any rocks big enough to account for those head injuries. The M.E. thinks it's possible that someone deliberately finished him off."

So, there could be a bad guy still out there, I thought. A *very* bad guy, who had coldly bludgeoned an injured man to death.

"Did someone think Franco screwed up the clinic robbery?" I asked Bonelli. "Maybe by leaving Sam alive to talk?"

"Anything's possible. We pulled Nardone back in for more questioning, but he claims he never met or even heard of Franco. Whether or not that's true, he acted scared to death . . . and I don't think it was because of me. He may have some info about whoever is running the drug ring, even if he never got a name. Now that he knows what that person is capable of doing, he's clamming up tighter than ever."

Great, I thought. Instead of shedding some light on the clinic robbery, Franco's death might just make the situation murkier.

"No way, I guess, to tell if some other vehicle ran Franco off the road?" Mark asked.

"The only skid marks were made by his bike, and the other tracks on the road came from lots of different vehicles, including tractor trailers. No way to even tell when they were made, because they're overlapping and worn down by now."

Yes, I could see where isolating any one set, on a roadway with lots of truck traffic, would be hopeless.

"Franco lives down that way, which explains the location of the accident," Bonelli went on. "A passerby reported seeing the motorcycle laying in the ditch, almost hidden by dead leaves, but that wasn't until early Friday morning. The M.E. says he probably died shortly after midnight, so it's not surprising that no one witnessed the actual crash."

"Could one of those big trucks have driven him off the road?" I asked. "Maybe the driver was tired, and didn't even see him until it was too late."

"Be pretty heartless not to call nine-one-one, if Franco was still alive."

"Even more heartless to bash his head in," Mark added. "That would have to be one homicidal trucker."

"Exactly." The detective sighed into the phone. "Mark, I'd like to reassure you that your colleagues and employees are off the hook, but there still might be a co-conspirator inside the clinic. Or even a supplier who comes there often and knows where you keep the narcotics. Now that there's been a murder, we'll need to talk to everybody again."

Although his broad shoulders sagged, he told her, "You know Maggie and I will cooperate in any way we can."

Once he got off the phone, a cloud of gloom descended on what had been our cheerful, relaxing morning together. I finished dressing and apologized for having to get back to my responsibilities at the shop and keep my lunch date with Mom and Harry. Mark reflected that he also should phone the tech who was minding the clinic and make sure nothing unexpected was going on there.

"Even though we've restocked everything, at least we're not likely to get robbed again," he reasoned, as he saw me to the door. "Franco won't be back, and we've upgraded our security with motion-sensitive lights, outdoor cameras, and a new code system so complicated that even Maggie and I could get shut out." He gave me a parting kiss. "Anyway, have a nice lunch with your mom and Harry."

★ ★ ★

I walked to The Firehouse and arrived just as the two of them emerged from Harry's BMW sedan in the restaurant's parking lot. We'd all dressed in neat-but-casual clothes— Mom in slim pants and a coral cowl-necked sweater that set off her wavy auburn hair; Harry in his customary polo, blazer, and khakis. Over the past year, his blond locks had thinned a bit more, but he still kept himself trim, probably through his favorite sport, fussing over trivialities. All right, maybe that wasn't such a bad trait for an architect, but he sometimes carried it too far.

After they greeted me, Harry paused for a minute to size up the building's exterior against the backdrop of scarlet-and-gold maple trees. The brick, two-story structure had indeed started life as a firehouse, around the turn of the twentieth century, and retained the corner turret that once concealed the firemen's pole. Hook-and-ladder trucks used to emerge from the three large front bays, which were now fitted with tall, oak-trimmed glass doors.

Harry squinted his gray eyes against the noonday sunshine as if taking in every detail. "Nicely done," he murmured, mostly to himself. We stepped inside.

Weekday and Saturday evenings, working folks and dating couples would have filled the bentwood stools along the polished front bar. On a Sunday afternoon, though, the tables and booths saw most of the action, with older folks and families more visible. Harry had made reservations, of course. While the hostess showed us to our booth, he seemed to scan the restaurant's period touches, such as the industrial-style ceiling fans and the pressed-tin ceilings.

"I do like this," he pronounced, after we'd all slid into place on the leather-like seats. "Have to hand it to this Lathrop fellow, he's got style. I wonder if he uses an architect or designs these places himself."

"You should see what he's done with the Paragon," I said.

"Oh, we did," Mom told me. "Since we got to Chadwick a little early, Harry suggested we drop by there on the way. No movies today, but the lobby was open, I guess for the pet costume contest. You and Mark helped judge that, right?"

"We sort of pre-judged it, just to weed out the really lame entries. Did you vote?"

"Harry didn't, but I did." She laughed. "I do think there's one entry who's kind of a sure thing."

"That Maine Coon!" Harry shook his head, in awe. He had brought his purebred Sphynx cat to several shows, so he knew his breeds pretty well.

"Yes, I think Quentin's bound to score one of the three prizes," I agreed. "Nancy Whyte's actually got him, now." Harry and Mom had met her that spring at a local show, when Nancy and her two cats occupied a benching spot near theirs. I explained that she had taken in Quentin for a friend who'd become too ill to manage him.

As we looked over our menus, I warned them that The Firehouse tried to live up to its name by offering a lot of spicy selections. Some recipes came from south of the border; others leaned toward Thai ingredients. Harry opted for the "breakfast tacos" filled with black beans, chiles, and cheddar, with sausage on the side, while Mom ordered an avocado—two halves—stuffed with corn, green chiles and shredded chicken, served with ranch dressing. Avoiding the hottest choices, I went for a lime shrimp salad with spicy Old Bay potato chips on the side.

We got our iced teas first, and Mom finally brought up the subject of the veterinary clinic robbery. Harry had gotten wind of it, too, if mostly from her, but knew few details. Our local paper reported that the thief had stolen narcotics, but Bonelli had taught me well, and I remained cautious about how much more to reveal.

"It still worries me," Mom said, "that if the robber is after animal medications he might also try to break into Cassie's shop."

I decided that one more bit of information might be enough to put her mind at rest. "We might not have to be concerned about that. Did you read about the guy who died in a motorcycle crash on Route 94 last night? Bonelli has reason to believe it was the same person who attacked Sam and broke into the clinic. If that's true, he's gone now, where he won't be a problem anymore."

That surprised Mom. "Really? How can they be sure it's the same . . ."

"Forensics, Mom. The cops have their ways."

Harry sniffed. "Would explain the crash, too, if he was on drugs at the time."

Since this train of thought reassured both of them, I said nothing more to derail it.

Harry excused himself to use the men's room. On his return, he enthused about the way the restaurant's performance area, quiet today, had been retrofitted into the fire-pole turret. "This place and the old theater are very different structures, but they're both excellent updates that keep the original character."

Our lunches arrived, and we spent a few minutes sampling and raving about them. Harry noted that The Firehouse's food matched its ambience in quality.

"I got to talk with Lathrop quite a bit, when he came to my shop and when Mark and I went through photos for the pet contest," I said. "He's a pretty imaginative guy."

"Also kind of an enigma, I understand," Harry added. "Doesn't belong to any professional organizations, vague about his background and credentials, very picky about whom he associates with or hires. That rankles some of the other architects around here, because Lathrop sometimes beats them out for high-profile jobs. On the other hand, he also takes on projects none of them would want."

"Like this place and the Paragon?" I asked.

"Exactly. It's very romantic to think of renovating an old building, but it's often a nightmare, and much more expensive than building a new one from scratch."

It was on the tip of my tongue to launch into the tale of woe about my worn-out heating system and to ask Harry if he thought the estimate I'd gotten from the HVAC guy was reasonable. But I bit my tongue in time. He might be able to advise me, but then either he or Mom might insist on footing the bill for a new unit. I didn't want to take that kind of handout from either of them, even as a loan, unless things got really desperate. I was a big girl and a semi-successful businesswoman; I should be able to cover the cost of maintaining my own home and business.

Mom, meanwhile, continued the thread of the conversation. "I guess for a place that needs so much updating, the permitting process alone would be time-consuming." A paralegal herself, she added, "You'd probably need to hire an attorney."

Harry nodded. "Everything would have to be brought up to code, such as the wiring and the plumbing. Usually, there's also some asbestos or even mold to be abated. Those issues can hold a project up for months, even years, but Lathrop has a reputation for getting the work done efficiently. There's talk that he greases a few palms, but who knows?"

"Well, at least in Chadwick he's preserved a couple of

beautiful landmarks and repurposed them for new uses," Mom defended the developer.

"And while The Firehouse has been very successful, the Paragon probably struggles a bit," I pointed out. "Even though Mark and I love the vintage screenings, not many people our age even go out to the movies anymore. Its main audiences are older folks who like the convenience of staying downtown, or enjoy the nostalgia of seeing those classic films in an old-fashioned setting."

"Yes, I'm sure Lathrop didn't expect that theater to be a big moneymaker." Harry had finished the first of his upscaled tacos and eagerly started on the second. "No one is really sure where or how he gets his funding, but he must have plenty."

"He doesn't have a company?" Mom asked.

"Doesn't seem to. In an interview once, he referred to his 'partner,' but that might have been a personal, not a business, relationship." Harry smiled as if this were a somewhat naughty assumption. "Of course, he could have family money—I heard he hails from someplace in the Midwest. Or, some people just have a knack for getting grants and working all the angles. Anyhow, he's as much a philanthropist as a developer . . . and definitely an eccentric."

Silently, my mind began running along another track. An architect or contractor renovating a building for a new use would have to know its layout and systems inside and out. The veterinary clinic also had been renovated, from a private home. That project had been just a year or two before I'd opened my shop in town . . . probably about the same time as The Firehouse redesign.

The architect who refitted the old firehouse had to adapt it to function as a restaurant. Whoever redesigned the white colonial on Laurel Street to serve as an animal hospital must have made a lot of changes, too. Had the secure storage for the anesthetics been part of the original plan, requested by Mark and Maggie?

If so, that would be a few more people who'd know which closet held the narcotics—the architect, the contractor, and whoever installed the security system. I wonder if Angela thought to check out any of those folks!

Back at my shop that afternoon, I checked again on my boarders and turned out a couple of the younger cats who seemed itching for more exercise. Since I never let two loose in the playroom at once unless they came from the same household—because unfamiliar cats tend to fight with one another—Sarah and I had to keep rotating animals in the space throughout the day. A couple of our boarders at the moment were older and more sedate, but others would start climbing the wire mesh doors of their tri-level condos after a while, letting us know they needed to stretch their limbs.

Even after Sarah had gone for the day, I lingered in the playroom to cat-sit one frisky Abyssinian. I sat in the space's token "human" chair and used my laptop to note down my latest ideas about the clinic robbery. I figured the CLOSED sign, turned outward on the shop's door, should give me privacy after sunset, even with some of the shop's lights turned on.

I wanted to share my new suspicions with someone, but leaving a message for Bonelli felt almost like going over Mark's head. In case he and Maggie already had covered this ground with the cops, I'd just send him an email. He could reply, or not, when he had some spare time.

I explained that, during my lunch with Mom and Harry at The Firehouse, the topic of updating a building for some new use had come up. *What firm worked on the clinic, for you and*

Maggie? Would they know about the secure storage closet? No rush to get back to me, just curious.

Enough, I thought. Possibly, Bonelli had already looked into those angles. And poor Mark deserved at least one night off from racking his brain over such questions.

I hit send, then set my laptop aside.

I caught the Abyssinian without much trouble—she seemed happily tired out from running and climbing. After returning her to her condo, I switched off the shop lights and climbed the stairs to my apartment.

There, Cole, Mango, and Matisse ganged around me, wailing for their dinners. I took care of them, and silence descended, except for the chewing. In my usual gourmet-chef style, I microwaved a frozen pizza and ate three slices while watching the seven o'clock news and then an episode of a BBC mystery on the living room TV.

The hour-long show had wound up, and I was contemplating a wedge of honeydew as a bedtime snack, when my cell phone rang.

I expected the screen to show Mark's number but saw Dawn's. Why would she be calling, after nine p.m.?

She sounded breathless. "Cassie, I'm so glad you're home. There's some *freak* prowling around outside my place, and I'm scared to death!"

Chapter 15

My longtime friend does not give in to hysteria easily, so I asked her to explain.

"It happened just now," she said. "I was taking out the trash, for tomorrow's pickup. Y'know how there's kind of a wide alley between the stores? This guy suddenly lurches around the corner, coming off the street, and just stands there, staring at me! It felt that way, anyhow—with the streetlight behind him, he was mostly just a silhouette. But from what I could see, he looked like a monster!"

Again, though Dawn has plenty of imagination, she usually doesn't exaggerate or make fun of people's appearances. "Big, you mean?"

"Tall, big shoulders, and hunched over. But he had an animal's head! Even in silhouette, I could make out pointed ears, and when he stepped closer and the back door light fell on him, he had a snout!"

I was still digesting all this when Dawn interrupted herself. "Oh, good, a cop car's pulling up outside. I called them right away."

"I'm coming over, too," I said.

"Drive here, don't walk! I know it's only a couple of blocks, but this weirdo could still be prowling around."

When I arrived at Nature's Way, Dawn stood near the big oak display counter, telling her story to Officer Steve Jacoby. The square-jawed, blond young cop, who also had an older brother on the force, held an open notepad. They both looked up when I knocked on the glass front door, and Dawn had to unlock it to let me in.

"I called Cassie right after you guys," she explained to Jacoby.

"Glad you had your priorities straight." With a crooked smile, he glanced around at the shop's seasonal decorations. "You do realize, Ms. Tischler, that this was just some bozo in one of those full-head Halloween masks? And that Halloween is less than a week away?"

Though his questions were more lighthearted than condescending, I saw Dawn bristle. "Of course I realize that. But how many grown men do you see walking around the streets in full wolfman getup, a week before Halloween? And why would someone see a woman alone in a dark alley and deliberately stalk her like an animal? I mean, he *growled* at me."

"A very mean trick, I agree. But maybe he went to an early Halloween party, left a little drunk, and just did it on a whim. You said he never came close or made any real move to attack you."

"No, but he stood there a long time, like he was considering it. I backed toward my door, keeping him in sight, and when I screamed, he finally took off."

Jacoby nodded, as if taking the threat more seriously. "Okay. Can you think of anyone who might want to get back at you for something? A nasty ex-boyfriend, maybe?"

Dawn shook her head. "Not really. All my breakups have been pretty low on drama."

I smiled to myself at this. When it came to her love life, Dawn did maintain a rather neo-hippie attitude of going with the flow. She didn't play the kind of head games that would make a man insanely jealous. Anyway, she'd been exclusive with Keith for several contented years.

Jacoby straightened his shoulders, poised to leave. "We'll have a cruiser go around this block for the next couple of nights, in case the guy shows up again. I guess, aside from his height, you can't really describe him?"

Dawn shrugged. "He had on a light blue work shirt and dark pants, probably jeans. The shirt was open at the top and his neck area looked dark, though that could have been the long fur from the mask. His hands looked dark, but also large and hairy—he probably was wearing gloves, to go with the costume. I guess the mask could have made him look a little taller, too, because of the pointed ears."

After jotting down these final details, Jacoby turned to me. "You planning to stay with her tonight?"

"I'd be happy to." I hadn't brought any clothes along, but my cats had eaten enough to hold them until morning.

Another arrival through the shop door, however, resolved this question. Keith wore gray sweats and a hooded jacket, as if he'd dashed out of his apartment, and his lean, brown-bearded face was creased in worry. He crossed immediately to Dawn, took her in his arms, and asked if she was okay.

She smiled. "Untouched by human hands . . . or any other kind."

I was glad she'd at least regained her sense of humor.

Before leaving, Officer Jacoby also reassured Keith that the prowler was probably just some jerk trying out a new

Halloween costume by scaring a few strangers. He promised, though, that the Chadwick cops would keep an eye out for the rest of the night.

The rest of us took seats around the shop's wood-burning stove. Dawn repeated the details of her frightening experience for her boyfriend's benefit, and reviewed the questions Jacoby had asked her.

"The creep seems to have taken some pains to make sure he wouldn't be recognized," Keith pointed out.

"Well, it's easy enough to get a wolf's head and matching paws," I said. "You can find them online or, at this time of year, in any pop-up Halloween store. I guess Jacoby could be right. The guy could have tried them on, looked in the mirror, and thought, 'Hey, I'm pretty scary!' So, he decided to wander around downtown like that, and couldn't resist surprising a woman in a dark alley. Almost like role-playing a scene from a movie."

Dawn ran a hand through her luxuriant hair. "I hope that's all it was. If he'd popped around the corner and said 'Boo,' then maybe laughed and kept going, I'd buy that explanation. But I can't forget the way he just stood there, staring at me. Completely silent, except for that growl!"

Keith's frown deepened. "You told Jacoby that no one could have a grudge against you, Dawn. But that's not really true, is it? What about that little undercover job you and Cassie pulled last week at The Roost?"

She faced him with startled eyes. "No . . . it couldn't have anything to do with that. Could it?"

"I'm the one who blew Nardone's cover," I reminded him. "Not Dawn."

"You came in together," Keith said. "It wouldn't take a genius to figure out that she was in on it, too."

And Dawn is more recognizable, I realized. There were lots of medium-tall women out there with shoulder-length brown hair who favored boring, classic clothes. But Dawn was five-nine, with that wild copper mane, and had really stood out in her crocheted midi-dress. Anyone who asked around town, and described her, could have been told, "Sounds like the lady who runs the health-food store."

And she'd used the alias "Donna," pretty close to her real name.

My heart sank as I remembered something else—Dawn had told Tanith about our escapade at The Roost. Had the goth girl carelessly mentioned it to someone she shouldn't have? But now didn't seem the right time to say *I told you so,* especially with Keith so agitated.

"Nardone's still in custody, isn't he?" Dawn asked me.

"I don't know. Even if he's not, he's got a trial coming up, so I'd guess the cops are keeping a close watch on him."

"There were those two guys we talked to, Joe and Gary. After you spilled that woman's drink, and then MacDonald showed up, they both left in a hurry. Maybe because they smelled something fishy?"

"And were afraid they'd get caught up in the net," I finished, then gave her an apologetic smile. "Sorry, I really stretched that metaphor!"

Normally good-natured, Keith did not appear to find anything funny about our speculations. "Damn it, you two! That was supposed to be just a little innocent surveillance of the bar scene, nothing to attract the attention of any bad guys. Now you might have gotten yourselves on their radar!"

Dawn, bless her, jumped in to defend me. "Well, what was Cassie supposed to do, let that poor woman toss down a spiked drink? As it turns out, our instincts were dead-on, and the cops made a good arrest, with fresh evidence."

Tensely, Keith massaged his short beard. "I know, but—"

"Look, there's nothing more we can do about it tonight," I told them both. "In the morning, I'll call Bonelli and get her advice. I'll find out, first, if they picked up the guy in the costume. If not, I'll ask whether it could have been Nardone, or whether they want to look for the guys who talked to us in the bar. For now, though, I'd better get back to my place and make sure everything is still kosher there."

"That's right!" Dawn's amber eyes widened. "If someone at the bar found out who I really am, they probably know about you, too . . . 'Cathy.'"

Yeah, not much difference from the name on the front of my shop. Maybe Dawn and I weren't quite ready yet for the big leagues of undercover investigation.

Keith rose from his bedspread-shrouded armchair. "Not going to walk back, are you?"

"I brought my car, thanks. And I'll keep my wits about me. You stay here with Dawn."

My commonplace, seven-year-old CR-V stood at the curb, still locked and unmolested. Driving the two blocks home, I did spot a Chadwick PD patrol car idling on a side street, which bolstered my courage.

Everything seemed fine inside my shop, too, the alarm still set and the boarder cats all dozing peacefully. Just to be safe, I retrieved the canister of pepper spray that I normally kept behind the front counter, and brought it along as I climbed the stairs to my apartment. But I found nothing amiss there, either. I gave each of my three pets a small scoop of dry food to compensate for leaving them alone all evening. Finally, I went to bed, though sleep was still a long time coming.

Officer Jacoby was probably right, I thought. Dawn's boogeyman had just pulled a prank on the first, easiest victim he'd found, but never really intended to harm her. Even she admitted that if not for his odd behavior, she might have laughed it off.

We're all on edge because of the clinic robbery, still looking for suspects everywhere. Even though the actual thief, the one who parked his motorbike behind the building, is no longer around to hurt any of us.

Could the cops be sure of that, though? They had IDed him from the bike, the info in his wallet, and his general build, but Sam never got a good look at him. The guy who was killed had short hair, but Sam had thought that, from the reflection he saw in the door glass, his attacker's hair seemed longer . . .

Dawn's prowler wore a mask with fur down to the collar, even hiding the front of his neck. She said he also could have had on gloves.

Sounded like he was taller than the person who had accosted Sam, even if you allowed for the pointed ears. But the clinic robber probably didn't act on his own. If that had been Enrique Franco, the cops seemed to think someone higher in the ranks had run him off the road and beaten him for good measure. As a punishment, and maybe a warning to the rest of the dealers. Bonelli suspected a ring, active in at least three states.

Could Dawn have encountered another member? Or maybe even . . . the boss?

Chapter 16

By the time I called Bonelli on Monday, from my shop, one of her guys had already questioned Nardone.

"He said on Sunday night he always visits his folks," she told me. "Now, as good Italian parents, would they lie for him, or not? I personally got the sense they were shocked that their son tried to drug a girl in a bar, are mortified that he'll have to go to trial, and are keeping him on a tight leash from now on."

An appropriate figure of speech, I thought, if he was the beast that had menaced my friend. "Do you think there's a chance it was somebody else with the narcotics ring?"

"No way to be sure, of course, but I'd say that's a stretch. Doesn't mean Dawn wasn't in any danger, though, and we're still watching out for any perv who might be preying on women around town."

I relaxed a little. "I guess she and I tend to relate everything scary that happens, these days, to the clinic robbery."

"That's natural, and I very much hope I didn't put you two in any danger by sending you to The Roost that evening. I'll check up on those two guys who talked with you, though we haven't got much to go on besides first names and general descriptions. Where did they work, again?"

"Gary told Dawn he was a 'barista,' which just means he makes fancy coffee drinks; you could check with the Best Beans shop out on the highway. Joe said he was in 'medical supplies,' and I wonder now if that was a euphemism. Even if it's a legit firm, he still could have access to pharmaceuticals."

"Usually that title would mean he dealt with the hardware, the medical equipment. But like you said, it could just be his cover story." A beat of silence suggested that Bonelli was taking notes. "MacDonald saw the two guys from a distance, when you were chatting with them. He was doing his own surveillance, though, so he couldn't get too close. He told me he wasn't sure he'd even recognize them again."

"I guess by now everyone at The Roost knows MacDonald is a cop."

Bonelli chuckled. "You got it, so we've had to replace him, anyway. But I'll tell our new guy on the scene to keep a lookout for Joe and Gary, just in case they're regulars."

I didn't hold out much hope. "Even if they were with the ring, they bolted out of the restaurant that night at the first sign of trouble. They'll probably be too gun-shy to return, at least for a while."

The detective was not so easily discouraged. "We can try asking the bartenders. Those guys probably hear and observe a lot. The only trick will be getting them to open up."

I sensed that Bonelli wanted to move on to her other duties, but I had to sound her out on one more theory. I told her about my lunch the previous day with my mother and Harry at The Firehouse, and what he'd said about adapting buildings for new uses. "Any professionals who worked on the veterinary clinic probably knew which storage room was going to be used for the anesthetics, right?"

"Mmm, not necessarily. The key factor was the locked case, itself, which was anchored to the wall. It's practically a safe. That would have been installed by a security company, maybe the same one that handled their electronic door locks. I suppose there's always a chance that a former employee of the company went rogue, and pulled the break-in, but those firms usually screen their people well. Dr. Reed told me she did hire a different company to change all of the locks and codes after the robbery, to be on the safe side."

I thanked the detective for bringing me up to speed, and hung up feeling I'd done everything I could for the present.

Sarah, with a little time on her hands, had been decorating our front window for the season. Nothing as elaborate as Tanith had done at Nature's Way, and leaning more toward cute and funny.

She'd used stretchy gray stuff to create spiderwebs in the two upper corners, and had embedded green, yellow, and orange catnip mice like little mummies. She'd also wrapped a skeletal hand around a hair dryer and aimed it at the silhouette of a bristling black cat. I watched while she propped up these things, invisibly, by taping them on the inside to clear plastic easels.

Though it was a rather bleak day with a light drizzle, I stepped outside to admire the finished scenario. "That's terrific!"

At my side, Sarah laughed. "You don't think it will scare away our customers?"

"Nah. Most cat owners don't scare that easy."

So my assistant would be alert to any possible trouble, I briefed her on Dawn's weird encounter of the night before. Sarah admitted that, like the rest of us, she would not take it too seriously except for the attack on Sam, the robbery at the clinic, and the not-so-accidental death of Ricky Franco. "But of course, there could be no connection at all."

"Let's hope not." Back at the front desk, I checked our schedule for the rest of the day. "Ms. Leibowitz is coming for Godiva at eleven, right?"

Sarah nodded. "Diva had her breakfast, and I gave her a quick brushing this morning, so she's ready to go home."

When our front door opened, ten minutes later, I think both of us expected Irene Leibowitz. It surprised me to see, instead, a tall, gray-bearded figure who looked as if he might have just stepped off a fishing trawler: Dark jeans, navy pea-coat and ribbed turtleneck, black watch cap. On closer inspection, I noticed the peacoat was a rich tweed, the knit cap also pristine, and the beard conspicuously well-groomed.

Avery Lathrop seemed to be a man of many faces . . . or at least, many roles. His wide grin told me that he enjoyed my reaction.

"Mr. Lathrop," I said. "What a pleasant surprise . . . again!"

"People always seem startled to see me out and about in the daytime," he said, "instead of lurking in the shadows at the Paragon, or some other building even more elderly than I am."

This was another bit of theatrical exaggeration, I told myself, since the man probably hadn't reached seventy yet and seemed in good shape. "Maybe that's just because we associate you with those wonderful restorations."

He slipped off his cap and tucked it in his coat pocket. "I won't take much of your time, Cassie. I wanted to confirm that we'll be awarding the prizes for the werewolf look-alike contest on Halloween, around five p.m., and to ask if you and Mark would help present them."

That flustered me a little. "Oh . . . us? I assumed you'd want to do that yourself."

"Well, there are three awards, so why not have three presenters?" He half-leaned on my front counter and half-sat on one of the stools. "Admittedly, I do have a practical reason. The owners of the winning pets will come with them, of course. But just in case any of the creatures become camera shy, and give even their owners trouble, it might help to also have a couple of professional animal handlers on the scene. They will be up on the stage, in front of an audience, and we wouldn't want any to escape or be injured."

I had to give him credit for thinking ahead. "Saturday night? That should be no problem for me. Mark's schedule is less predictable, but things at the clinic have quieted down these days, so he should be able to make it."

"Oh, I'm glad to hear that," Lathrop said. "A shame that his clinic has had such problems. Did the police ever find out who was responsible?"

Guarded these days with everyone beyond my inner circle, I resolved to tell Lathrop nothing he would not have learned already on the news. "They haven't made an arrest, no."

"I supposed the place will have to review all of its security measures. If they need help, tell Mark to give me a call. I've got an excellent company that installed alarms for me at The Firehouse and a couple of other projects in this area."

"Thanks, though I think he and Maggie have already taken care of all that."

"They probably have."

I saw a chance to satisfy my curiosity about some things. "The clinic, like the Paragon and The Firehouse, was adapted from another type of building. Over the weekend I was talking with a family friend who's an architect. He said a renovation like that is more difficult than building something new, because of all the things that have to be brought up to date."

"Oh, it's true, it's true." Lathrop unbuttoned his peacoat and eased farther onto his high stool. "When I discuss my projects with town planners, and even the contractors, they think I must be crazy. Only now that I've had a few successes do they trust me to be able to deliver what I promise."

"How did you decide, though, to specialize in restoring old buildings?"

"Nostalgia, I suppose. I grew up in a very small town in Illinois; a bit like Chadwick, with a lot of solid brick buildings that were meant to last. I went to the UIC School of Architecture, and after graduation I took the conventional jobs, designing modern corporate headquarters." He scrunched his face. "Bored me senseless! So, once I no longer needed the work that badly, I started seeking out my own projects. Residences and commercial buildings that were sitting neglected, blighting their communities, but had great character and could be given new life. Along the way, I became a connoisseur of small towns, and gradually worked my way East."

Ms. Leibowitz—white-haired, but still slim and athletic—arrived at that point and greeted us all with a rosy-cheeked smile. Since handing over Diva to her and collecting payment was a straightforward transaction, Sarah took care of it without interrupting my conversation with Lathrop.

I tried to keep him on the subject of restoring old structures. "I get a sense that the Paragon was a particular favorite project for you."

"Oh, I adore movie theaters. They always take me back to my childhood. Growing up in that sleepy town, I spent many hours with my friends, or even alone, watching cartoons, adventure stories, and yes, even horror movies in our downtown theater. I like to think I'm recreating a little of that feeling for people here in Chadwick." He shrugged philosophically. "Maybe I'm fooling myself, maybe those days are gone forever. Lord knows, the Paragon will never make money for me! But I don't worry about that."

His dismissal of any need to make a profit caught my attention. "It must cost you a lot, though, to even undertake one of these restorations."

"I try to work with local contractors and I bargain-hunt for architectural salvage. Sure, we face a budget crisis almost every time. But somehow, the money we need always shows up." He waved his hand in the air like a stage magician.

I couldn't help wondering if he "found" his money through grants, or possibly some under-the-table sources. Then I felt ashamed for having such suspicions.

Ms. Leibowitz departed with her cat, and that seemed to tip off Lathrop that he might be occupying too much of my work time. With another broad smile, he got to his feet and buttoned his peacoat. "Anyhow, Cassie, I do hope to see both you and Mark on Saturday. We should have a decent audience for the presentations. I'm happy to say, people have been voting at a great clip. I have to clean out the ballot box at the end of each day so it doesn't get too filled up!"

I couldn't resist asking, "Any sign yet of who the winners will be?"

"From what I've seen, every contestant got at least one to two votes, but by now a few have pulled out in front of the pack, so to speak. I'm going to start checking with some of the owners, to make sure they'll be free to come on Halloween. Without tipping my hand too much, if possible!"

"Of course," I agreed, matching his sly tone. "Wouldn't want to let the wolf out of the bag too early, right?"

This made him chuckle. "I'm sure I can count on your discretion, but you may want to let your friend Nancy Whyte know that her presence, and Quentin's, probably will be requested at our little soirée. If the gentleman can come in his evening dress, all the better."

"I'll convey the message." A daunting thought occurred to me. "I don't have to wear a costume, do I? Or Mark?"

Lathrop looked intrigued by the idea. "No one will mind if you do—might add to the fun! Just as long as we don't scare the real stars of the evening."

As he started for the door, I remembered his very professional Santa Claus getup from the holiday-movie marathon the previous Christmas. "Are you planning to wear one?"

He paused. "I may succumb to the temptation. Something tasteful, of course . . . suitable for the occasion."

During lunch break, I did shoot Nancy a pseudo-mysterious text message, to tell her that she and Quentin might want to keep their Saturday evening open for a visit to the Paragon. Then Sarah and I spent a couple of hours tidying up a messy Manx. When I checked my phone afterward, I had a call from Becky at FOCA and returned it.

"Thanks again for coming to the parade Saturday," she said. "Sorry you and I didn't get to talk longer. We had so many entries this year, Chris and I had our hands full with the paperwork—making sure everyone was legit and had the right entry numbers."

"You had a terrific day for it, and it looked like a big success," I said.

"It really was. Between the entry fees and some new donations, we raised thousands for the shelter! And we also raised our profile, as they say in marketing. With all of the people who entered their pets and the ones who just came to watch the parade, more folks have heard of us now. We were closed Sunday, of course, but in the last few days we had a bunch of new visitors drop in to look around, and half a dozen new adoptions."

"That's great! I got one of my cats, Cole, about six years ago around Halloween. It was before I moved to Chadwick—the shelter was just outside Morristown. They had a Black Cat Adoption Special, trying to counteract the superstition that black animals are bad luck. I gather, though, that shelters have stopped doing that."

"We have," Becky said. "It seemed like a good idea for a while, but there are too many creeps out there who want black cats at Halloween for abusive reasons. Every shelter tries to check out their adopters carefully, of course, but people can lie, and at this time of year it's just too risky. FOCA still has a special adoption day for black cats and dogs, but we've moved it to the springtime."

We chatted a little more about the progress of the were-wolf look-alike photo contest at the Paragon before Becky had to get back to her shelter chores. Remembering that a week ago she had been so frightened and depressed over the death of her estranged friend Karin, I was glad to hear Becky sounding like her usual, cheerful self again.

I told Sarah about the success of the FOCA fundraiser, and she smiled. "This is turning out to be quite a Halloween season, isn't it?"

"For Chadwick? Yeah, more excitement than usual—of the good kind and the bad." I recalled Dawn's spooky encounter in the alley, then tried once again to convince myself it hadn't been a serious threat. "And the fun's not over yet. Tomorrow night, the famous cable TV psychic, Ripley Van Eyck, appears in person at Nature's Way! Want to come and find out what the future has in store for you?"

Sarah responded with an ominous chuckle. "I don't think I want to know."

"Don't blame you," I said. "The way things have been going lately, I don't think I want to, either!"

Chapter 17

I called Mark the next day, during my lunch break at work, and was glad I also caught him at a slack time.

The news that Lathrop wanted us to help present the awards at the Paragon didn't throw him too much. "By Saturday night, my schedule should be pretty clear. Maggie, lucky woman, is on call this weekend for any emergencies."

But when I added that we should probably wear some kind of costumes for the occasion, Mark's defenses went up. "Aw, jeez. I wouldn't mind if it was a private party, with friends. But I don't want to look like a fool in front of a bunch of strangers, or maybe even some of my clients!"

"A bunch of strangers who were willing to dress up their cats, ferrets—and yes, even a cockatiel—to look like werewolves? I don't think any of them will be in a position to criticize us."

His pause suggested that he saw my point. "Lathrop doesn't expect *us* to come as werewolves, I hope."

"No, I don't think so. In fact, I sensed that he might be co-opting that costume for himself. I'm sure you and I can do something lower-key."

"Easiest thing would be to just wear my scrubs. Maybe you could be my patient. Do some kind of cat outfit, and bandage one paw? That could be good for both our businesses."

"Too predictable. Listen, I've already given this some thought. Why not come as your alter ego?"

A surprised chuckle on the line. "I didn't know I had one!"

"Sure you do—you're a jazz musician. Professional, even, since you sat in a couple of times with your teacher's combo. We could go as 1950s beatniks, and we probably have most of the clothes already. You've got a black turtleneck and black jeans, right? We can get berets, that's easy. And you'll need a goatee."

"What's that?"

"You know, a little beard, like a soul patch."

"Sounds okay," Mark relented. "Not too expensive or labor-intensive. But shouldn't it relate to the animal theme?"

"Ah, but it will! We'll paint whiskers on our faces and call ourselves the Hep Cats."

He laughed again. "You have thought of everything! That'll be practical, and also won't interfere with us handling the animals, if we need to. Okay, I'm in. I'll go through my closet and rustle up some black stuff. Don't know if I can grow much of a beard by Saturday, though."

"I'll get you something to stick on," I promised. "And also the berets."

As I hung up, I thought, *Even if that does mean battling the crowd at a highway party shop, just a few days before Halloween. Why do I get myself into these things?*

Sarah knew I planned to drop in on Dawn's big promotional event that evening with Ripley Van Eyck. My assistant also found his name outrageous, though from what I'd read online, he'd had it from his birth, about fifty-five years ago.

"What does this guy actually do?" Sarah asked me. "Does he predict things, or does he just tell you that your dead relatives are watching over you, that kind of stuff?"

I appreciated the hint of cynicism in her tone. "I don't really know. Guess I'll find out."

"Girl, you could have a *lot* of dead people trying to get in touch with you," she warned.

"You make it sound like I killed them," I protested. "If they send me any messages at all, they should thank me for bringing their murderers to justice."

Sarah nodded. "That's a fact."

"If we do contact The Beyond, want me to give anyone a message from you?"

"Not really. My Charlie's been gone five years now, but I still have conversations with him all the time. Not that I *really* see or hear him," she hurried to explain. "But I don't think this Ripley can tell me much about my late husband that I don't already feel to be true. I know Charlie's in a good place."

When I arrived at Nature's Way at ten of six, most of the two dozen chairs in the area facing Dawn's big display counter were taken. I found a seat toward the back, near the end of a row. Even so, I doubted that I could sneak out of the session without being noticed, and I didn't want to hurt Dawn's feelings. However weird or hokey things got, I would try to stick it out until the end, through sheer loyalty. After all, the woman had accompanied me on that daredevil visit to The Roost, which might even have provoked the creep who had frightened her in the alley on Sunday night.

Dawn stood near the display case, talking with Ripley. Maybe I was psychic, too, because I'd guessed right when I'd pictured him as *elfin*. He stood a head shorter than her, about the same height as the third person in their group—Sue

Brookings, the mature, sharp-nosed Lifestyle columnist from the *Chadwick Courier*. Van Eyck's wire-rimmed glasses complemented his fluffy silver hair, and in lieu of wizard's robes he'd opted for an outfit worthy of Mister Rogers: wool pants and a subdued plaid shirt, topped by a gray cable-knit cardigan. Far from mystical, aloof, or otherworldly, he seemed positively cuddly.

I noticed Tanith also standing a few feet back from their cluster, possibly in awe of the psychic. She didn't look too much witchier than usual tonight, in a short rust-colored skirt, black tights, and platform shoes. With these, she wore the same black leotard top as when I'd first met her, but kept a big, orange-paisley shawl draped around her shoulders.

I heard Keith's voice from above me. "Hey, Cassie, ready to get your fortune told?"

I smiled up at him. "Just here to support Dawn and the shop. And you?"

"The same." He dropped into the empty seat next to me—the last in the row—ruining any slim chance I might have had to sneak out early. But at least now both of us would be in the same boat.

Quietly, he added, "Although Dawn swears this guy predicted, over the phone, that I'd make a big sale through my gallery show. Maybe I owe him something for that?"

"Well, you made your own luck by inviting Dez Mitchelson. Did you have any idea that he could afford something like your daylilies painting?"

"I never really thought in such mercenary terms," Keith said, "but he did tell me that he's got one of the big units on the top floor of Public Storage. And I know those places have vaulted ceilings, an extra loft area, lots of light . . . and acres of wall space. Wish I could afford to be up there!"

"I met him briefly in the park Saturday, during the pet parade. He was walking his dog."

Keith's smile had overtones of a wince. "Ah, yes, I've met Hero . . . and kept my distance. He took that beast to a park full of other animals?"

"There were some tense moments, but Dez seems able to handle him. Anyhow, he said something about his dad being an art collector, too."

"Mm-hmm. He also mentioned that to me, once. Sounds like no love lost, though, between those two. Dez said when he was in school, he wanted to be an artist, himself, but his father shot down the idea. Even though I guess they had plenty of money, he told Dez he didn't intend to support him while he frittered away his time at something so useless."

"Wow, that was harsh."

"Of course I thought so, too. But Dez made light of it, saying that he'd found a steadier line of work and still satisfied his creative leanings by being a patron of the arts."

I wanted to tell Keith that I'd seen reviews online under Mitchelson's name, but hesitated. So far, I had not found any critique of the October three-person show at Eye of the Beholder. *I shouldn't get Keith's hopes up, in case Dez has decided not to write about the exhibit, or couldn't find a media outlet for the piece.*

We broke off our conversation then, because Dawn stepped in front of the oak display case to face her guests. She drew herself up to her full, queenly height, and projected her voice clearly to get everyone's attention. "Okay, since we seem to have a packed house, we probably should get started. Can you all take seats, please?"

A few people still browsing through her merchandise, or admiring the Day of the Dead knickknacks, obediently filed into the last empty chairs.

While the guest of honor stood modestly by her side, Dawn read off his credentials. Ripley had noticed his intuition as a small child, but only gradually realized that most other people thought it strange. His grandmother had the same ability, and after she passed, Ripley found his talents grew stronger. He kept them mostly to himself while studying philosophy, psychology, and theology in college. He considered the ministry for a while, but after conducting private readings for some friends and relatives, decided he could help more people that way. He held free grief-support groups and PTSD clinics and had occasionally helped law enforcement profile elusive criminals.

"Mr. Van Eyck has a total of thirty years' experience as a psychic consultant, with a reputation for a high degree of accuracy," Dawn added. "Many of you probably are familiar with his cable TV series, *Second Sight with Ripley Van Eyck*, and he's also written a book, *Messages from the Spirit World*. He swears that he has not talked to any of our audience members in advance, and any impressions that he receives or advice he gives will be honest and spontaneous. So please welcome Ripley Van Eyck!"

Hearty applause by some of those in attendance suggested they were regular fans of the psychic's show.

The guest speaker thanked Dawn for inviting him to Nature's Way and the audience for attending. In a quiet voice, which somehow still resonated well through the barnlike space, Van Eyck began by explaining how he worked during his public appearances. "I will be happy to answer questions, but I don't predict the future. I can't tell you at what age you're going to get married, but I may be able to guide you on how to find the right partner. I won't tell you whether or not to hire a particular person, but perhaps I can advise you on the type of worker you should be looking for. Does that make sense?"

While most people in the audience nodded, in my view the approach gave the psychic more credibility. At least he didn't seem likely to steer anybody wrong, advising them to do something stupid or even dangerous. If he was willing to take questions, it also reduced the chance that he had planted certain accomplices in the audience to make him look good.

Van Eyck's first few "readings" were not earth-shaking. A man who looked to be in his early forties, and gave his name as Robert, said he'd recently lost his job and had interviewed for a couple of positions since without success. "Should I switch to another field?"

Ripley answered promptly but thoughtfully. "You could try, but that won't solve the whole problem. You were fired because of an argument with your boss, correct?"

The man stiffened but admitted, "Yes, I was."

"Robert, you're uncomfortable with authority figures. Sooner or later, no matter whom you work for, you'll run into difficulty unless you first solve that issue. Possibly people can even sense it, in your job interviews. I'd suggest that during your time off you work on this trait, either alone or with a professional. If you do, you should start to have more success."

For a second, Robert almost looked ready to argue with Van Eyck. Then maybe he recognized the irony of such a response, because he simply swallowed his pride and thanked the psychic.

A middle-aged woman in full makeup, whose red V-neck sweater made the most of her formidable chest, sounded on the verge of tears when she asked if her last boyfriend would ever come back to her. "I really thought he was the one, but a couple of weeks ago he walked out, and now he won't even return my calls."

True to his promise, Ripley did not predict the future for her. "Even if he doesn't come back, Jeanette, that may be for the best. I sense that you ought to develop your own self-confidence and independence before jumping into another relationship. Is there a skill you've always wanted to develop or a sport you've always wanted to try? Find a way to pursue something like that, and don't worry if you're not terrific in the beginning. Do it for the love of it, until you get good at it. Once you can be passionate about something besides a man, maybe you'll attract the type of partner who really deserves you."

That answer made Jeanette smile and drew applause from the rest of the audience. Off to the side, Sue Brookings snapped a couple of flash photos, no doubt for her newspaper article.

Soon after, Ripley did pick out one individual—a thin, sad-eyed woman with wavy white hair named Teresa. "You lost your husband recently," he told her.

She nodded. "Last month. He had cancer."

Ripley frowned in sympathy. "It was a long siege, and you took care of him. He's here with you now. He wants you to know how much he appreciates all you did for him."

When Teresa's face crumpled and she started to cry, the psychic added, "You weren't with him when he died. You thought he was sleeping, and you had to run an errand. When you came back, he had passed. He wants you to know it's okay. Our loved ones sometimes do that, Teresa. They choose to pass when we're not around, because they think it will spare our feelings. So don't feel guilty. He doesn't blame you and he wants you to know he's watching over you every day."

She thanked Ripley and much of the audience murmured approval. In whispers, Keith and I agreed that the psychic could be using a combination of smart guesses and basic psychology to come to these conclusions. He wasn't going out on too many limbs. On the other hand, his advice couldn't do these folks any harm, and the effect was good theater—it was emotionally moving.

Tanith sat in the front row, and now she rather shyly raised her hand. "How can I stop fighting so much with my mother? She finds fault with everything I do, and she just doesn't trust me. Even though I did a little wild stuff in the past, I've really straightened out and I'm trying to be responsible. But she still finds fault with my friends, the music I like, how I dress . . . she won't let me be *me*."

Ripley smiled. "Yes, I can see that. Your mother had a tough upbringing, herself, and she doesn't want you going down the same road. She doesn't understand that you're not rebelling in a bad way, you're just artistic. And you're drawn to other creative people, too, aren't you?"

Her face lit up. "Exactly!"

"Maybe you can try explaining it to her that way, or ask another adult to help you." He sent a meaningful glance in Dawn's direction but did not put her on the spot. "It's good that you've found a job where you can express your talents, at least to some extent. And since we're all friends here, and it's almost Halloween, why don't you let Clyde out from under wraps?"

The rest of the audience showed little reaction to his question beyond mild curiosity. Only two people looked completely stunned—Dawn, and Tanith herself.

The young, goth woman didn't ask how Ripley could have known. She just stood up, turned her back, and let her paisley shawl drop, so we all could see the colorful dragon spreading its wings between her shoulder blades.

A few people smiled and chuckled, as did the guest

speaker. "There, I'm sure the old fellow is glad for a breath of fresh air!"

With her gaze fixed on Ripley in fascination, Tanith thanked him and took her seat again.

Keith leaned toward me. "Think that was a setup?"

"Not unless he knows Tanith from some other context. I can't believe Dawn would take part in any trickery, can you?"

"That's what I was thinking; not a chance!"

Ripley's appearance was supposed to end at nine, but though a few guests left promptly, others lingered to try for personal readings. Sue took a couple more pictures and interviewed the psychic briefly. Then he patiently explained that Dawn needed to close her store, but anyone who wished could contact him privately through his website. While Tanith and Keith folded and stacked the chairs, Dawn and I were left alone with Van Eyck.

"I hope that I successfully brought a few new visitors into your beautiful store tonight," he told my friend.

"Yes, I saw many fresh faces, thanks," she said. "And everyone seemed to find your readings very helpful."

He sobered a bit. "Before I leave, I also have some advice for you that I was not going to mention in front of all of those people." With a glance at me, he added, "For both of you."

I saw Dawn swallow in apprehension. "Does it have anything to do with what happened a couple of nights ago? What I saw outside in the alley?"

"I'm afraid it does. The two of you did a good deed recently, but it angered someone very dangerous. That scare was a warning to you, and I'd advise you to heed it. From here on, leave matters to the police."

"We will," Dawn assured him. "But . . . can you possibly tell us anything more that will help us?"

"Remember that this is a season of masks," Van Eyck said.

"The danger involves someone you know, who has made a good impression on you. I can't see any more than that, not even whether it's a man or a woman, because this person is adept at hiding their true nature. But as the old saying goes, watch out for a wolf in sheep's clothing."

Chapter 18

Thursday morning at work, while Sarah and I were cleaning out the boarders' condos, she asked me how the event with Van Eyck had gone. I filled her in on Ripley's apparently successful insights concerning the audience members.

"Frankly, if he's just very shrewd at reading people, he could have come up with most of his responses to their questions," I said. "From their body language and their tones of voice, even I could tell that the one guy had a chip on his shoulder, and the flashy middle-aged woman thought she desperately needed a man."

Sarah nodded. "And it's not all that hard to guess that a woman in her seventies who looks worn-out and sad might have recently lost her husband, after caring for him a long time."

"The thing that did impress me," I admitted, while scooping out a litter box, "was that Ripley didn't have to fish for information. He didn't just say, 'You recently lost someone . . .' and let the other person supply the details. He committed himself about who it was. Plus, the business with Tanith's tattoo! Both she and Dawn swore that Ripley could not have seen it beforehand. Sure, he might have guessed someone like

Tanith would have some body art, but he knew where the dragon was and what she called it—'Clyde,' of all things!"

"That would have been quite a lucky guess," Sarah agreed, pouring fresh litter for another boarder.

"He also seemed to know that Dawn and I went to The Roost together." I explained what the psychic had said about the two of us "doing a good deed" that had attracted the attention of someone dangerous.

"A 'wolf in sheep's clothing'?" Sarah straightened up and gaped at me. "Almost sounds like he also knew about the character who scared Dawn the other night!"

"Seems like way too many coincidences, doesn't it? And Tanith knew about all of those things. At the very least, he could have contacted her and persuaded her to feed him information ahead of time."

"Maybe Ripley is the wolf in sheep's clothing, himself," my assistant suggested.

Closing the door of the freshened condo, I considered this only briefly. "He wasn't the man in the alley. Dawn kept saying that guy was tall, and Ripley's almost a head shorter than she is. Besides, why would he play such a mean trick on someone who was hosting him at her store, paying him to appear, and giving him an opportunity to promote his books? Unless my own instincts are way off, Van Eyck came across as a very modest, gentle kind of guy."

"He could just be a good actor. But you're right, that wouldn't make a lot of sense. I guess it all depends on whether you *Believe It or Not*. Get it? 'Ripley'?" She waved a hand. "You're too young."

"I've heard of it." I smiled. "It was a comic book, wasn't it, about weird facts?"

"Yes, but also a TV show, and I think they even have a string of museums now."

"Interesting. But I don't think Van Eyck is any relation to *that* Ripley."

If he did have psychic abilities, though, and really foresaw some danger to Dawn and me, we both ought to watch our backs.

It was a cool, gloomy day, and I noticed that Sarah had come dressed for work in a sweatshirt over a turtleneck. It was a ladylike sweatshirt in a flattering pumpkin shade, and her dark green turtleneck matched the embroidered design at the neck. Still, I got the silent message that, to an outsider, my shop was *cold* these days. I'd instinctively bundled up, too.

When I caught Sarah rubbing her upper arms for warmth, I told her, "I know, sorry! The heating system really is on its last legs."

"Does this Ripley have any healing powers?" she asked, with a glint in her eye. "Maybe you could ask him to 'lay hands on' your furnace."

"He didn't make any claims along that line. But I should at least have asked him where I might find enough money to replace the thing, without committing myself to long-term financing through the HVAC company. Guess one of these days, I'll just have to bite that bullet."

While Sarah and I groomed an elderly Abyssinian boarder, whose owner was picking him up that afternoon, my mind drifted to other questions. I hadn't talked to Bonelli lately, though I figured if she'd discovered anything more about Dawn's back-alley visitor or about the clinic robbery, she probably would have called me. I wondered if she'd done any more checking with the firm that had installed the new security system during the clinic's renovation.

That reminded me of my recent conversation with Lathrop. There was a guy who knew all the quirks of old buildings, and probably had associates well-versed in security. He'd also hinted that he was working on a costume for the award presentation Halloween night.

The contest did follow a werewolf theme. And Lathrop was tall!

Was there any chance he put on the costume and went skulking around town looking for people to scare? That would have been pretty childish, especially for a man of his age. But he was eccentric, with a definite theatrical bent.

At least if it was Lathrop, Dawn should have nothing to fear. Unless . . .

Unless Avery is also part of the drug ring. The Chadwick cops interrupted one drug sale in back of The Firehouse, Lathrop's property. Bonelli said other ketamine arrests had taken place at bars and restaurants in nearby states. Could those buildings also have been Lathrop renovations?

I liked Avery and did not want to suspect him of being mixed up in anything so nasty, especially since it might have resulted in two deaths—the woman at the lake house party and the motorcycle guy. But I also remembered the breezy way Lathrop had brushed off my comment, about how all of those renovations must be terribly expensive.

"Somehow, the money we need always shows up!"

I called Bonelli and made an appointment to see her later that day; she said she'd be at her desk around six.

After closing my shop, I took a leisurely stroll around town to kill time. I felt safe enough because it was a brisk but clear evening, still light out, and with a fair number of people strolling the sidewalks. Plus, I kept my pepper spray handy in my pocket.

I took time to appreciate the Halloween decorations in the various shop windows. Towne Antiques always featured imaginative displays that changed with every holiday and season. Tonight, it showcased almost life-sized, jointed figures of a skeleton and an old witch that must have dated from the 1960s. The front corners of the window displayed smaller, light-up ceramic images of a ghost and a haunted house; what looked like a real, carved jack-o'-lantern; and a montage of vintage Halloween cards.

What chilled my blood most, though, was a central grouping of old dolls that had seen better days. In faded clothes, they'd originally been pretty, but now some were balding, or missing limbs, or had one eye drooping in a permanent wink. A dingy clown with orange yarn hair and a huge, red-lipped grin might have delighted some child several decades ago, but now sat in a small rocker as an extremely spooky centerpiece.

I had to grin. Philip Russell, owner of the antiques shop, had risen to the occasion once again, in spades.

Nidra had not embellished the front window of Eye of the Beholder, beyond adding just a couple of tall corn stalks. That didn't surprise me, and it was a good call. Any more would have taken away from the artworks themselves, still one for each participant in the current show. She generally stayed open a little later than the town's more mundane businesses, so people could browse after work, and I was glad to see her lights still on this evening.

I glanced at my watch. Only five-thirty. Plenty of time before I had to get to the police station.

The gallery's elegant proprietor greeted me with a wide smile. "Cassie, glad you dropped by. I was going to notify you, and the others who made purchases, about picking them up. I want to keep everything on the walls through the weekend, but even though I'm usually closed on Mondays, I'll be here next week for anyone who wants to get their pieces that day."

"That would be great, thanks. I'll try to come by during

my lunch break." I nodded toward the front window, which still displayed Keith's humorous portrait of the bug-eyed tabby cat. "I am looking forward to bringing home his painting of Tigger, though I'm not sure what my three actual cats will have to say about it."

"Just ask Keith to paint portraits of them, too!" Nidra joked.

I saw a chance to dig for a little more information. "If you're not sworn to secrecy, did he make any more sales since the opening?"

"Yes, two more. Also small ones, the park landscapes. Several people admired his portrait of Dawn, which of course wasn't for sale, but who knows if he might get some commissions along that line. The only large one that sold was the daylilies."

I nodded. "Did you know that he and Dez Mitchelson live in the same building? Public Storage, that renovated warehouse near the railroad tracks. Keith said they met when he was loading up his artworks to come here, and Dez saw a few of them."

"No, I wasn't aware of that." She made a puzzled face. "As I remember, Dez told me he'd come because of the ad I ran in the *Courier*."

It was that same explanation he'd given me. "He probably saw that, too. Maybe he didn't want to sound as if he had too personal an interest, just in case he decided not to buy anything."

Nidra laughed. "A lot of people do play it cagey, when they come into a gallery. Art is so personal, both for the artist and the customer; I guess you can feel 'guilted into' buying something that's not your taste, just out of friendship."

"He might have had another reason for keeping a low profile. Did he tell you he's done art reviews?"

She gave me a crooked smile. "No, he didn't, but after meeting him, I did some research and found a few online. Of course I was hoping he'd write something about this show, but so far I haven't seen anything."

"Me, neither. It would have been such a boost for Keith to get a good review, for his first show." I knew it must be getting near six, and I should be on my way to the police station. "Maybe when Dez comes to pick up his painting, you shouldn't mention that we saw his critiques, or that I told you he lives in Keith's building. Just in case he's trying to keep those things quiet?"

Nidra tilted her head and shrugged agreement. "Sure, though I can't imagine why he would. Unless he's wary about giving out his personal information, in general."

"Do you think he's that wealthy?" I speculated.

"Or there could be other reasons. I have a cousin in India who's an actor. He's pretty successful and, like Dez, very handsome. He's been in some of those Bollywood movies. If he's not doing an actual public appearance, he keeps a very low profile; sometimes he even makes reservations using an alias. He lives very modestly, and when he goes out it's always with his girlfriend. Otherwise, the fans would never leave him alone!"

I laughed. "Must be a nice problem to have, I guess. Anyway, have a great week, with even more sales, and I'll see you on Monday."

Walking on to the Chadwick police station, I wondered if Dez Mitchelson also was evasive about his address and personal life because he'd been chased so often by random women. Since he wasn't also a celebrity, like Nidra's cousin, that seemed a bit far-fetched. Besides, at the reception and again in the park, he seemed to be hitting on me! He even accused me of inventing a boyfriend, to dodge him, and only backed off when Mark actually showed up.

Something else Nidra had said about her cousin stuck in my mind, though—that he sometimes went by an alias. If Dez Mitchelson also used that trick, it would explain why I wasn't able to find any information about him online besides the art reviews. Maybe he ran a whole different, more lucrative business under another name.

I could have asked Nidra whether he used a check or a credit card to leave a deposit for the painting, and if it also said "Dez Mitchelson" on that. Of course, then she'd really know I was fishing!

At the police station, I checked in as usual at the front window and said I had an appointment with Detective Bonelli. I was buzzed in and started down the hall to her glass-walled office. Meanwhile, I heard a commotion from the far end, toward the rear of the building, where the cops processed people recently arrested. Then Officer Jacoby came into view, shepherding a dark-haired young man who grumbled and resisted.

"Man, what is this crap? You guys already . . ." The prisoner broke off when he made eye contact with me, and his scowl deepened. "Oh, terrific—*you* again!"

Only then did I fully recognize Pete Nardone, who looked scruffier than he had at The Roost. Jacoby didn't give his prisoner any further chance to menace me, but steered him sharply toward one of the interview rooms. The door shut behind them.

That rattled me. I'd forgotten Nardone was out on bail. Could he have been the one terrorizing Dawn in the alley on Sunday? He wasn't a very big guy, but she'd admitted that the upright ears of the mask could have made the wearer look taller.

Angela must have heard the exchange, too, because she put her head out of her office doorway. "Cassie? You all right?"

"I'm fine." In her office, I took a seat in the straight wooden visitor's chair that faced her desk. "Nardone is back in custody?"

"We have new information. Someone identified him as having attended the party at the lake house where Karin Weaver died."

"You think he was responsible for that, too?"

"We don't know if he killed her, and we may never be able to prove that, but he's got to know something about the ketamine. Of course, whether we can get anything out of him before his lawyer shows up . . ."

"You don't think Nardone could be behind the whole ring, do you?" I asked.

The detective made a skeptical face. "He's acting more like he's scared of someone higher up, especially since Franco was killed. Besides, he's not smart enough. Whoever's behind this ring has been covering his tracks pretty well."

Bonelli knew about my interest and college training in psychology, so I dared to ask her, "What would be the profile for someone like that?"

"Oh, there's nothing cookie-cutter, for sure. Some drug dealers start as users, themselves, just making connections for their friends. But after they start making money, that becomes the main attraction. Many stop using entirely, because it would cut into their profits. They run it like a business."

"Does it make a difference whether they're dealing typical street drugs, or the prescription kind?"

"Very perceptive!" she commended me. "Pushing pharmaceuticals to a suburban clientele is a lot less dangerous than dealing something like heroin, cocaine, or meth. These guys don't encroach on the turf of any hardcore drug lords, so things rarely get violent—no messy shoot-outs in the street. Franco's bike crash, if it was murder, would be an anomaly.

But that *was* made to look like an accident. If it was meant as a warning to other dealers, it was done discreetly."

The idea of such a cold, calculating act made me shudder. "So, the kingpin, if we call him that, could come across as a good, clean-living, solid citizen."

"Absolutely. They often have some other, legit source of income, though usually it doesn't quite explain their lifestyle. A guy out in Utah ran a multimillion-dollar opioid ring out of his home in the suburbs. At the time, he was about the age you are now. Dozens of his customers died from overdoses, though the cops were only able to charge him with one death. He was a former Eagle Scout and a chess whiz."

I measured this description against both Lathrop and Mitchelson. The older man was certainly an individualist and secretive about his background.

Reluctantly, I mentioned Avery's connection with The Firehouse and other renovation projects in town. "I don't know if he could be connected to any of the other restaurants or bars in nearby states that have had trouble."

Though she looked surprised by the suggestion, Bonelli made a note on her computer. "I admit, I don't know much about Lathrop. Just met him once, very briefly, at a town meeting. He's an older guy."

I nodded. "Hardly seems like the type to be dispensing party drugs to millennials and Gen-Z kids. Though he'd probably recruit younger types, like Franco, to do that for him. And maybe also to eliminate Franco for screwing up."

Bonelli shot me an appraising look, as if maybe she thought I'd become hardened by my amateur sleuthing over the past couple of years. "We did talk to Franco's contacts. He was estranged from his father, who suspected Ricky was into some shady stuff. His landlord saw some sketchy people come and go from the guy's apartment, but didn't know their names.

Franco worked as a stock boy at a big-box store, but the boss there was ready to fire him for too many absences."

"So, nothing too helpful, eh?" I asked.

"Not much. Forensics is still checking some fibers and other things from Franco's place. But if he had a cell phone, and he must have, that's gone, too. Wasn't on his body or anywhere in the apartment. The killer probably took it." With a discouraged shake of her head, Bonelli typed a few more words onto her computer screen. "We also found out a bit more about those two guys you and Dawn talked to, Gary Eckhart and Joe Bailey."

I was impressed. "At least you got their last names, which was more than we thought to do."

"They had their reasons to avoid attention that night, though I don't know if there was any criminal connection. Gary has a popular 'weed blog' devoted to the topic of cannabis legalization, which is probably coming any day now in New Jersey. He offers advice on how to start a legal weed business, etcetera. Whether he thought our cops might hassle him, or whether he's also into promoting harder drugs, I can't say."

"And clean-cut Joe?"

"He does have a medium-level job selling medical supplies, but I think his real secret is that he was at singles' night under false pretenses. He's separated, but not yet divorced, and his wife has charged him with desertion of her and their two small children."

I shook my head. "Lucky thing that I didn't fall madly in love with him."

"Very lucky." Bonelli smiled. "Anyway, thanks for the tip about Lathrop. I'll see what more I can find out about him . . . discreetly, for now."

"One more suggestion, though it's probably also a very

long shot." I told her what little I knew about Dez Mitchelson. "I really have no reason to suspect him, except that he's a mystery man. After he bought one of Keith's most expensive paintings, and said he was a collector, I tried to look Mitchelson up online. All I could find were some freelance art reviews. Of course, maybe he comes from such a wealthy family that he doesn't have to work, and moving to a converted warehouse in Chadwick is slumming, to him."

"That's always possible." Bonelli also didn't seem to feel there was much to support my suspicions of Dez. "As long as you know his current address, I can try to investigate how he's paying his bills. Everyone these days has a bank account, a couple of credit cards . . . an electronic trail."

"He brought his dog to the veterinary clinic recently for a checkup. Unless he paid with cash, you might get some information from them."

Behind her glasses, Bonelli's dark eyes grew keen. "I very well might. Again, thanks for the information, Cassie."

Standing to leave, I scanned the hallway outside, through the glass walls of her office.

"Don't worry about Nardone," she added, with a smile. "I think he'll be staying with us a while longer, this time."

That made me think of one more question. "What did Ricky Franco look like? Anything unusual about him? I'm sure he wasn't in great shape after the accident, but . . ."

"No, he wasn't, but we got a picture from his driver's license." Bonelli pulled up the image on her screen. "Nothing special about him, but he was a decent-looking kid. Why?"

"That woman who saw a motorcycle driving away from the clinic said the driver was 'really ugly,' right?"

"Very true," Bonelli recalled. "Either she was pretty nearsighted, or it wasn't the same guy."

"Or she has very high standards!"

We both laughed at that.

That detail continued to nag at me, though, while I headed back to my shop to get my car. Pete Nardone also was pretty good-looking, if in a slicker way. And unlike the person whose reflection Sam Urbano had glimpsed at the clinic, both Nardone and Franco had short hair.

Chapter 19

The next morning, I ducked out of work for a few minutes to hit the pop-up Halloween store on the highway, which opened at ten. I hoped to make it a quick trip, but unfortunately, I didn't realize that Frightful Fun had moved into the same strip mall as the already well-established Best Beans café.

I parked a short distance from my destination and hoofed it briskly toward the entrance. On my way, I barely noticed the shaggy-haired fellow in the apron who leaned against the façade of the coffee shop, talking on his cell phone. He spotted me, though. Just as I reached the sidewalk in front of the Halloween store, he yelled out, "Hey! Hey, you, *stop!*"

I did, mostly from surprise. Finally I recognized Gary Eckhart, from my "wild" night out at The Roost.

He stuffed his phone in his pants pocket and strode toward me angrily. "Hello, 'Cathy.' Or should I say, 'Cassie'?"

Could Gary possibly be this upset because things didn't work out between him and Dawn at The Roost? After all, he and Joe Bailey had ditched us, not the other way around.

Whatever the reason, his long, somewhat hound-dog face looked ruddy with rage at the moment. I couldn't pretend I didn't know him, but I didn't have to put up with this hostile treatment. "Hi, Gary. You have a problem of some kind?"

"You're the one who has a problem, sticking your nose into other people's business!"

He stepped between me and the parking lot, virtually pinning me against the wall of the Halloween store. The Best Beans barista was more scrawny than brawny, and at the moment, his bib apron defused some of the menace. If he put his hands on me, I wouldn't hesitate to knee him in the crotch. Although there weren't too many people around outside the store, I still could attract plenty of attention if I decided to scream.

All of my survival instincts vibrated on high alert. Outwardly, though, I tried to stay cool and play innocent. "What on earth are you talking about?"

"You sicced the cops on us, me and Joe. I mean, what the *freak*, lady? What did we ever do to you?"

After a second's thought, I decided to admit at least part of the truth. The report of the roadhouse bust had made the papers, anyway. "Look, the cops made an arrest at The Roost the night we were all up there. If they questioned you and Joe, they probably did that with everybody who was at the bar that night. They talked to me and Donna, too."

Gary sneered. "Her name's not 'Donna,' and she doesn't work at a furniture store, either. She's Dawn, from the health-food shop in Chadwick. I realized she looked familiar because I went in there once, with some friends. I just saw her from a distance then, and thought she was kinda hot."

I nodded, an admission that he'd caught on to our scheme. "All right, we did tell the police about the people we talked to at The Roost, but we didn't accuse you or Joe of doing anything wrong."

"You weren't just up there looking for dates that night.

You're narcs! Joe had a feelin' about that, after you spilled that girl's drink and suddenly the cops showed up. So, he and I asked around. You're the Cassie McGlone who helped bust a weed farm last year, up on Rattlesnake Ridge. I hear the guy's doing hard time now!"

If Gary knew that story, I couldn't bluff any longer. His intel left a lot to be desired, though. "That sentence had nothing to do with his marijuana crop. He also . . ."

"And you worked with the cops on something to do with the cat expo at the convention center, last fall. You nailed some poor dude there, too."

Gary was wasting his sympathy on a couple of very bad people, but now did not seem the time to go into any lengthy explanations. I just stiffened my spine, glared back at him, and spoke quietly. "It's true, I do occasionally work with the Chadwick police. And I've faced down tougher customers than you, Gary. So, I'd suggest you take a few steps back before I start yelling my head off. If a security guard comes out here, which of us do you think he's going to believe?"

That got through to the shaggy-haired barista, and he did retreat a few steps. Already, passersby had begun to slow down and stare. Just a word from me, and one of them would probably go for help—or might even come to my rescue, personally.

Still fuming, Gary tried to heap more guilt on my head. "Y'know, it doesn't even bother *me*, so much. My blog and my business are totally legal; I got nothing to hide. But you really messed things up for Joe! First, his witch of a wife threw him out of the house, and told Social Services he's not supporting their kids. But now that he got questioned over this drug bust, which he knew *nothing* about, Joe could lose his job. You oughta *think* sometimes, lady, before you go destroyin' people's lives!"

A gray-haired, bulky fellow, in a WORLD'S GREATEST GRANDPA T-shirt, suddenly appeared at my side. Glancing from me to Gary, he asked in a meaningful tone, "Everything all right here, miss?"

"Yes, sir, but thank you for asking," I said. "Now, I've got some shopping to do. If you'd make sure this gentleman doesn't follow me inside, that would be a big help."

Gary deflated; hands raised in surrender, he backed in the direction of Best Beans. "I'm going, honey, I'm going. I said my piece."

Even so, the stranger waited until I had stepped inside the Halloween store before he departed, with a smile and a nod.

It was now close to ten-thirty, and even at that hour of the morning, the big store's aisles had grown crowded. Well, Halloween was only two days away, and who'd want to leave their shopping until the last minute? Maybe having the holiday fall on a weekend meant there would be more parties and parades than usual, even for adults.

My heart still pounded from my confrontation with Gary. I also felt pressure to finish my errand quickly and get back to my own job.

At first, though, the sensory overload inside the store bewildered me. How to find the few small items I needed, among the looming blow-up props for yards, roofs, and porches, or looming mannequins of the Grim Reaper, the Joker, and a ram-horned demon? The areas for adult costumes were separated from the kids', but I needed to narrow my sights even more than that.

With my nerves still jangling, I hurried past a whole section of bloody severed heads, limbs, and hands, and an array of weapons from all eras. At least the plastic guns all had been replicated in neon colors, so they couldn't possibly be mistaken for the real thing. Villainous plastic visages included the ghostly *Scream* face, Jason's hockey mask, Michael Myers, and the Mummy.

When I spotted an alcove featuring makeup, wigs, and accessories, I knew I was on the right track. It still took some searching, because they weren't among the hottest items, but at last I scored two black felt berets for myself and Mark. A little more poking around turned up a "Beatnik Beard" he could stick on his chin with spirit gum, and a black makeup crayon we both could use to draw cat whiskers on our cheeks.

Wending my way back out of this corner, I resigned myself to a fairly long wait to check out. Meanwhile, in the corner of my eye, I noticed a wall grouping of full-head dog, cat, gorilla, and wolf masks, all embellished with fake fur. I remembered that Dawn thought her boogeyman in the alley had worn something like that, with an animal snout.

I stopped in my tracks.

A mask like that would make anyone, from a distance, look "really ugly." And, in a murky reflection, as if he had longish hair.

Why hadn't I, or anyone else, thought of that before?

Still in the checkout line, I whipped out my cell phone and called Bonelli. When I got a recording, I lowered my voice to leave her a message. "The guy who robbed the clinic and rode away on the motorcycle probably was wearing a Halloween mask," I said, explaining why it made sense. "Maybe even the same kind as the creep who scared Dawn. Don't worry about getting back to me—I just wanted you to know, in case it helps."

I returned to my shop later than I'd planned, but Sarah had no complaints. She told me Nancy Whyte had called, bubbling over with glee. "Lathrop gave her a heads-up that Quentin has definitely won Scariest in the photo contest!"

"Great! I figured he was a shoo-in, especially with those

great shots Nancy submitted. Is she bringing him back to us for another fluff 'n' fold before his big appearance?"

"She didn't mention that. Probably, she thinks he still looks okay. Get what you needed for yourself and Mark?"

I showed her my purchases, and she laughed, probably picturing our normally clean-shaven vet as a fifties hipster. "You're sure to be the 'heppest' cats at the Paragon."

"I dunno. From what I saw in those pictures, we'll have some tough competition. That female Lykoi in the cape was gorgeous—I'll bet anything she gets Cutest."

While I put on my green CCC apron and tied back my hair to tackle some chores, I explained why I'd taken so long to run my errand at the strip mall. Sarah frowned to hear that one of the guys Dawn and I had talked with only casually at The Roost had accosted me so rudely in public.

"The nerve!" my assistant said. "Once he suspected you were working with the police, it would've made more sense for him to just avoid you."

"Well, Gary strikes me as kind of an anti-establishment type. He was more upset that the bust drew too much attention to his friend Joe, who's been trying to duck out on his fatherly responsibilities."

"What's this Joe like? Now that he knows who you really are and where you work, I hope he doesn't decide to make trouble for you."

I realized it wasn't an idle concern for Sarah—anyone who might come looking for me at the shop could be a threat to her, too. "I don't think that will happen, but I'll mention it the next time I talk to Bonelli."

While we turned a pair of Siamese littermates free in the playroom, Sarah asked how my conversation had gone last night with our favorite detective.

"It was . . . informative," I told her. "Frankly, I don't want to say too much about it, because we discussed a couple of new suspects whom I don't really like to . . . well, suspect."

She raised her eyebrows above the rims of her glasses. "Not me, I hope."

"Oh, you're top of the list! You don't fool me, with all of your churchgoing and charity work," I teased. "No, none of my longtime friends, I'm glad to say. But Ripley told me and Dawn to watch out for someone who had made a good impression on us. Maybe I'm putting too much faith in his clairvoyance, but that made me think twice about a few people."

My assistant did not pry any further. I decided not to tell her, for the time being, about my insight that the clinic robber might have worn a mask. Bonelli never liked me to spread too many details about police cases among my friends. She would get my phone message, and that was more important.

That afternoon, Sarah and I worked on beautifying a black Persian, Midnight, just in for the day and being picked up by his owner at five. While I detangled his mats, my mind drifted back to our possible suspects.

I hoped Lathrop would not turn out to have any connection with the local drug ring. Could that be one reason why he'd involved me and Mark with the Paragon's Halloween contest—to keep an eye on us and monitor how much we knew? In all my contacts with him so far, Lathrop had been funny, smart, and likeable, if mysterious.

Was there anyone left I could trust? I didn't want to become paranoid about all of my male acquaintances!

At the end of my work day, just after Sarah had gone, Mark called on my cell.

"I can't talk long," he said. "Just wanted to bring you up to speed on something that might have bearing on our robbery case. I guess you had a sit-down with Bonelli yesterday, about Dez Mitchelson."

"Well, it wasn't totally about him," I said, "but he did tell me he'd brought his dog, that big mastiff, to your clinic, so I told her about that."

"Anyhow, she called Maggie today and asked her impression of the guy. Maggie thought he seemed very nice, conscientious about his dog's care and all. She thought it was odd that Bonelli would suspect him, and mentioned it to Lily, the tech who assists Maggie most of the time."

"And?" Mark had to be building up to something pertinent.

"Lily said that while his dog was getting routine blood work, Mitchelson stepped out of the exam room and wandered down the hall. When she asked if he needed help, he said he was looking for a restroom. But she saw him try the locked door of the secure-storage room, after walking right past the restroom door, which is clearly marked."

"This is the first time Lily told this to anyone?" I asked.

"I guess it was such a small detail that it slipped her mind. She says at the time she figured the guy was just embarrassed and didn't want to ask for help. Besides, right after the robbery, we were all looking closely at our staff, people with inside knowledge, and not at our clients."

It could have been an innocent coincidence, I thought. Barely enough to bring the guy in for questioning. But if Bonelli wanted to do that, I supposed she could say they were talking to everyone who had visited the clinic shortly before the night of the robbery.

"I hope she gets to the bottom of it soon," I told Mark. "Meanwhile, I hit the Halloween store today and got all the tools necessary to turn you into a retro hipster for tomorrow. Want me to bring them over tonight, so you can do a dry run?"

"Yeah . . ." He paused, as if checking the time. "I'll probably be tied up here for at least another half hour. Want to drop by the clinic, just to give me the beret and the goatee? Since I've never worn either, I might need some practice with them beforehand."

"Good thinking. After all, you wouldn't want to look *silly*, around all those costumed animals! Not to mention whatever Lathrop will be wearing."

He chuckled. "Yeah, I suppose there's not much danger of that. Besides, you'll look as goofy as me, right? Okay, babe, see ya soon."

It would be a short errand, and under normal circumstances, I might have just walked the four blocks to Mark's clinic. But I was still shaken by the attack on Sam, Dawn being menaced in the alley next to her own store, and the news that Joe Bailey now blamed me for ratting him out to the cops and destroying his whole life.

At least I didn't have to worry about Franco anymore, but I remembered too well the venomous glare Nardone had given me at the police station. *Heck, if his lawyer got him out on bail again, he could come looking for me!*

Until we got to the bottom of all this, even for short hops around town, I'd take the car. I pulled on my pleather jacket with my sweatshirt and jeans, my hair still tied back the way I'd worn it all day for work.

I had parked the CR-V toward the back of my small, gravel lot, half-hidden behind my grooming van. The floodlight over my back door helped me see my way, although the vaulted roof of the van kept the car in shadow. But even on my own property, I kept it locked these days. As I approached, I clicked the remote on my key fob; the front and back brake lights flashed in response, unlocking all the doors.

I opened the driver's side and tossed my bright orange bag from the Halloween store onto the passenger seat. As I faced front again, to slide in behind the wheel, something thick and heavy dropped over my head, cutting off both my vision and my air.

I twisted and kicked, but someone very strong held me fast. With my arms trapped against my sides, I felt my left jacket sleeve shoved up a few inches.

Then a sharp pinprick just above that wrist.

The thick covering over my face, which smelled like a wool blanket, loosened just a little. I could breathe, but still not well enough to muster a decent scream.

Suddenly, I went slack.

I heard the rear car door creak open and felt myself being wrestled backward. Drowsy and mellow, I barely even wondered what might be happening to me, much less why.

My captor set me on the rear seat of my own car, and I slumped forward. Even when my arms were tugged behind my back and tied with some kind of cord, I couldn't rouse myself to struggle. Released from my captor's grip, I sprawled sideways, and I felt the loose blanket being spread out to cover all of me.

As if from underwater, I heard a mocking male voice say, "There you go, Cassie. Just relax, now. We're taking a little ride."

Chapter 20

I was back at my parents' house, on a hot summer day. My dad was still alive, and we were all swimming in our small, in-ground pool. Actually, I was just floating on my back, and not very well, because I'd sunk below the surface. I knew that because I couldn't breathe right, though somehow I wasn't drowning, either. The water also felt oddly scratchy against my face and hands.

Passive, I just rode the riverlike current and rocked with the waves, not even wondering why a backyard pool would have that kind of movement. Now and then came a jounce; maybe one of my parents had jumped in at the other end. After a while, I also felt a shift in gravity, as if the pool had tilted uphill.

Though drowsiness weighed heavily on my eyelids, I forced myself to open them.

Saw red. Not water enveloping me; a blanket.

My arms started to cramp, behind my back, but I couldn't budge them. Still struggling against sleep, I rubbed my head against the nearest surface to push the blanket away from my face.

A blast of golden light struck my eyes. Scintillating, beautiful. An overwhelming sense of peace, of oneness with nature and the universe, swept over me. I didn't even mind being so immobilized, didn't fear or even question my situation.

A few minutes passed before my rational self began to recover some control and to make sense of what I felt and saw. Auburn sunset refracted on a beautiful fall evening. Golden treetops streaming past a horizontal window. I was in a car—my own car?—and probably headed west.

Driving through woods. Was the car driving itself? *Did I start it and then lose control of it?*

I shifted some more until I could see the driver's headrest. The head that poked above it was dark, but not like Mark's hair. Threaded with gray, it also bristled out below the headrest, where the driver's collar would be.

I don't know anyone with hair like that! A stranger?

The driver must have heard me squirming around, because he muttered something. I couldn't understand it, though—his voice was muffled. He swiveled his head to peek at me.

My heart seized up, and I shrank back against the seat.

Not human! Some kind of monster!

In a panic, I thrashed and kicked at the car door. At least my feet were still free.

He called out louder, then, so I finally understood him. "Shut up, back there! If I have to gag you, I will."

Just his mention of the word *gag*, combined with my shock, made my gorge rise. Now I felt nauseous and could barely keep from messing up the back seat of my own car. As I tried to calm myself, the eerie relaxation stole over me again.

I dozed off for the rest of the trip. Dreamed about Quentin Collins, the handsome son of a wealthy old family, who turned into a wolfman under the full moon.

The car slowed. I began to make out distant voices, a crowd. We drove around slowly for a minute, then stopped. My driver got out and yanked open the back door.

By now, I had already accepted his gray wolf's head—pointed ears, wiry fur, snarling fangs, and all—as normal. Oddly, though, he carried my shoulder purse in one dark paw.

"Out." With the other hand, he grabbed my arm.

Once I was on my feet and showed I could still walk, he tossed the red blanket over my head as before. He left the front just loose enough so I could see where I was going.

"I've got the syringe right here," he murmured close to my ear. I felt the merest prick against my arm, which was still bound. "Make one sound, and I'll put you to sleep . . . permanently."

We started walking together, downhill.

The crowd voices came back, a little louder now. One guy hooted from a distance, "Oooh, Little Red Riding Hood! Better not go in the woods with *him!*"

Several other voices laughed at this, wildly, drunkenly. I turned my head enough to glimpse a large, raised, wooden deck, above and to our right, crowded with nightmarish figures. A few leered down over the wooden railing—an ugly clown, a heavily made-up Egyptian princess, a helmeted superhero, a busty female pirate.

None of them seemed to have any idea that I might be in real trouble. If they even would care.

In another brief flash of sanity, I put it all together. *We're at The Roost. A Halloween party. It's Thursday, singles' night. They see me and the wolfman, but they think we're wearing costumes. And that we're going into the woods to . . .*

If I'd been myself at that moment, I might have done something clever and resourceful, or taken a reckless chance.

Stuck out my foot and tripped my captor, so he'd drop the syringe and I'd have a chance to scream my head off. I'd done risky things in the past to get out of a tight spot.

But I wasn't myself. I'd become this passive, detached creature. Dimly aware of what was going on, but sleepwalking through it, as if it were a dream . . . or a dark fairy tale.

Now he marched me down a flight of stone steps. I'd left my shop in jeans and a sweatshirt, but he kept the blanket over my head and shoulders as a hood. Even though I wore sneakers with good traction, the steep angle made me dizzy; I tripped, and my stomach lurched again. Heard more laughter, farther behind us this time. I guessed the gawking spectators thought I was drunk.

If anyone recognized me, I'd have quite a reputation at The Roost when all of this was over. If I even survived.

My captor—and by now, I had a pretty good idea of who he was—yanked me upright again with a snort of disgust. Finally, we reached a level plateau, the lower patio of The Roost. Maybe because the sun was going down and the air had turned chilly, or maybe because there was more excitement closer to the restaurant, we had that rustic lookout spot to ourselves.

Wolfman took my purse and gave it a mighty heave over the edge of the precipice. I heard it land somewhere out among the dense bushes, far down the incline. With it, I supposed, went my cell phone, my wallet, and my ID. I had no idea whether or not he'd hung on to my car keys.

"Okay, Cassie," he told me, "I have good news and bad news." He pulled out a small, disposable-sized syringe. "The good news is, in a minute I'm going to untie your arms, so you'll be more comfy. The bad news is, you're also going back to sleep."

I tried to struggle again, which might have affected his aim. Nevertheless, even in my semi-anesthetized state, I felt another pinprick in my lower arm.

Enough to put me out "permanently"?

Maybe, because once he'd finished with the syringe, he also threw that, as far as he could, down the darkening ravine.

In less than a minute, my head began to swim again, and I sank down on the cold paving stones. Soon, though, that relaxing warmth spread through my veins once more. By the time my captor spread the red blanket over me, I hardly needed it. He did that more to conceal me, I'm sure, than to keep me comfortable. But I felt him untie my arms, and I lazily brought them forward to my sides.

Then I dropped off into a truly "dead" sleep.

If I dreamed at all during that stretch, I don't remember. I'd received light anesthesia in the past, for that nasty dental procedure. This was the same experience—I went out like a shot, dropping into a deep, black well.

When I came back to consciousness, it seemed as if no time had passed at all.

But it had. By now, night had fallen. Though my sense of pain was still muted, I could tell I lay in a very awkward position. The air had turned chilly, and a light drizzle prickled my skin. I no longer heard any voices from the restaurant's big deck, now somewhere far above me.

I rose on my elbows. Looked straight down into a bottomless, black abyss.

My sleepy serenity morphed into full-blown hysteria. *Where the hell am I?* Cold leaves brushed my face. I twitched away from them, and my fingers closed around a rough branch.

Did I roll off the edge of the patio? Or was I pushed?

I looked up and saw the lip of the stony plateau several feet above me. I lay propped half inside some kind of bush or small tree. But when I tried to straighten, shifting my weight, a twig snapped beneath my foot.

To crawl back up seemed impossible. One wrong move, and I could plummet the rest of the way down the ravine instead.

What did Tanith call it? "Going down the K-hole"?

Some small and distant noises now sounded deafening— the eerie calls of night birds in the woods, the throbbing dance music and laughter from the restaurant far above me. Frozen in place, I also picked out one more familiar sound.

The tinny notes of "Stray Cat Strut." My cell phone's ringtone.

Very far away, though. I remembered Wolfman heaving my purse down the ravine. My smartphone, my twenty-first-century lifeline, lay down there somewhere. And it was ringing. Someone was trying to reach me.

But could I reach *it*? Much too dangerous to grope my way down that steep hillside in the dark!

If I just had some kind of light . . .

Yeah, that would be on my phone, too.

I wondered why Wolfman had left everything of mine behind. He probably wanted this to look as much like an accident as possible. I could be tracked by my phone, though, so leaving that seemed dumb. Along with my car, my purse . . . and the empty syringe.

On the other hand, no one had seen *him* with me, just a guy in a wolf mask. And wearing those "paws," he wouldn't have left prints on anything.

It might look as if I drove out here myself, shot up, and fell over the edge of the lookout. But that would only work if . . .

If I were dead. He must have intended that final shot to finish me off. Maybe he misjudged the dose? Or maybe my attempts to wrestle free did some good, after all!

As I gazed down into the velvety blackness, it beckoned like a giant maw, eager to gobble me alive. Now it seemed to pulse in time with the blood that pounded in my ears. I dimly remembered something about another young woman having a heart attack at a party, from some kind of drug . . .

I jerked back from the hypnotic view and commanded myself to get a grip. Reminded myself that I wasn't insane or under some dark spell—I'd just been drugged. As long as I could keep it together, I might be okay.

The light rain made the tree's branches and even the nearby rocks slippery. I still wore my somewhat waterproof brown jacket, but it hung open, and the damp started to trickle down the neck of my sweatshirt. Shuddering, I looked around for the red blanket, but it was nowhere in sight.

For the moment, though, whatever shrub I sat propped against seem to be holding me securely enough. Worst case, I could wait until the sun came up and a maintenance crew arrived. I could scream for help, then, and maybe they'd be able to rescue me.

If I can just keep my wits about me and stop imagining things!

And if I can just stay awake that long . . .

The second challenge wasn't easy, though. I'd almost drifted off again when I thought I heard a very welcome voice calling my name, though from far, far away. Another hallucination?

"Cassie?" Mark sounded on the verge of tears. "Dammit, are you out here?"

That blew most of the cobwebs from my brain and shocked my survival instincts back to life.

"Yes," I screamed back. "Down here!"

I shifted a little on my perch, to look upward, and felt another small branch snap under my other foot.

"She's in the ravine!" he hollered to someone, in a raw voice. I heard feet jogging over the fallen leaves. Then Mark's head, backlit from the low lights of the deck area, peered down from the stone patio. "Oh my God, are you okay?"

"I am," I lied just slightly. "But there's no way up from here!"

A second figure peered down over the stone edging. A strongly built, young guy with a buzzed haircut, he wore an orange prison jumpsuit. When he spoke, though, I half-recognized his voice. "It's okay, Mark," he said. "Between me and you, I think we can get her out of there."

That sounded reassuring, anyhow. When the second man disappeared briefly, I realized that, despite his misleading costume, he must be Officer Jim Gardiner of the Chadwick force, who'd helped me out of another close scrape that spring. He quickly returned, holding something I'd hoped never to lay eyes on again in my lifetime—the red wool blanket.

"Mark, I'm gonna hang onto this tree up here," he explained. "I'll also hold one end of this blanket and you hold the other. Then it should be safe for you to creep a few more feet down the hill and grab Cassie's hand. You up for that?"

Mark nodded, though I worried that both of us still might plunge down the ravine. *At least we'll go together!* But my life sort of flashed before my eyes, and I thought of other people I loved that I might never see again.

It could work, though. I'd seen Gardiner up close in the past, and he had muscles on his muscles. Good thing, because he might have to drag us both back up! I noticed that even he struggled to keep his footing on the incline's large, slippery rocks.

Mark gave me confidence. Dark hair plastered to his forehead, he edged downward through the bushes, with a death grip on his end of the blanket. "It's okay, Cassie . . . almost there."

I tried not to move a muscle, in the meantime, for fear that the last branch supporting me would give way. Finally, I felt Mark's strong hand close around mine, and could see the determination in his eyes and clenched jaw.

"I got her!" he yelled up to Gardiner.

"Great!" the other man called back. "You guys start climbing, and I'll pull up on the blanket."

My head mercifully clearer by now, I used every foothold I could find to boost myself upward, and Mark slowly retreated to pull me along. After what was probably fifteen minutes, but seemed much longer, the two of us half-crawled back onto the safety of the stone patio.

Relieved, Gardiner started to toss the blanket down into the ravine.

"Don't!" I stopped him. "That's evidence. My purse and all its contents are already down there. I don't know how far, but if you come back in the daytime, you ought to be able to find them."

Mark hugged me tightly. He was breathing hard, probably from fear as much as exertion. "What in God's name happened?"

"I was abducted, probably by the same person who ran Franco off the road and scared Dawn outside her shop. And I should warn you, he shot me up with something, probably ketamine. Right now, I'm as wobbly as one of your patients after surgery." I nodded toward the ravine. "The syringe is down there somewhere, too."

With a deep frown, Gardiner pulled out his radio. "Then morning will be too late to search. I'll get a team out here tonight. They should be able to hike up from the lower level."

"Meanwhile, I'm taking you to the E.R." Mark kept one arm around me, his face slack with horror. "Who was it? Who the hell did this?"

I hesitated. "Before I tell you, Mark, remember that Officer Gardiner is standing here as a witness. You can't take matters into your own hands! The last thing I need now is you getting locked up for murder."

Chapter 21

I spent the rest of that night in a bed at the nearest medical center, St. Catherine's, under observation. The staff considered giving me medication to reverse the effects of the drug but decided against it. Since I was not a habitual ketamine user and seemed to be recovering gradually on my own, they just kept an eye on me and monitored my vitals while I slept it off.

I was grateful for the supervision, because I did keep slipping into a doze. In at least one of my nightmares, the leering masks and gory severed limbs that I'd seen at the Halloween store beckoned to me from that dark, seemingly bottomless ravine. I felt they wanted me to fall in—or leap in—and join them. More than once, I woke suddenly with my heart pounding. It reassured me to remember I was hooked up to a monitor, which would alert a nurse if my ticker reacted too badly. Even though the hospital room was comfortably warm, now and then I still shivered.

And of course, the more the sedation wore off, the more I began to feel the aches in my arms from having my hands tied behind my back, and bruises from being rolled off the stone platform downhill into the shrubbery.

When I was first admitted, the staff had checked me out thoroughly. More thoroughly than was necessary, I'd thought at first. Only gradually did it occur to me that they wanted to make sure Dez had not taken advantage of my spells of unconsciousness, the same way men usually do after drugging their female companions.

Fortunately, they found no evidence of that. I suspected my captor had been far too eager to get rid of me, in the most expedient way possible, to let himself be distracted by anything so trivial as lust. Even though that might have made me look even more like just another "loose" female, out carousing when I'd fallen off the overlook patio to my death.

After I was assigned a room and put to bed to recover, Mark explained how he and Gardiner had located me. When I didn't make it to his condo and didn't answer my phone, he asked Dawn to check my home and shop. She reported back that I wasn't there, and my car was gone. That panicked Mark, and he called the Chadwick cops, who tracked my cell phone to The Roost.

"At first I thought you might have gone back up there, spur of the moment, on some mission for Bonelli," he told me, sitting at my bedside, "but she said you two hadn't discussed anything. She called Gardiner, who was at The Roost undercover to keep an eye on the Halloween party. She asked if he'd seen you, or anything at all suspicious. He said not so far, but he'd ask around. Meanwhile, I just headed up there."

By the time Mark reached the roadhouse, Gardiner had heard about the couple who went down toward the lookout, the guy wearing a wolf's-head mask. No one saw them come back out, but then no one was really paying attention. Besides, everyone assumed they wanted privacy.

"When I got up there and saw your car, I felt hopeful and scared at the same time," Mark went on, his voice thick.

"Gardiner dialed your number, and we could hear the phone ring, somewhere down that ravine. I knew you must be there, somewhere, but in what condition . . . !"

I reached out my hand, and he gripped it almost as fiercely as when he'd been pulling me back up that dark, slippery hillside. I saw him trying to blink away tears, and we switched roles, me reassuring him, "It's all over now, babe, really. I'm going to be okay."

We hugged as tightly as we could without setting off any of the monitors.

My doctors may also have reassured Mark that I'd been unmolested, but if so, he never brought up the issue. That night, he stayed in my room, sleeping in the well-padded guest chair. By morning, I could sit up without swooning and told the nurse I probably could face a breakfast tray.

Now that my head had cleared, I remembered it was Friday. "Oh my gosh, the shop . . . Sarah will wonder where I am! And my poor cats . . ."

Mark, looking relieved that I'd made it through the night and seemed on the road to full recovery, managed a tired smile. "Relax, Dawn's got it covered. I only told her as much as I had to, but she'll feed your upstairs cats and let Sarah know why you're not there this morning. They both have keys to your place, right?"

I nodded. "Thanks so much. Don't *you* have to go in to work, though?"

"Maggie's taking over my patients for today. She realizes you only ended up this way by trying to save the clinic's reputation." He pulled his chair closer to my bedside again. "Now, are you up to telling me exactly what happened? Or are you saving the gory details for the cops?"

"No reason why I can't tell you . . . seeing as you probably saved my life last night."

I explained how I had figured out that Franco probably wore a full-head werewolf mask when he accosted Sam, robbed the clinic, and rode away on his motorcycle. But for some reason, his boss, the Mr. Big of the operation, found fault with the robbery. He ran Franco off the road and delivered a few more killing blows while the thief was lying in the ditch.

"I'm betting Mr. Big provided the mask to begin with, and maybe Franco returned it to him," I guessed. "When he found out that Dawn and a female friend went undercover at The Roost, he used the same mask to try to frighten her off the case. Then he realized I was the person who actually spilled Judy's drink, and decided to use stronger measures with me."

Mark worked his jaw angrily. "And you're sure it was Dez Mitchelson?"

"Had to be. He knew about my shop, that I was friends with Dawn, and that I lived alone. He had the same build as my attacker, and even though the mask muffled his voice, I recognized it."

What I didn't tell Mark, but might reveal to Bonelli, was that I also recognized Dez's spicy aftershave. He'd worn it at the gallery reception and also when we'd met Saturday in the park. He did not think to erase that telltale clue . . . or maybe he just didn't think I'd survive to tell anyone about it.

The Chadwick cops had found and retrieved my purse from the steep hillside, the night before, and brought it to the medical center. They'd also found the syringe, and kept it and the blanket for evidence.

"I told Gardiner that Mitchelson lives in Public Storage," Mark said, through gritted teeth. "I'd love to know if they've caught the S.O.B. yet."

He glanced toward my purse where it rested on the night-stand, and we had the same thought.

"Yeah, let's see if I've gotten any calls," I said.

He fished out my phone and handed it to me.

I had plenty, including messages from Dawn, Keith, and Sarah. Luckily, my mother would know nothing about this latest escapade . . . yet. *If my previous adventures were hard on her nerves—!*

The name that jumped out at me most urgently from the small screen was Bonelli's. Like Mark, I needed to know if my abductor, the mastermind of our mysterious local drug ring, was finally behind bars.

The detective's level contralto voice steadied me, as usual. "Unbelievable, Cassie, but you did it again. If you hadn't raised our suspicions about Mitchelson, and even told us where to find him, he might have gotten away with this. He must have phoned one of his other dealers last night to give him a lift back to his apartment. When we nabbed him back there, he was *real* surprised. Still had the mask and gloves lying around, too. Call me when you're feeling up to it, and I'll tell you the rest."

I reported the good news to Mark, then got back to Bonelli. When she picked up, I first reassured her that I was feeling fine. I told her Mark was with me and put her on speaker.

"You animal lovers may be glad to know," she said, "that however heartless Mitchelson might be toward his fellow humans, he does seem to care about his dog. When our guys forced their way in, this huge Hound of the Baskervilles charged them. They raised their guns to shoot it, but Mitchelson begged them not to and called it off."

Mark sniffed. "More feeling than he showed for Cassie."

"He probably got that beast for protection, because he's been running quite an operation out of his fancy digs. We seized his computer. Of course, the files are all protected, but we'll get into them, even if we need help from the feds. I suspect we'll find that Mitchelson has been doing business all over the state, and beyond."

"Wow," I said. "How did he decide *I* was a serious threat?"

"Nardone. After we picked him up the second time, he was allowed one phone call. A smart guy would have called his lawyer, but instead Pete tipped off Dez that you were helping us investigate the clinic robbery. I guess Mitchelson figured it would take more than showing up in the alley in his wolf costume to scare you off the case."

"He left me for dead," I told her, "but he also left my car, my phone, and my ID at the scene. Any idea why?"

"Maybe by leaving that stuff, plus the syringe, he could implicate you in the clinic robbery. You *and* Mark."

"He must have been getting pretty desperate," Mark muttered.

"Probably lucky for us that he was. And lucky for Cassie that he underestimated the dose of ketamine that would kill a healthy young woman."

"Oh, I put up a decent fight before that second shot." For the first time during our call, I smiled. "He might have spilled some."

"Thank God he didn't bash your head in for good measure, like he did with Franco," Mark pointed out.

"But that wouldn't have looked as much like an overdose and an accidental fall, which I guess is what he wanted. I'm lucky, though, that he didn't roll me a lot farther downhill."

"Might have been tough to do," Bonelli pointed out. "That slope was densely covered with trees and bushes, even hard for our guys to navigate. You wouldn't just roll, and for

Dez to carry you farther down and then get back up, himself, would have been quite a chore. Besides, like you said before, it might not have looked as much like an accident."

Still, I shuddered to imagine how long I might have lain out there if he had accomplished that. I seized the chance, then, to raise another delicate topic. "Um, Angela, you can keep my name out of this, can't you? When you talk to the media?"

She had no problem with my request. "Don't we always? Frankly, Cassie, in this case you were almost a CI for us—though unpaid. We wouldn't expose a civilian informant, and we wouldn't do it to you, either."

I relaxed. "Thanks, I appreciate that. My mother would lose her mind if she knew about this."

"I'm sure. Your poor mother—!" Angela groaned, though with a hint of humor. "All I'm telling the press is that our investigation of the clinic robbery and the death of our best suspect led us to Dez Mitchelson, a newcomer to our area, as the mastermind of a tristate party-drug ring. I'll refuse to supply any more details because our investigation is ongoing."

A silver-haired neurologist, Dr. Gupta, stopped by then to check my vitals. I got off the phone, and Mark stepped out of the room to give me privacy. The doctor listened to my heart, took my blood pressure, and tested my reflexes and my balance. He also asked a series of questions that seemed designed to assess my mental state.

Finally, he smiled and said, "Well, Ms. McGlone, you seem to have come out of this pretty well. I'm sure it helped that you don't dabble in drugs otherwise and that you're in overall good health. I'll authorize your release."

I thanked him and agreed that I felt well enough to go home.

"Just take it easy for another few days," Dr. Gupta added.

"Avoid alcohol and driving, and if you have any problems with coordination or memory loss, call my office right away. Otherwise, I think you're good to go!"

Mark, of course, was delighted to hear that news. I changed back into my sweatshirt and jeans, which at least had dried overnight, and a nurse gave me my signed release and discharge details. Then Mark helped me gather my things and drove me home.

In the rear lot of my shop, I found my own car, returned by the Chadwick PD and no worse for wear. The orange bag from the Halloween store still lay on the passenger seat, and I retrieved it.

Sarah and Dawn waited inside for the two of us and overwhelmed me with sympathetic attention. I must have still looked fatigued, because my assistant fetched the chair from the playroom for me. Everyone else balanced on the tall stools in back and in front of the sales counter.

Suddenly, the full impact of what I'd been through, and how badly it could have ended, crashed down on me. I felt drained, more emotionally than physically. My eyes brimmed and, knuckling away a tear, I turned to Sarah and Dawn. "Thanks so much, both of you, for pitching in here on such short notice."

"Nonsense," said my assistant, patting me on the shoulder. "We're just so glad you're all right! It sounds like you had a terrifying ordeal."

"Let's just say, I have a lot more sympathy now for Mark's surgical patients," I quipped.

"Hey, no fair," he protested gently. "We're very careful with our doses. The animals are 'out' for a very short time and recover quickly, with no ill effects. Nothing like what you went through!"

"I'm sure that's true. After all, you're not *trying* to scare them out of their wits . . . or to kill them."

"Speaking of animals," Sarah began in a cautious tone, "you had a phone call from Mr. Lathrop. He was double-checking to make sure you and Mark are still coming to the awards presentation tomorrow afternoon. He wanted to remind you that it's at five, between the matinee and the evening movie, but he'd like you to get there by at least four-thirty to get oriented."

Mark frowned. "No way is she going to be up for that! Cassie, I can call Lathrop, tell him you've been sick, and that you're just out of the hospital and still recovering."

I considered this option but rejected it. "No, please don't. I'm much better already, and by tomorrow I'll probably be fine. We can still go."

"Are you sure?" Dawn asked me, also looking concerned.

I straightened in my molded-plastic chair. "Absolutely. It's not like I'll be doing any hard work. Besides, Mark, I shelled out almost thirty dollars for our berets and your beard. I can't let them just go to waste!"

He smiled faintly at my mock outrage. "I'll reimburse you, really."

"No, if our props survived this whole ordeal, it's a sign that we're meant to go." Reaching for the plastic bag from Frightful Fun, I snatched out a beret and planted it, askew, on my head. "Seriously, we talked Lathrop into this contest. We can't let him down now."

When Mark opened his mouth to protest some more, Dawn cut him short. "Face it, Cassie's so stubborn even a murderous drug kingpin couldn't keep her down. Sounds like she's going to the theater tomorrow, and so are you."

"Oh, if she's going *anywhere*, I'm definitely coming along," he vowed. "Maybe every single minute of every day, for the next year or so!"

My cell phone rang, and when I saw the screen, I announced, "Bonelli."

"Answer it," Dawn urged me. "Let's see if she's got any updates since this morning."

I put our favorite detective on speaker, and she filled in some gaps concerning my near-death experience at The Roost.

Gossip at the roadhouse, following Nardone's bust, had gotten back to Dez through his personal grapevine. Someone remembered that "Cathy" had come in with "Donna," and the two women were not regulars. A little prying revealed that "Cathy" had been drinking virgin cocktails, so she probably wasn't as inebriated as she had acted.

After "Cathy" spilled the doctored drink, someone recognized "Donna" as the tall redhead from the health food store. That inspired Dez to throw a scare into her with his werewolf getup. But since he knew the two women were friends, he suspected Cassie was the one who actually got Nardone arrested, and that was bad for Dez's business.

The detective guessed that when Dez ran into Cassie at the pet costume parade, he saw an opportunity to find out more about her and whether she might be working with the police. What he hadn't expected was her connection with Mark Coccia of the veterinary clinic, and then all of the pieces fell into place for him. Cassie might know enough to cause him real trouble. So, Dez made a plan to get rid of her, make it look accidental, and maybe tarnish her wholesome reputation in the process.

"Cassie, your instincts were good when you suggested that Dez might be going by an alias," Bonelli told us. "His real name is Mitchell Desmond. You still won't find much on-line about him, but his father, Bryan Desmond, is a successful investor with his fingers in a lot of pies. His M.O. is buying up struggling, undervalued companies, cleaning house ruth-lessly, and reshaping them from the ground up. He's known in the business world as kind of a shark, but his tactics have been mostly successful. And he always stays—just barely—on the right side of the law."

"Interesting," I said. "A guy like that could cast a long shadow over his son, I imagine. From some things I heard from Keith, and from Dez himself, I suspected he had major Daddy issues."

Bonelli paused for a beat. "Funny you should say that. His digs at the warehouse were impressive—high ceilings, big windows with views of the mountains—and he also had a pretty sophisticated library, for a drug lord. Lots of expen-sive art books, plus a whole bunch of those self-help 'success' manuals for entrepreneurs. Looks like Dez studied every pos-sible trick to get ahead, make big bucks, and create the image of a prosperous go-getter."

"Any sign of a wife or girlfriend at the apartment?" Dawn asked. "He was so good-looking, I'd expect that."

"No, and that's another interesting thing," said Bonelli. "There were no personal photos around the place. Not of Dez himself or of anybody else, male or female."

I flashed back on the moment in the park when the *Courier* photographer had veered in our direction, taking pictures of one of the prizewinners. Was it just coincidence that Dez had picked that moment to retreat with his dog, quickly, to the less-crowded riverbank?

"He had some nice artworks and sculpture," the detec-tive continued, "but nothing that was obviously a gift or a memento. Through his computer files, we tracked down a couple more of his dealers, and it seems like even they only knew him as Dez Mitchelson."

"He couldn't let anyone get close enough to know his real story," I concluded.

"Probably not. So, for a smart, educated, handsome, and successful guy, he must have been incredibly lonely."

Mark's scowl made it clear that he felt no sympathy. "Well, he ought to make plenty of new friends in prison."

Even over the phone, Bonelli heard this and chuckled. "Really, Dr. Coccia! And I've always thought of you as such a *humane* kind of guy."

"He's calmed down," I said. "Last night he kept threatening to take the law into his own hands, in pretty vivid terms."

"Don't worry, Rambo," the detective told him. "We'll make sure Mitchelson gets what he deserves. Meanwhile, you all can relax. And Cassie, just concentrate on getting well. Ketamine can have some unpleasant aftereffects, and you got a serious dose."

After we hung up with Bonelli, Dawn's face clouded over. "Well, I guess this screws up Keith's big sale. Doesn't sound like Dez will be picking up that painting on Monday, after all."

"Talk to Nidra," I advised her. "She said other people who came through the gallery admired the daylilies. If they left their information, maybe she can let them know it's still available."

"There's an idea. Strange, though, to think someone who appreciated art so much, and wrote about it so well, could also be so cold and ruthless. Maybe I'm just biased because both my mother and my boyfriend are professional artists."

With a shrug, Mark reminded us, "Adolf Hitler supposedly was a frustrated architect. Maybe Dez, or Mitch, would have been happier as a poor, unsuccessful painter. I doubt it, though."

Even Dez had doubted it, I remembered. He'd told me he didn't have the patience to be a struggling artist, and shared his father's desire for "the good life." Clearly, he'd meant "good" in the material, not the ethical, sense.

A few caterwauls from the rear of the shop reminded me that it was time to feed our boarders, and though Sarah and Dawn offered to tend to them, I insisted on doing my share of the work. "You should get back to your own shop," I told Dawn. "And Mark, I'm sure they need you by now back at the clinic."

Both got to their feet, but Mark lingered a minute. "Cassie, I still think we'd better pull the plug on the gig at the theater tomorrow night."

Maybe I *was* suffering from memory loss—I'd almost forgotten about the awards presentation at the Paragon. "No, don't. I can handle it."

"Really? Dressing up in costume, running around on a stage, and wrangling other people's animals? You shouldn't put yourself through all that. Lathrop can give out all three awards himself. Or if he really needs a helper, I can still go."

"I doubt that we'll need to do much wrangling, with only three winners coming." I jutted my lower lip in a pout. "Besides, I'd miss all the fun. I want to go!"

Dawn smiled at my enthusiasm, on her way out the door. Mark, close behind her, just sighed, as he often did when I resisted his attempts to coddle and protect me.

My mother could have told him, by now, how futile those efforts usually turned out to be.

Chapter 22

Saturday was pretty slow at the shop, with no one picking up or dropping off cats on Halloween. Our front door opened mainly for groups of trick-or-treaters, who were making the rounds of all the downtown businesses. Some were young kids accompanied by an adult, and others were teens. Former schoolteacher Sarah had thought ahead, stockpiled wrapped candy for them, and kept it in a plastic pumpkin on the sales counter. Still, by the end of the day, we almost ran out.

Around lunchtime, my mom called. I was afraid she somehow had gotten wind of my near demise at The Roost, but she only wanted to apologize for not being able to come to the awards presentation at the Paragon that evening.

"One of Harry's colleagues is giving a Halloween dinner," she said. "No costumes—we're all a bit too old for that. More of a harvest theme. But he was invited, it's mostly couples, and I think I should go with him. You don't mind, do you?"

At first, I thought she was asking if I objected to her socializing with Bock's colleagues as his date. Then I realized that she meant she'd miss the pet photo contest. Truthfully, I'd never really expected her to drive all the way out from

Morristown just to see three animals and their owners collect awards, and I had to appreciate her thoughtfulness. "Not at all, Mom. Go have a good time."

"Thanks for understanding, Cassie." Mom sounded about to hang up when she thought of another topic. "Oh, by the way, I saw on the news that they arrested someone in connection with a big New Jersey drug ring. Could that have had anything to do with the robbery at Mark's clinic?"

I needed to keep my wits about me, here. "Yes, Mom, they're pretty sure it was connected."

"Well, that's good news, isn't it! Was he the man who broke in?"

"No, it was someone working for him. But the cops got that guy, too." I didn't add that they "had" Franco in the morgue.

"Wonderful! It must be such a load off your mind, and Mark's. Did our friend Detective Bonelli break the case?"

"You guessed it, Mom. You know Angela—sooner or later, she always brings in the bad guys." I needed to get off the line before I ended up telling any outright lies. "Gotta go now, but you have a good time tonight, and give Harry my best."

When I hung up, I caught Sarah stealing a glance at me, and mimed wiping my brow in relief.

"I gather that poor woman still has no idea of what went on with you Thursday night?" she asked.

"No, and with any luck she never will."

Sarah shook her head. "Boy, I'd hate to think of my kids keeping those kinds of secrets from me!"

I laughed; Sarah's daughter and son were both in their early thirties, and married with children. "You probably don't need to worry. From what you've told me, both Marla and Jay sound much more sensible than I am."

A little later, Dawn checked in by phone to say that she and Keith definitely would be in the audience at the Paragon. "We figure you'll need the moral support . . . if not physical support!"

"I'm fine, really. Sarah and I had an easy day today, so I'm all rested up. Even my furnace has been on its good behavior, sort of." I told Dawn about the brief conversation with my mother. "I'm surprised she wants to go out on Halloween at all, with all the trick-or-treaters around. Mom does *not* like to be scared."

A pause on the line. "So, you're saying you're adopted? No, that can't be right, you look too much like her!"

"Ha-ha. I don't like to be scared, either—not *really* scared, the way I was Thursday night. No one would! But when I see something bad going on, and I can do something to stop it—"

"I know, Cas. Just ribbing you."

"Mom must *never* know about that. We're all conspiring to keep it from her."

"I'll tell Keith. Just as well, though, that we won't have to make small talk with her at the theater tonight."

Mark and I got to the Paragon just before five, dressed in beatnik black from our sneakers to our berets. I'd even used a bar of soap to scrawl *The Hep Cats* in white on our turtleneck sweaters, and of course we'd drawn whiskers on our faces, and Mark wore the goatee.

Lathrop loved our retro getups. Defying my expectations, he'd assumed the persona of Dracula—more Christopher Lee than Bela Lugosi, because of his imposing height. He'd even covered his balding pate with a dark toupee that included the iconic widow's peak.

His manner was still too kindly for his character, though,

and when we arrived, he immediately asked if I was feeling better.

"Much, thanks," I said. "An extra day was all I needed." The theater owner also would remain in the dark, I resolved, as to the cause of my temporary "health problem."

My head still spun a little as I climbed the five steps to the theater's shallow stage, but over the past forty-eight hours, that was happening less and less. Behind the curtain, Mark and I conferred with Lathrop, usher Dave, and a curly-haired man in his forties, Thomas, whom Lathrop introduced as his partner. The winning pets and their owners would come in by the back entrance, Avery and Thomas explained, while a small audience gathered in the first few rows of the theater.

"We kept it down to about two dozen people," Lathrop said, "mainly family and friends of the pet owners, a few of our benefactors and subscribers, and a reporter from the *Courier*."

"No sense in getting the animals too riled up," Thomas added, with a smile. "At least they'll all have their pictures in this week's paper."

First the three winners arrived backstage, and the choices fulfilled Mark's and my predictions. The Lykoi moon goddess, named Ava, squirmed a bit as her handler struggled to keep her silver lamé cape in place. It was decided that Mark would present her with the award for Cutest Werewolf. I would hand over the prize for Funniest to the ferret, Slinky, who again wore his doll-sized shirt and pants. So ferocious in his photo, he seemed perfectly mellow that night in the arms of a doting teenaged girl.

A suspenseful hush fell over us when Nancy arrived with her humongous wheeled pet carrier, and I realized neither of the other owners knew what to expect. They might have seen the photos of their rival contenders, but Quentin's headshot didn't prepare them for his size. There were nervous murmurs as I helped Nancy unload the Maine Coon, holding him by his leash and harness, while she added his Victorian stand-up collar and cravat.

Meanwhile, Lathrop grinned from ear to ear, exposing short but realistically pointed vampire fangs. "He's incredible, isn't he? What a star!"

Thomas furrowed his brow in concern. "We have a table set up out front where we can pose the animals, but I'm not sure it will hold that guy!"

Nancy peeked through the curtains at the table and reassured them. "It's big enough, and he's a cat-show veteran. He'll be okay."

Dave went out to the lobby to let in the audience, and once they were seated, Lathrop stepped out through the velvet curtains. He managed to enunciate well around the fangs as he welcomed them to "the First Ever Werewolf Look-Alike Contest for Non-Canines."

"I hope that some of you have enjoyed our marathon of spine-tingling films this week," he added. "If you are new to the Paragon, I hope you will become a regular visitor and perhaps even a supporting member!"

Once he'd finished his opening spiel, he called for Mark and me to join him in front and introduced us. "Both Ms. McGlone and Dr. Coccia are expert animal handlers," he added dramatically. "I felt that with these wild, unpredictable creatures of the night in our midst, it might be wise to have assistants who are prepared to deal with . . . the unexpected."

Lathrop was playing it to the hilt, but as Mark whispered in my ear, "He doesn't know the half of it!"

I had to grin, but for a second I flashed on that horrible face peering back from the driver's side of my car, with its crazed, yellow eyes and lolling tongue. I remembered how I'd believed my captor was a real monster . . . and how close I'd come to falling to my death in that ravine . . .

Mark must have seen me sway on my feet, because he put a hand against the small of my back. "You all right?"

I pulled myself together. "Fine. Just my ferret phobia." When he looked genuinely sympathetic, I laughed. "Kidding!"

After that, I suffered only a bit of normal stage fright, but overcame it by focusing on Dawn and Keith, who smiled at us from the third row of the audience.

As things turned out, I went first, to announce Slinky as the Funniest werewolf look-alike. The movie screen behind me showed a blowup of the ferret's scary winning photo, which drew laughter and applause, but he behaved well as his teenaged owner, Viv, accepted her prizes. They would be the same for each winner—a gift certificate for a dinner for two at The Firehouse, and tickets for four to any movie at the Paragon. Viv explained that she'd had Slinky for three years and loved his antics, which included riding around on her shoulder and nibbling her ear.

Mark did the honors for Ava, who had settled down enough to look exotically elegant once more, as the Cutest Werewolf. After accepting the certificates, her handler, Ron, put in a plug for his Lykoi breeding business. He also explained that the Lykoi's sparse coat was a natural mutation and, unlike some, involved no special health risks for the cat. "And though werewolves can be nasty, our Lykois are sweet, friendly, and make great pets!" he finished.

Lathrop himself introduced "Quentin Collins" as the winner for Scariest. The Maine Coon also drew the biggest round of applause, though as a seasoned pro, he held his seated pose on the stage's small table and accepted the ovation as his due.

Our black-cloaked emcee handed the gift certificates to Nancy, who acknowledged with regret that Quentin's real owner had been too ill to attend. Just in case any younger audience members didn't get the reference, she also explained about the *Dark Shadows* origins of his name. Still, the cat's massive body, devilish ears, and glowering expression would have earned him the prize even if he'd been named Mickey Mouse.

Sue Brookings made notes and took photos of the whole presentation, and even after the audience dispersed, the rest of us hung around for a few more shots. Mark joked that although posing in cat whiskers would probably help *my* business, his credibility as a serious medical professional was probably shot forever.

Nevertheless, I could tell he was having a pretty good time. And why shouldn't he? The threat to his clinic had been eliminated and he and his staff cleared of all suspicion. Even the late Karin Weaver's parents had called off their lawyers after learning that other well-managed veterinary clinics in the region also had been robbed of drugs. At any rate, the Weavers now had a more appropriate and loathsome target for their anger in Mitchell Desmond.

Mark and I both had reasons to celebrate that evening. I also was relieved that I wouldn't have to suspect Lathrop anymore, and could go back to thinking of him as just an unconventional older guy who enjoyed reviving picturesque landmarks for new uses and making people happy.

Around seven, as our audience began to leave, Lathrop asked me and Mark, "Are you staying for tonight's movie? It's the last in the marathon, *An American Werewolf in London*."

Mark and I glanced at each other; he grimaced, and I chuckled darkly.

"I'm sure it'll be fun," I told Lathrop, "but we've both had *really* crazy weeks. Mark's been working a lot of overtime, and . . ."

"That's right, you've been ill, Cassie." The older man frowned in sympathy. "I forgot that for a minute, I guess because you look so well tonight."

"This *was* a lot of fun. But you know how it is when you can rise to the occasion, and afterward you're suddenly pooped!"

"I remember well, from my amateur-theater days." He reached into some hidden pocket of his vampire cape and pulled out two printed coupons. "Before you go, though, I must give you both these—free passes to any and all Paragon showings for the rest of the year. It's the least I can do, after all of the work you put in to this contest."

"Thanks very much," Mark told him with a smile. "It was our pleasure, and we definitely will use these passes."

Lathrop waved a hand. "You two go now, and get some R and R. Again, thank you both!"

Dawn and Keith had been watching from across the lobby, so we told them about our payment. Half-joking, Mark suggested they use our passes for that evening's flick.

She shuddered. "A week ago, I might have taken you up on that, but now—! It'll be a while before I feel safe at night again, even going into the alley to empty my garbage."

"I don't blame you a bit," I told her. "Y'know, Bonelli emailed me a picture of the mask they found in Mitchelson's apartment. It was actually a pretty cheap one, with bulgy eyeholes and bristly gray fur. But I was so out of my mind, I thought 'Dez' was a real monster."

"You were right about that part," Mark reminded me.

It suddenly struck me that Ripley's prediction had come true—someone Dawn and I liked and trusted had turned out

to be a villain. I also realized that in spite of Mitchelson's su-
perficial appeal, something about him always had made me
uneasy. It was that "mystery," rather than any strong romantic
attraction, that drove me to find out more about him.

As we all drifted toward the theater's main exit, Keith
shook his head. "I can't believe that S.O.B. was living right in
my building, running a drug ring, and then acting like Mr.
Charm at the gallery opening. If I'd had any idea . . ."

Dawn interrupted her boyfriend. "Well, he would have
gotten away with it a lot longer if not for Cassie. The Chadwick PD should give her a medal."

"No, please!" I protested. "They're playing down my involvement as much as possible, which I appreciate even more."

As we left through the theater's front doors, I spotted a
few late trick-or-treaters strolling past the lighted storefront
of Cottone's Bakery, which of course was also decorated with
autumn leaves and pumpkins.

Dawn and Keith said their good nights and kept going on
foot to her place, while Mark and I got into his RAV4. He sat
behind the wheel in silence for a minute, and I braced myself.
By now he had taken off the silly goatee, and his grave expression troubled me.

Leaving the car in park, he began, "I have to admit something, Cassie. What happened Thursday night at The Roost
really shook me up. You've tangled with some bad guys before, and every time I've told myself it probably would never
happen again. Maybe this time was different, though, because
you really couldn't have saved yourself! If Gardiner and I
hadn't come along . . . I hate to imagine how things could
have ended up."

I figured now was not the time to argue that, by morning,
I *might* have caught the attention of the restaurant's cleanup

crew. Mark was right, though. Who could say if my perch in the flimsy hillside shrub would have held me that long?

"Anyway, this incident has made me do some hard thinking about our relationship," he went on, not meeting my eyes. "It wasn't easy, but I've come to a decision."

Oh, God, he's breaking up with me! I can't believe it! After all we've been through—

In hopes of heading him off, I began, "Mark, you're not telling me anything I don't already know. If it wasn't for you and Officer Gardiner, I probably would have fallen out of that tree and plummeted down the ravine. But I really don't set out to take these crazy chances! It's not as if I went up to The Roost of my own accord. I wasn't even chasing after Mitchelson when—"

He leaned across the car's console and put a finger to my lips, with a softer expression. "I know all that. When you start investigating a case, I guess you just can't give up until you see it through."

But did he consider that a good or a bad thing? Maybe a trait he just couldn't deal with, long-term? I felt on the brink of a fall just as frightening as the one into that dark ravine, and suddenly, I couldn't breathe.

"It still drives me crazy," Mark went on, "to know that psycho could have done *anything* to you, that I even could have lost you! But I realize something now. If I insisted that you never, ever get involved with a police case like this again . . . I'd lose you anyway. You could never promise to give that up completely, Cassie—it's too much a part your nature. So, I guess I'll just have to accept you, and love you, the way you are."

Dizzy with relief, I watched him open the car's glove compartment and pull out a business-sized envelope.

"The Chadwick PD may not be able to pay you for your services—which this time really went above and beyond the call!—but Maggie took up a collection from the staff of the veterinary clinic," he said. "They know you risked your life to clear the clinic's name, and they're grateful to you. So am I."

Astonished, I opened the envelope. The string of three zeroes on the check blew my mind. "Oh, Mark, I can't accept this. The clinic probably needs it more than I do!"

"Not really. We finally got reimbursed by our insurance company to cover the theft, and a couple of our regular clients actually sent us donations to show their support." He passed an arm over my shoulders. "I know how you've been suffering with that decrepit heating system, and Dawn told me you'll probably have to arrange financing to replace it. I also figure you probably wouldn't accept a loan from either me or your mother." With a sideways smile, he added, "She's the one you really have to think of, Cassie, if you keep on with this police work. The next time something goes wrong, if you're not so lucky, I don't want to have to tell that poor woman . . ."

I cut him off with a long kiss, then swore, "I hear you, really, about Mom. She and I *will* have to have that talk, I guess, someday soon. It won't be pretty, though. Like I said, she scares easily!" Relenting, I tucked the envelope into my purse. "Thanks, Mark, and I'll thank Maggie tomorrow. It is good to know I won't have to get through this winter with those rattling ducts and banging pipes. My nerves these days aren't what they used to be."

"Gee, I wonder why," he wisecracked. "Neither are mine!"

We drove the short distance back to my shop in silence. At this hour, we passed few costumed strollers, but lights on the neighborhood porches still illuminated swinging skeletons, giant spiderwebs, lawn tombstones, and window jack-o'-lanterns. Some images made my skin crawl, for the first time, and that disturbed me. Maybe, in some small corner of my brain, I truly was my mother's daughter? Halloween always had been one of my favorite holidays, though. I hoped Mitchelson, aka Desmond, hadn't ruined it for me forever.

Mark pulled in behind the shop next to my CR-V, which had been graciously returned by the Chadwick cops. It was my first time stepping out into the lot after dark since my abduction, and I suppressed another shiver.

But I had nothing to fear tonight, I reminded myself. Franco was dead, Nardone and Desmond were in jail, and I had Mark here to protect me. I knew now how far he would go to do that.

Even the balky furnace wouldn't frighten me tonight. And next week, I could use my gift from the clinic to make a sizable down payment on a new, energy-efficient system.

We stood for a second in the parking lot, partially lit by the security light over my back door. Mark started to pull me close again, beneath the night sky. Suddenly, he laughed out loud and pointed upward. "Boy, doesn't it just figure? Maybe *that* explains this whole insane, scary week!"

I followed his gaze. Above us, a bank of purple clouds parted, like the Paragon's velvet stage curtains, to reveal a full, brilliant Halloween moon.

Connect with Us

Visit us online at
KensingtonBooks.com
to read more from your favorite authors, see books
by series, view reading group guides, and more.

for sneak peeks, chances to win books and prize packs,
and to share your thoughts with other readers.

facebook.com/kensingtonpublishing
twitter.com/kensingtonbooks

Tell us what you think!

To share your thoughts, submit a review,
or sign up for our eNewsletters, please visit:
KensingtonBooks.com/TellUs.

Connect with